***To Sam Lavelle, it looked like
Captain Picard had made his
decision. . . .***

The captain turned off his padd and set it firmly on an empty console.

"It appears we have to depend upon this makeshift crew, despite our doubts. Now I have to go talk to the Romulan."

Sam Lavelle blinked at him. *"Romulan?* There's a Romulan on board?"

"A wounded Romulan," answered Picard. "He lost an arm when we recaptured this ship, and he's recuperating. You have the conn, Mr. Lavelle. Ro, you're with me."

Sam couldn't help but watch Ro and Picard walk off the bridge—they were two of a kind, calm and controlled on the surface and wild-eyed gamblers underneath. *My life is now in the hands of those two.* He would have disobeyed anybody else in the universe who ordered him to go back to that monstrous collider and the slave pens, but he had to follow Captain Picard. If anyone could get them through this insane war alive, it would be him. . . .

THE
DOMINION WAR

BOOK THREE

TUNNEL THROUGH THE STARS

John Vornholt

POCKET BOOKS
New York   London   Toronto   Sydney   Tokyo   Singapore

An *Original* Publication of POCKET BOOKS

POCKET BOOKS, a division of Simon & Schuster Inc.
1230 Avenue of the Americas, New York, NY 10020

STAR TREK is a Registered Trademark of Paramount Pictures.

A VIACOM COMPANY

This book is published by Pocket Books, a division of Simon & Schuster Inc., under exclusive license from Paramount Pictures.

ISBN: 0-671-02500-7

First Pocket Books printing December 1998

10 9 8 7 6 5 4 3 2 1

Printed in the U.S.A.

For all the Tanque Wordies

TUNNEL THROUGH THE STARS

Chapter One

SAM LAVELLE STRODE onto the bridge of the *Orb of Peace,* hardly able to believe that he had given up a spacious Cardassian antimatter tanker for this austere Bajoran transport. He was sure he had gotten the worst of the deal, especially considering that he *thought* he was going to be rescued and sent home. His last voyage had been a perfect example of Murphy's Law, and this one promised to send him from the frying pan into the fire.

The cramped bridge had a strange viewscreen with Bajoran writing all around it. He was able to translate two phrases: "The devout will enter the Celestial Temple," and "The Kai holds the lantern of Bajor." Even without the platitudes, the stars glimmered enticingly on the screen, making him wish that he were going home.

But Sam knew there was no escape from this war—not until the Dominion was driven back to their part of the galaxy.

He spotted the slim Bajoran, Ro Laren, seated at the conn. Both Captain Picard and Geordi La Forge looked Bajoran—with nose ridges and earrings—but Ro was the real thing. Sam remembered hearing stories about her on the *Enterprise,* but he had only seen her once, in Ten-Forward, just before her ill-fated mission to infiltrate the Maquis. Now she was captain of this Bajoran vessel.

"I'm your relief, Captain," he said, keeping his voice low in the dimly lit bridge.

"Thank you." Ro Laren rose from her seat and stretched like a willowy lioness, shaking her short-cropped mane of dark brown hair. She was wearing a Bajoran uniform which hugged the lanky contours of her body, and Sam looked longer and harder than he should have. Ro caught him staring at her, and her eyes drilled into his. Sam knew he should look away, but it had been a long time since he had gazed lustfully at a woman, and he wasn't anxious to stop.

"I'm sorry," he said, managing a shy smile. "I don't know what got into me. It's funny what even a small taste of freedom will do to a man."

Her face softened, and she looked sympathetic if still annoyed. "How long were you a prisoner of the Dominion?"

"About two months, I guess," answered Sam. "It's hard to say, because we were never allowed to see any chronometers, except when we were on work detail, building that damn collider. And then, we only saw shift timers. We were kept segregated from the women. I saw them every now and then on the worker transports, but that was it."

"I know the Cardassians—it must have been bad."

He nodded slowly. "Yes, it was, and a lot of good people are still there. I wish we could do something to help them."

"There's no chance for a mass escape?"

"I don't see how," Sam answered glumly. "The complex where the prisoners are housed is near the collider, but each pod of prisoners is isolated. There's no way to get hold of a ship like we did—that was a fluke. No matter when you do this, thousands of prisoners will be working. If your mission is to destroy the artificial wormhole, your mission is to destroy them, too."

Ro crossed her arms and wrinkled her ridged nose. "You know, that's exactly what I've been telling Captain Picard. And it sounds even worse coming from you, because you've been there."

"Yes, I've been there, and I can't believe I'm thinking about going back. This isn't exactly the way I envisioned my escape—going back to that place, on purpose." Shivering, Sam sunk into the chair at the conn and studied the unfamiliar instruments.

"I'm sure Captain Picard would offer you a chance not to go, if he could," said Ro. "But we only have this craft, and no way to split up."

Sam snorted a laugh. "Yeah, if you don't mind me saying so, your demolition squad is a little short-handed."

"We had a whole crew and more than one torpedo. But we lost five torpedoes fighting our way through the Dominion border patrol, then we got shanghaied by pirates in the Badlands, and hijacked by Romulans—"

"Pirates and Romulans?" asked Sam with boyish curiosity. The smile faded from his lips when we saw how upset Ro was about these incidents. "Hey, I'm sorry if we lost more good people, but I'm sort of burned-out on death. I can't even think about it, if you know what I mean."

"I know what you mean," admitted Ro, staring down at the deck. "The *Enterprise* is supposed to take us home, but only if we alert them with a subspace beacon."

"But how quickly could they get here?"

"That's a good question." The Bajoran hovered over Sam's shoulder and pointed at his console. "You'll want to watch the hull pressure—right there."

"Okay, thanks." Sam took some time to scan all the readouts, finding them fairly easy to understand. It wasn't nearly as complex as the antimatter tanker. He tried to concentrate on his duties, but the Bajoran's presence was bringing back memories and emotions he had tried to push away, without much success.

"I had a good friend who was Bajoran, Ensign Sito Jaxa," he said with a wistful smile. "Her death was the first casualty I really experienced in Starfleet, and it hit me pretty hard. She was killed by the Cardassians, and that act started the war for me a couple of years early. I was gung-ho to get at them."

"I followed Sito's career," said Ro, "but I never got a chance to meet her. I think I was away at Tactical Training while you and your friends were serving aboard the *Enterprise.*"

Sam chuckled. "You couldn't help but to follow Sito's career—she was full of zip. She got into a lot of trouble at the Academy."

"Along with Wesley Crusher," said Ro with a smile.

While they shared an unexpected moment of nostalgia, Sam glanced at the striking Bajoran. It was too bad that his life expectancy was so short, or he would have been tempted to pursue the former Starfleet officer. Of course it was wartime, and anything could happen.

Returning his mind to his duty, Sam adjusted the viewscreen, and a brown-magenta cloud coalesced into view, still some distance away. Pulses of light blinked on and off within its murky depths, which gave it an oddly cheerful glow, like a surreal Christmas wreath.

"The Badlands," he mused. "Is it all that bad?"

"Worse," muttered Ro. "I wouldn't go back there, except there's no other place to hide."

"Well, if it's any consolation, you're within striking distance of the artificial wormhole from here. It's just that there's a fleet guarding it, and it's ten kilometers long."

"So I gather," replied Ro solemnly.

They heard footsteps, and Sam turned to see Captain Picard come striding onto the cramped bridge. He looked odd with his Bajoran earring, nose ridges, and tufts of white hair; but his voice, bearing, and stern demeanor left no doubt who was in charge. Immediately, Sam stiffened in his seat and studied his readouts until he was caught up.

"Status?" asked Picard as he consulted the small padd in his hands.

"Estimated arrival time at the Badlands: one hour," reported Sam. "No sign of enemy craft."

"Thank you, Lieutenant. I haven't had an opportunity to say how good it is to see you again, although I wish it were under better circumstances."

"Me, too, sir."

The captain looked somber. "I've talked to your

crew. I realize that we ruined your escape attempt. I'm sorry. I'm sure you expected to get farther away than the Badlands—"

"I wasn't really expecting to escape," replied Sam honestly. "I just wanted to die like a Starfleet officer, not a slave. I don't want to go back to that place—and I doubt if this mission will work—but it's still a good chance to die as a Starfleet officer."

The captain's lips thinned. "I wish there was an alternative, but there isn't. We can't allow the Dominion to ever use that artificial wormhole."

"I know, sir," admitted Sam. "I thought the same thing every day, even while I was building it."

Picard consulted his padd and looked around to make sure they were alone. "I need an honest evaluation of every member of your crew. You know what we have ahead of us—a major sabotage mission with a high degree of risk."

Sam frowned thoughtfully. "The only member of the crew I really know is Taurik, and I would trust him with my life. As for Woil, Shonsui, Horik, and Maserelli—they're all career Starfleet officers, who ought to be fine in a crisis. But they've been through some rough times lately, and they may be close to cracking. I'm sure you could say that about all of us, except for Taurik, of course. Many times during our imprisonment, I wished I were a Vulcan."

"I've often wished that I were a certain android," said Picard with a wistful smile. "What about the scientist, Enrak Grof?"

Sam winced, trying not to show his doubts. "Until today, I would've said he was a traitor and a collaborator—and an unpleasant one at that. He could've stopped us but didn't, so I guess he's on our side. As I'm sure he'll tell you, he's basically in it for the science and the glory. Grof knows that artificial wormhole backwards and forwards—he helped design it."

"So he told me," said Picard. "None of the rest of you have any in-depth knowledge of its workings?"

"No," answered Sam. "Taurik knows some of the theory, but we were grunt labor, only told what was needed. Grof was right in there with the Vorta engineers, on a buddy-buddy basis with our resident changeling."

"You saw a changeling?" asked Picard with interest.

"Only once, when they put me in charge of the tanker." Sam smiled nostalgically. "To tell you the truth, Captain, I remember more about the food than anything else. It was the first decent food I'd had in weeks."

Captain Picard allowed him a slight smile. "I know this has been difficult for you, Lieutenant, and I wish I could relieve you of further burden. But you know our situation."

"Not really," answered Sam. "Taurik and I were captured early on, defending the outer colonies. We volunteered for that service, if you can believe it. I've heard rumors—if this ship is any indication of what Starfleet can spare, I guess we're in a lot of trouble."

The captain looked grave as he explained, "If the Dominion manages to bring through reinforcements from the Gamma Quadrant—either by clearing the mines from the Bajoran wormhole or through their new artificial wormhole—the situation will be desperate. We didn't even know about the artificial wormhole until we encountered Ro and her passengers. There wasn't enough time to do anything but gather intelligence, which is why we're using this ship. We've done that, we know it exists, and now it's time to take the next step."

The way Picard said it almost convinced Sam that they could pull it off. He tried not to think about what few resources they had at their disposal, even if the *Enterprise* was out there somewhere. *These people have no idea what they're up against.*

After a few moments of uneasy silence, during which no one voiced their obvious concerns, the captain turned off his padd and set it on an empty console. "It appears we have to depend upon this makeshift crew, despite our doubts. Now I have to go talk to the Romulan."

Sam blinked at him. *"Romulan?* There's a Romulan on board?"

"A wounded Romulan," answered Picard. "He lost an arm when we recaptured the ship, and he's in the captain's quarters, recuperating. Had I known we would have all these casualties to deal with, I would've brought Dr. Crusher along."

Hesitantly Sam asked, "Is Alyssa Ogawa still serving on the *Enterprise?"*

Picard smiled. "Yes, we've managed to hold on to Ogawa. She's now chief nurse in sickbay, and that's quite a job in wartime. Do you feel confident with the Bajoran conn, Lieutenant?"

"Yes, sir. I'll contact you if I have any questions."

"Good. Ro, will you please accompany me?"

"Yes, sir."

Sam couldn't help but watch Ro and Picard walk off the bridge—they were two of a kind, calm and controlled on the surface and wild-eyed gamblers underneath. *My life is now in the hands of those two.*

He would have disobeyed anybody else in the universe who ordered him to go back to that monstrous collider and the slave pens, but he had to follow Captain Picard. If anybody could get them through this insane war alive, it would be him.

As Captain Picard descended the spiral staircase to the lower deck of the *Orb of Peace,* he wondered what he should do with their Romulan prisoner. Some would say it was practical to execute him on the spot—it was no less than he deserved—but such actions were not in Picard's nature. Essentially, the Romulan had been doing the same thing they were doing, pretending to be someone he wasn't in order to gather information about the artificial wormhole. His methods were much different, however, in that he and his comrades had murdered a dozen innocent people trying to hijack the *Orb of Peace.*

Picard turned to glance at Ro Laren, who was striding behind him, a determined look on her angular face. He wondered if *she* thought they had a chance to destroy the artificial wormhole, to get out of this alive. But what could she tell him that he didn't already know? They were behind enemy lines, confronting overwhelming odds, and they had no choice but to continue.

Ro smiled at his concerned expression. "It's all right, Captain. I've given up the dream of living to an old age and retiring on a Starfleet pension."

"I don't think anybody is enjoying their pension at the moment," remarked the captain.

With a rush of heavy footsteps, a burly figure bolted from the mess hall and planted himself in front of Picard and Ro, blocking the corridor. His eyebrows and beard bristled, and the brown spots on his forehead, temples, and neck seemed to pop out of his skin, like mountains on a relief map.

Enrak Grof scowled angrily. "Captain, I just heard that you expect *all* of us to go with you on this insane mission to destroy the wormhole! I can understand why you and your crew would feel a need to sabotage it, but it's simply impossible that *I* go. I'm the only one in the Federation who understands this technology—the only one who could possibly duplicate it. It's imperative that you send me back to Starfleet headquarters immediately!"

The captain tried not to grit his teeth as he calmly replied, "Believe me, Professor, I would like nothing better than to send you back to Starfleet, but this vessel and the people aboard it are all I have. You *are* the only one who understands the technology of the artificial wormhole, which makes you the most essential member of the party."

"I can't argue with that," snapped Grof, "but the information I possess in my head cannot *die* with me. You must find a way to return me safely to Starfleet!"

While Picard clenched his fists, and carefully considered his next words, Ro stepped in. "What if we could find a way to return the information you possess but keep you here with us—to help? Would that be satisfactory?"

"If this is your only ship, how could you do that?" asked Grof skeptically.

"I don't know yet," answered Ro, "but soon we'll be in the Badlands, where almost anything is possible. Let's keep our options open, because there must be a way to safeguard your knowledge. In the meantime, I suggest you go to the science station on the bridge and start recording your notes."

The Trill nodded thoughtfully. "Yes, I suppose I should do that, anyway. What if I had an accident or something? Good thinking. What did you say your name is?"

"Ro Laren, captain of this vessel."

"Well, Captain Ro, I sincerely appreciate your willingness to accommodate me. I am not exaggerating when I say this technology is crucial to the future of the galaxy."

Reluctantly, it seemed, Enrak Grof shifted his attention from the attractive Bajoran to Captain Picard, and his scowl returned. "Captain, you just don't understand the import of the situation like Captain Ro does. You want to destroy the greatest invention of our times, but I won't let you destroy the knowledge as well."

"We'll find a way," promised Picard.

"You had better." The Trill stomped toward the spiral staircase and headed toward the bridge.

The captain watched him go, then lowered his voice to say, "Insufferable man."

"I know that kind," said Ro. "Maybe if he does a good job of transcribing his notes, we won't need him."

The captain nodded appreciatively, then grimaced. "But we still have him, plus a murderous Romulan and a handful of ex-prisoners who should be in sickbay, not on duty."

Ro gave him a smile. "This is how we assembled crews in the Maquis—whoever showed up. Sometimes it works."

"I'm glad you're here," said Picard gratefully. "Now let's go see our prisoner."

He led the way into the captain's quarters, the only private cabin on the whole ship. Since the *Orb of*

Peace was a civilian transport, it had no brig or interior force-fields, so they had turned the captain's quarters into a temporary cell, with only a mattress. A Cardassian prisoner had managed to escape, but so far the Romulan prisoner had been docile. Of course, he had lost an arm and a considerable amount of blood; he had to be extremely weak.

Nevertheless, Ro drew her Bajoran phaser as they approached the door. Geordi had disabled the circuitry which opened the door from the inside, and the Romulan had been alone in there for several hours. They had to be prepared for anything—from a dead prisoner to a berserk prisoner.

The captain nodded to Ro to be ready as he touched the wall panel. The door slid open slowly, as if it were still slightly damaged by the Cardassian's rampage. Soothing red and turquoise lights lit the cabin, which appeared empty except for a sleeping figure on the mattress.

The figure on the bed stirred slightly as they entered. Ro stationed herself in the doorway, her weapon leveled for action, and Picard took a step forward. The Romulan rolled over, gripping the bandaged stub of his arm. Lying there helplessly, he looked younger than Picard had remembered, the equivalent of a human in his early thirties. Picard knew, however, that appearances could be deceiving with these long-lived races. The prisoner gazed at them not with hatred or fear, but resignation.

"How are you feeling?" asked Picard.

He sighed. "Weak and ashamed over my capture. I assume now you will execute me."

"Don't tempt us," said Ro.

Picard's jaw tightened. "I still don't see why you

had to kill my crew and hijack my ship, just to get away from Shek and Rolf."

"You don't know that Ferengi and his Orion henchman," muttered the Romulan. "We would have done *anything* to get away from them, even if our mission hadn't been almost finished. You happened along, and we knew we might not get another chance to escape. I sincerely doubt if you would have *given* us your ship."

"Perhaps not," answered Picard, "but we might have given you sanctuary, if you had asked. What is your name?"

"You can call me Hasmek, if you need a name for your reports, but I refuse to be interrogated."

"We know all about your mission," said Ro. "You talked while you were in shock. You and your confederates enlisted with the pirates to get close to the artificial wormhole. Now that you know it exists, you were going to advise your superiors to give up neutrality and ally themselves with the Dominion. Have I left anything out?"

Hasmek sneered at them. "Only that I also know *your* mission—to destroy the artificial wormhole. I realize the Federation is given to fits of fantasy, but do you have any idea how impossible that will be?"

"We don't have much choice," replied Picard. "At the moment, our problem is what to do with *you.*"

With a grimace, the Romulan sat up and stared at him. "You mean, you haven't decided to kill me?"

"That's not Starfleet practice," said Picard.

"However," added Ro, hefting her weapon, "not all of us are in Starfleet."

"You're Bajoran, technically neutral like us. Or are you a fake Bajoran, like him?" asked Hasmek.

Ro shook her head with disgust. "We're getting

nowhere with him. I say we maroon him somewhere in the Badlands, somewhere he'll never be found."

The Romulan's cheerful disposition turned sour. "Yes, leave me to starve to death—that's the humane Federation way. If you don't execute me properly, I'll make an escape attempt and force you to do it."

Ro asked, "I wonder what the Dominion would do with a Romulan spy?"

"Probably the same thing they would do with a Federation spy," answered Hasmek. "But they wouldn't have the qualms about it that you seem to have."

"We can't let the Dominion find him alive, and he knows it," said Picard. "We could conceivably give him back to Shek and Rolf, if we could find them."

The Romulan stuck his jaw out and assumed an arrogant pose. "That would be as good as an execution, probably for all of us."

The captain heard footsteps in the corridor, and he turned to see the Vulcan, Taurik, slip through the door. Even in the subdued light, Picard was surprised by the similarity in the facial appearance of the Vulcan and the Romulan. They were similar in age, too, and both men had straight black hair that was uncharacteristically long after their adventures in Cardassian space.

Hasmek was momentarily stunned to see his double, then he slumped weakly back into bed. "A Vulcan lackey."

"Captain," said Taurik in a low voice, "we don't wish to alarm the crew by using the comm system, but Sam has detected a ship. They may be in pursuit."

"What kind of ship?" asked Picard.

"It appears to be Cardassian."

The captain exhaled as if he had been punched in

the stomach. Relying on Bajoran neutrality, they had talked their way past Jem'Hadar and Vorta sentries, but not Cardassians, who couldn't resist harassing Bajorans whenever the opportunity presented itself.

"I'll check on it." Ro shouldered past Taurik and headed for the bridge, with the Vulcan right behind her. Left alone in the room with his prisoner, Picard turned and gazed at Hasmek.

"The Cardassians have no qualms about torture and execution, especially for spies," he said somberly.

"I know," answered Picard grimly.

Chapter Two

PICARD REMAINED in the captain's quarters, watching his Romulan prisoner, who was watching him in return. A crazy idea was percolating in his mind, and he might have to act on it, depending on what Ro discovered.

A few seconds later, Picard's combadge chirped, and he answered it with his code name, "Boothby here."

Ro's normally resolute voice sounded disheartened as she reported, "A Cardassian Galor-class warship is on an intercept course with us. Contact in approximately twenty minutes."

"Any chance that we can make the Badlands in time?"

"None."

We have one photon torpedo at our disposal, the

captain reminded himself. *We'd be lucky if we could take out an unarmed shuttlecraft.*

"Replicate two Romulan uniforms," ordered Picard. "Put one on Taurik and send the other one down to the captain's quarters."

"Yes, sir," answered Ro in a quizzical tone. "Out."

Hasmek sat up in bed and looked suspiciously at him. "What are you planning, Boothby?"

Picard strode toward him and said, "I know you're weak, but do you think you could remain on your feet for a few minutes and do some talking?"

Hasmek grinned at him. "Very clever. You're planning to put me and the Vulcan on-screen and say that Romulans are in charge of this vessel. I didn't know Federation captains could be quite so devious."

"I'm learning," muttered Picard.

"How do you know I won't betray you?"

"You have nothing to gain and your life to lose. Bajoran neutrality works with the Jem'Hadar but not necessarily with Cardassians. I'm hoping that they'll respect Romulan neutrality. There's hardly any bad blood between your races."

"Not yet," answered Hasmek. "Have you been so foolish as to come here with no permission at all?"

The captain's eyes narrowed—he wasn't used to being addressed in this fashion. "We have documents of passage in our computer, given to us on our first stop. I don't think they've expired yet."

With a flurry of footsteps, Sam Lavelle burst into the room clutching a thick gray jumpsuit in his hands. He looked quizzically from Picard to the wounded Romulan and held out the bundle of clothing. "Is this what you wanted, sir?"

"Yes. Remain here to help me get Hasmek to the bridge. Hasmek, this is Sam."

"Charmed," drawled the Romulan, doing a comical impression of a human accent.

"Yeah," answered Sam doubtfully.

With his good hand, Hasmek gripped the back of the conn chair and held himself steady. His empty left sleeve was tucked under the armpit of his uniform. The moody lighting on the bridge of the transport had been arranged so that only he and Taurik, at tactical, were visible. Picard and Ro crouched in the forward shadows, phasers in their hands, both aimed at the one-armed Romulan. Everyone else was below.

At his console, Taurik actually had command of the ship and was poised to fire his lone torpedo and go to warp if the Cardassians tried to board or attack. They probably wouldn't get far, but escape was their only option if talking failed . . . or the Romulan betrayed them.

Right now, a massive, bronze Galor-class warship filled the small viewscreen and commanded everyone's attention. It looked like a manta ray caught in shallow waters under golden sunlight.

Ro Laren told herself that she had to watch the Romulan and not be distracted by the enemy, who stood poised to vaporize them. As her sweaty hand gripped her phaser, she glanced at Captain Picard, who nodded to the Vulcan and the Romulan. She leveled her weapon and waited for Taurik to send commands from his console.

"Gul Dubarok is on screen," said the Vulcan.

Ro had seen enough Cardassians in her life to know that she didn't have to turn to look at this one. She could imagine the thick, muscular neck, pallid gray complexion, severe black hair, and sunken eye sockets which gave a cadaverous look to the haughty face. Luckily, the one race which could match the Cardassians in sneering arrogance were the Romulans, who considered themselves vastly superior to everyone, including the Dominion.

Disdainfully, Hasmek declared, "I am Captain Hasmek, and this is the *Orb of Peace,* under the command of a Romulan crew. We have broken no law—why have we been stopped?"

Ro heard a woman's voice reply, "You are in a war zone. State your business, and know that we have scanned you. Why do you have such a mongrel crew?"

The Romulan drew himself up indignantly. "We have a multiracial crew because we are a joint scientific mission, sponsored by governments which are neutral in this war, principally Bajor and the Romulan Star Empire. Our people have been studying the Badlands for years—you can see that we're virtually unarmed. In our opinion, the Dominion has total control over this sector, and the Badlands are safer than they have been in years."

"You've had no contact with Federation vessels or Federation sympathizers?"

"Federation vessels?" Hasmek sneered and motioned toward his empty sleeve. "I lost this arm fighting the Federation. If you think Romulans would aid the Federation, your worries are baseless. You've beaten those sniveling do-gooders, and I for one am jubilant. By the way, we have traveling documents, which we would be happy to transmit to you."

There came a pause, and Ro licked her lips nervously. The Romulan appeared unflappable, but she could see his knuckles whiten where he gripped the chair for support. There were also blood spots seeping through his folded sleeve—she hoped the Cardassians wouldn't notice.

Finally the Gul replied, "Begin transmission."

Hasmek nodded to Taurik, who plied his console. While the documents were being sent, the Romulan casually sunk into the chair at the conn. Only those on the bridge could tell that he had done so to keep from collapsing.

"Transmission complete," said the Vulcan.

There were several more long moments while the Cardassians digested the permits, and Taurik and Hasmek nonchalantly checked their instruments. They were both cool under fire, thought Ro. If the Romulan weren't a cold-blooded murderer, he would have made an interesting addition to this crew.

"Captain Hasmek," said the haughty feminine voice, "the *Orb of Peace* is cleared for passage. Any deviation in course from the Badlands will result in expulsion from Cardassian space."

Hasmek waved imperiously. "Understood. When we meet again, we will toast to your victory and dance on the bones of the Federation."

"We await that day," agreed the Cardassian. "Out."

The screen switched back to a view of the starscape, dominated by the sleek bronze warship. This time Ro watched as the Galor-class vessel glided slowly over their bow, turned in a graceful arc, and disappeared into warp with a brilliant flash. Only then did she begin breathing.

The Romulan slumped forward onto the conn and rested his head on his forearm. Picard holstered his phaser and approached the prisoner. "Well done," he said. "You have acted with honor."

"You mean, I lied with honor," murmured Hasmek with a weak smile. "If you think we want to ally ourselves with the Dominion, you would be wrong. Romulans are a proud people, and we aren't eager to serve *anyone.*"

Picard nodded resolutely. "Now I know what to do with you. I've got to take you with us on this mission to make sure that you see the artificial wormhole destroyed with your own eyes. Then I'll get you back to your superiors, so that you can tell them to remain neutral in the war."

Ro gaped at the captain along with the Romulan. *Could he be serious?* Although the Romulan had just shown his worth, how could they add a treacherous murderer to their already makeshift crew?

"You won't regret this decision," said the Romulan a moment before he closed his eyes and lost consciousness.

Will Riker stood in a nondescript corridor on Starbase 209, torn as to which direction he should go. One way led to the repair facilities, where the *Enterprise-E* lay in space dock, undergoing extensive repairs. In the other direction was the base commander's office, under Vice-Admiral Jack Torrance, a man younger than Riker.

In yet a third direction—below to the nineteenth level—were the medical facilities of Starbase 209. Riker was certain that members of his crew would be there, either receiving outpatient treatment or, in the case of Deanna Troi and Beverly Crusher, assisting the overworked staff. According to their logs, they had been helping out every day since the *Enterprise*'s arrival four days ago, while Riker had been attending tactical meetings. Those meetings had been terribly depressing, because there was no way to disguise the fact that they were losing the war.

To him, it seemed as if they had been at Starbase 209 for four months instead of four days. Even with the unexpected diversion of his romance with Captain Shana Winslow, he found it difficult to wait here while the war raged elsewhere. He felt helpless, guilty, and oddly relieved all at the same time.

Most of all, Riker wanted to know that his comrades behind enemy lines were safe, and he wanted to know that he would get his ship back in time to help them. As Shana had told him, Starfleet had no personnel to dispense hugs and reassurance, and that was what he needed most.

On top of that, he had something else to worry about—Shana's mental health. She was the cause of his quandary, his indecision over which way to go in the corridor. Riker took a few steps toward the base commander's office, but stopped, knowing that he couldn't go over her head without giving her a chance to defend herself. And he couldn't bring himself to go to her workplace and put more pressure on her, not knowing how she would react. He hadn't seen Shana for a day and a night, since she broke down and cried in his arms.

No, decided Riker, *I have to talk to Deanna Troi before I do anything else.* Feeling relieved with his decision, he strode into the nearest turbolift and requested level nineteen.

He emerged into a broad, busy corridor. Two occupied, robotic gurneys rumbled past going in opposite directions, following invisible magnetic strips embedded in the floor. A flock of medical workers emerged from one room and ducked into another, conversing in low voices as they walked. Two orderlies jogged past in a big hurry, and a man in an automatic wheelchair cruised slowly along the corridor.

Riker wandered the hall, glancing at signs denoting various departments, such as Surgery, Research, and Recovery. He took a chance and walked toward the door marked "Recovery."

When the door slid open, Riker was immediately plunged back into the war. Every bed in the immense room was filled—row after row of injured people from dozens of different races. Over each bed, digital readouts pulsed with cheerful precision, and workers carrying trays and hypos maneuvered through the rows like overworked honeybees. A few visitors clustered around individual beds, and Riker wandered in the direction of one such gathering.

He glanced at the patient, a blue-skinned Bolian; he was surrounded by uniformed officers, who were joking and kidding with him, obviously happy to have their comrade on the mend. Riker walked down the outer row of beds, seeing several patients who looked alert and well. But he saw many others who were badly scarred, unconscious, and still in field dressings and casts. The most disturbing were those who were awake but were staring vacantly into space—they were still at the battle site. A few patients who looked bored and disgruntled reminded Riker uncomfortably of himself.

The medical workers and volunteers paid no attention to him as they bustled past. Evidently, visitors were common in the Recovery section. Riker looked for a familiar face among the workers, but there were none until he reached the last bed in the last row. There he spotted Alyssa Ogawa administering a hypospray to an unconscious patient.

He walked closer to her and stood patiently until she finished. "Hello, Nurse Ogawa."

"Commander Riker," she said with some surprise. "Can I help you with anything?"

"Yes, I'm looking for Counselor Troi."

The nurse stepped away from her patient and pushed a strand of hair behind her ear. "I believe I saw her in the psychiatric section, which is out the main door and two doors to the right."

"Thank you," answered Riker with a friendly smile. "I'm amazed how many patients there are in this room. It's great to see so many people on the way to recovery."

"Not all of them are," said Ogawa sadly, glancing back at her patient. "There aren't enough beds for everyone. Some of them . . . we're just trying to make comfortable."

"I see." The smile faded from Riker's face. "It's very commendable that you're working here, when you don't have to be."

Ogawa sighed and looked around at the hundreds of casualties. "Oh, I definitely have to be here. They just keep coming in—and these are the lucky ones. Excuse me, Captain."

"Certainly." Riker watched the slender, dark-haired nurse return to her duties, then he wandered between two more rows of beds, feeling disheartened and ashamed. Here he was, worrying about a handful of close friends, when death and destruction were all around. It was hard to imagine that these people and the crew of the *Enterprise* had been lucky, but they were . . . when one considered the alternatives. According to Ro, thousands of Starfleet officers were toiling in slave labor camps, where they were treated worse than animals. He wanted to do something—anything!—but all he could do was to concentrate on his job, which at the moment meant sitting and waiting.

Riker almost didn't enter the door marked "Psychiatric Care," knowing he could be pulling Deanna away from patients. But he couldn't stop thinking about Shana Winslow, her torments, and her incredibly important position. He had to talk to *somebody*.

Taking a deep breath, he walked into the most depressing of the wards on Starbase 209, the place where the casualties couldn't be cured by skinbonding, blood transfusions, and antibiotics. The first room he entered looked like a typical recreation room, with Ping-Pong tables, video viewers, game tables, and a food and drink replicator. Two people were playing a game of three-dimensional chess, and two more people were watching a science program on the viewer. The only thing amiss was the two-way mirror by the door, through which the attendants were undoubtedly monitoring their charges.

A white-garbed attendant stood by the interior doorway, which led to a corridor and many doors beyond. He eyed Riker suspiciously and walked toward him. "I'm sorry, Commander, but we don't allow visitors here, except by special permission."

"Understood," said Riker. "I'm looking for Commander Deanna Troi, who's the counselor aboard my ship."

"She's a volunteer, right?"

"Yes. She's been here about four days."

"I think I know where she is. If you'll have a seat, I'll go look for her." The attendant hurried down the corridor, and the door whispered shut behind him.

Riker strolled over to the chess game and studied the layout of the three main boards and five smaller boards. Then his attention shifted to the players: an older Vulcan woman and a young Merakan with orangish hair. They were so intent upon their game that neither one looked at him or acknowledged his presence.

The Merakan reached out a fragile hand with slender fingers and moved a white knight from the center board to the top board. The Vulcan woman raised an eyebrow at this and said, "That is not classic Duranian Defense."

"Yes, it is," replied the Merakan huffily. He looked straight at Riker. "Isn't it?"

"I wouldn't know," answered Riker with a friendly smile. "Chess was never my game."

"Then why do you watch it?" asked the Vulcan.

Riker motioned around the almost deserted recreation lounge, then decided that he had better be extremely diplomatic with these people. "I wish to learn about it."

"Then take my place!" offered the Merakan, jumping to his feet. Despite Riker's protests, he was soon ushered into the seat across from the stoic Vulcan, who would undoubtedly crush him in three-dimensional chess.

"I'm not a very good player," admitted Riker.

"It matters little," answered the Vulcan. "We only

play games that have already been played. Famous games—"

"If we can remember them," added the Merakan. "We're not allowed to play *real* games, because—" He looked puzzledly at the Vulcan. "What is it we do?"

"We attack each other," she answered.

"That's right," said the Merakan cheerfully. "There's no dishonor in losing a game which has already been lost."

"Right," answered Riker doubtfully. He motioned to the Vulcan. "Your move."

The Vulcan stroked her chin. "At this point, black makes a fatal mistake, is that not correct?"

"That's it!" said the Merakan excitedly. "You mistake my retreat for an attack, and you break off your relentless offensive in order to castle with your rook. This moment of hesitation allows white to get the momentum. It goes on for another four days, but eventually you'll lose."

The Vulcan shook her head. "Durania is famous for beating such an incompetent?" Nevertheless, she made the necessary castling move to continue the game.

Riker was relieved to see Deanna Troi stroll through the doorway, brushing back a dark strand of errant hair. He jumped to his feet. "Thanks for the pointers. I'm Will Riker, and it's been nice to meet you—" His voice trailed off expectantly, waiting for them to furnish their names.

"And I'm—" The Merakan raised his finger as if to answer, then he looked puzzledly at his chess opponent. "Who am I?"

The Vulcan shook her head. "I have no idea. I only met you today."

Troi moved swiftly to Riker's side in order to rescue him from the awkward situation. "You're Lieutenant Anowon, and your friend is Captain Jobra. But it's been a very long day of playing chess—perhaps you should think about dinner, or a nap."

"But there's a war going on," said Jobra. Riker stared at the Vulcan, thinking that her answer sounded extremely coherent, until she motioned toward the chess boards. She meant the game.

"Absolutely!" exclaimed Anowon, dropping into the chair across from the Vulcan. In a matter of seconds, they were intent upon their game to the exclusion of the two visitors.

Troi ushered Riker toward the door, and he looked fondly at the beautiful Betazoid. Once the love of his life, now a friend for life, sometimes he felt that she would always be the only person who really knew him. It was good to have somebody in the universe with whom he could be totally honest and vulnerable. Of course, Deanna bestowed a feeling of trust and comfort to almost everybody, but he had also known her love. Although they had never been married, he often felt as if she were his amiable ex-spouse, with more than a few sparks of jealousy and physical attraction left between them.

When they reached the corridor and the door shut behind them, Troi shook her head. "It's sad to see those two," she whispered. "Head injuries gave them a rare form of amnesia which starts all over again every time they awaken. They can remember certain things, like old chess moves, but they can't remember that they know each other. We have to introduce them every morning."

"There's nothing you can do for them?"

"After the war, Jobra could probably get help on Vulcan, and there may be something the Merakans can do for Anowon. But we have no way to transport them, and no one we can spare to take them there. So they sit here, waiting."

"Just like us," muttered Riker.

Troi grabbed his arm and gaily tossed her black tresses. "But, Will, you didn't come down here to talk about depressing subjects, did you? You're going to whisk me away to someplace fun, make me forget that there's a war going on! Right?"

He shook his head glumly. "I'm afraid not. I will buy you dinner, though, in someplace private, if you'd care to hear what trouble I'm in."

She gave him a disapproving frown. "If you've been having fun, I'll really be mad."

"Well, yes," he admitted, "but it didn't last too long."

"I haven't seen the aquarium yet," said Troi. "I hear it's beautiful."

Riker gritted his teeth, thinking of his memorable date with Shana. "Let's go."

After staring at a proud lion fish, with its mane of frilly orange and white fins, Will Riker thought about what he had to do. Thus far, he and Deanna had talked shop, including the scheduled time-frame for repairs to the *Enterprise*, but he hadn't told her anything about Shana Winslow. It was time to summon his courage and open up.

Riker glanced around and saw that they were virtually alone amidst the bubbling turquoise tanks of the aquarium where he had last come with Shana. Deanna was staring into a tank of Vulcan eels, which slithered like flaming arrows through a sea of underwater volcanic ash.

"I've gotten involved with somebody here," he blurted out.

"You don't say," remarked Troi, without a shred of surprise. She stepped to another tank and looked at miniature jellyfish lit by phosphorescent lights. "Head of the repair facilities—very impressive."

He gaped at her. "You know all about it?"

"You don't think a juicy piece of gossip like that could stay secret. Commander Winslow is a remarkable woman."

"A remarkable woman with some very heavy responsibilities. She's in charge of us getting the *Enterprise* back in one piece. And she's deeply troubled—nightmares, unexpected chills, moodiness. On top of that, she has to cope with losing two limbs, a lot of grief, and tremendous stress from her job. I'm not sure she's coping."

"Most of us are barely coping these days." Troi stood up and fixed him with a sharp gaze. "Are you officially reporting to me that her ability to do her duty is impaired?"

"I don't know." Riker shook his head with frustration and tried to keep his voice low. "I don't want to do anything official, because I don't want to cause her more problems. Let's just say, her ability to have a personal relationship is badly impaired, and I want you to talk to her."

"All right. But, Will, I won't be able to discuss our conversations with you. She has to have her privacy."

"I know, I just want what's best for her," said Riker. "With any luck, we'll be gone in a few days, but she'll still be here, struggling with all of this. If I know you're taking over, I'll back off and stay away from her."

"Do you really think there's a problem with the ship?" asked Troi, now sounding more like a concerned command officer than a ship's counselor.

With a glance at the bubbling, turquoise tanks which surrounded them, Riker decided that they were alone. He leaned toward Deanna's ear and whispered, "I checked around, and her shop is always behind schedule. It's usually double the estimate, and she's already told us it would be a week. Of course, with supply lines down and all the shortages, it's quite possible that she's not at fault for the delays."

"Can't you get a status report?"

Riker frowned and tried to find the Saurian lungfish in a display of coral. "I did, and there wasn't anything on it. Shana won't speak to me, ever since the night when . . . well, she got very upset. If Geordi or Data were here, I'd send one of them down, and we'd know in ten minutes if everything was all right. Otherwise, I'd have to go over her head to the CO, and I don't want to do that. She simply won't talk to me."

"What makes you think she'll talk to *me?*"

"Because you're a sweetheart." He gave her his most winning smile.

Troi groaned, looking deeply troubled. "Of course I'll have a conflict of interest, too, because I'll be trying to get our ship released."

"I've tried to get the Admiralty to follow through on the mission," muttered Riker, shaking his head, "but the Kreel system is now in enemy hands. To even find Data's shuttlecraft would require a miracle, and I don't want to think about how hard it will be to spot that beacon. If we don't go soon, nobody will be there for the captain and the others."

Troi nodded grimly. "So we need the *Enterprise* back ASAP, no matter who stands in our way."

A phaser blast jarred the *Cook,* a small personnel shuttlecraft with one aboard, a unique artificial life-form modeled after a human. The android absorbed a number of sensory and digital inputs at once, and he knew that, although his shields and systems were failing, he had enough power left to reach the emerald clouds of the Class-F planet just below him. He was already entering the outer atmosphere, a murky soup of chlorine, chlorine dioxide, and chlorine oxide. The chlorine was poisonous and corrosive, and the chlorine dioxide was explosive—so he didn't expect many visitors.

Data knew that the planet's atmosphere could damage his hull, but he didn't have much choice with a Jem'Hadar attack ship on his tail. He had two photon torpedoes on his specially outfitted shuttle-craft, but he was determined to save them. This lifeless planet, called SK-739-6 in Starfleet nomenclature, would prove to be either his sanctuary or his undoing.

Another plasma blast grazed his hull, its energy dissipating in the thick atmosphere. The tiny craft shuddered and grew hot during re-entry, but Data never took his attention off his instruments. He didn't bother to stare in awe at the pea-green swirl of gases as a human would; instead he searched his instruments for solid ground amidst the shifting bogs. If the Jem'Hadar had been foolish enough to follow him into this uninhabitable world, then their presence didn't show up on his instruments.

More than likely, they had assumed an outer orbit and would look for life-signs—life-signs they wouldn't find. Twice before, he had eluded the Jem'Hadar by escaping to barren planets incapable of supporting life. Because Data wasn't a biological being, they had a hard time tracking him once he shut down the shuttle-craft systems. With any luck, they would assume he had crashed and died.

Unfortunately, every relocation like this brought an inevitable break in his search for the subspace beacon, the distress call from the away team. It also took Data farther away from the Kreel system, where he had left the *Enterprise*. If he could only find solid ground on this unfriendly planet, then he would once again set up his long-range scanner array to monitor the distant Badlands. If he couldn't, then he would have to make a break for it, before the Jem'Hadar attack ship could summon reinforcements.

After that it would be another mad dash to another unlikely refuge, with the resultant delays. The lives of Captain Picard, Geordi, and a dozen others—plus the survival of the Federation—depended upon his attention. He had to land and set up the array soon.

The android headed north to the polar icecap of the planet, peering from his instruments into greenish-yellow gloom. Although he found no level terrain, he was encouraged by the sight of white hills and plateaus pushing up through the clouds. It wasn't real ice, of course, but frozen chlorine dioxide, which should be solid enough to support the shuttlecraft.

Almost an hour of searching revealed an ice floe that was level and large enough for him to attempt a landing. Not wanting to melt any of the surface with prolonged thruster burns—or risk an explosion—he cut his engines several meters off the ground and came in hard with a resounding thud. Data remained perfectly still as the craft's runners melted into the dry ice with disconcerting cracking sounds. For a moment, he expected the ice to break and dump him into an ocean of chemicals, but the floe held the weight.

Data quickly shut down all systems. Geordi would say he was "playing possum." As soon as possible, he would resume his duty . . . and locate his friends.

Chapter Three

THE BADLANDS FILLED the viewscreen of the *Orb of Peace,* looking like a mass of dirty cotton candy filled with giant lightning bugs. Sam Lavelle shifted uneasily in his seat at the conn, trying to forget that the glimmering lights were in reality deadly plasma storms wreaking havoc in a vast dust cloud. He told himself the storms were far, far away, although he didn't know how far away they were. None of the sensors could penetrate the gloom a few meters beyond the ship.

But Ro had said that they were in a safe spot, a bubble, as she called it. No matter how far away they were, the random bursts of plasma were not conducive to relaxation, although they were eerily beautiful.

Finally Sam took his hands off the helm and rubbed his sore shoulder, telling himself that if they were hit by one of those charged bolts, it wouldn't matter what he was doing. In fact, he would rather die that way than be captured by Cardassians. He was sure he couldn't go through that ordeal again.

He heard footsteps, and he turned to see Geordi La Forge striding toward him. The blind engineer no longer sported the VISOR he had worn when Sam served with him aboard the *Enterprise;* instead he wore some kind of implants that covered only part of each eye. They must have been a big improvement, thought Sam, because La Forge had stuck with his VISOR for a long time. The Bajoran earring and nose ridges only made his appearance more bizarre.

"Hi, Lavelle," said La Forge with a friendly smile. "How does it look out there?"

"Weird. How does it look to you, Commander?"

The engineer squinted at the viewscreen and shook his head. "It's nice to know there are some things which look weird to *everyone.*"

"How is everything below?" asked Sam, worried that either Grof or the Romulan had caused an uproar by now.

"We're getting to know each other," answered La Forge. "To that end, the captain is assembling everybody in the mess hall for a shipwide meeting. I'm your relief, because he already knows me."

"Right now?" Sam stood uncertainly.

"Relax, Sam, he's not worried about you. But we've got to see where everybody stands before we make a bunch of plans that we can't carry out."

"Or trust people who we shouldn't trust," added Sam. "I don't know those people very well, except for Taurik."

"That makes two of us." La Forge sighed and took his seat at the conn.

"What's the captain going to do?"

"He'll have to trust his own judgment. Luckily, he's a good judge of character. I think he just wants to get everyone into one room and see how the group meshes."

Sam scowled. "With Grof around, we'll probably chafe instead of mesh."

Geordi smiled and turned to the swirling brown and magenta clouds on the viewscreen. "You'd better go below."

"Yes, sir."

Feeling as if he were invited to a party where everyone would be a stranger, Sam wandered off the bridge and down the spiral staircase. Upon reaching the lower deck, he spotted Tamla Horik and Enrique Maserelli lounging in the corridor outside the mess hall. They weren't exactly holding hands, but their affection for each other was more open than ever.

"Hello, Captain," said the Deltan female with a friendly smile. Although Sam was only a lieutenant, he had been the captain of their late, lamented Cardassian tanker. It was a measure of his crew's respect that a few of them still called him that.

Enrique gave him a grudging nod, and Sam knew that the materiel handler was still angry at him. At the height of their desperation, Sam had threatened to throw Enrique into the brig if he didn't cooperate. Now he regretted those harsh words, but there was no way take them back.

"Hi," said Sam, mustering a pleasant smile. "Ready for the meeting?"

"Why do we need a meeting?" muttered Enrique. "We know where the artificial wormhole is—let's send in the fleet and take it out."

Tamla gave Maserelli a smirk, as if he were a bit of a

simpleton. "It isn't that simple. *We* know about it, but I don't think the rest of the Federation does."

"They don't know anything!" growled a voice. Sam and his comrades turned to see Enrak Grof striding toward them from the aft hold. The burly Trill looked as belligerent and argumentative as usual, ready to tell the whole galaxy what to think.

He stopped in the corridor and regaled them. "They don't understand what we *built* out there! They don't know its value—they only want to *destroy* it. Although I doubt if they know how to do that."

"Oh, I believe that Captain Picard has a plan," countered Sam, not at all certain if that were true.

"A plan to take out a magneton collider ten kilometers long and protected by a fleet of ships? With an *unarmed transport?* If he does, he's the greatest military genius in the world. I think his plan is to get us all killed in a pointless display of hubris."

Lena Shonsui stuck her head out of the mess hall door and glared at Grof. Even though her arm was in a cast and one eye was blackened from a recent injury, the diminutive woman was livid. "Shut up, Grof! The last thing we need is to listen to a traitor like *you*. You're lucky we don't beam you into a bulkhead!"

The Trill whirled and glowered at her, his wiry beard and eyebrows bristling. *"You!* You nearly got us all killed, and your ineptitude cost us two probes!"

"At least I didn't kill hundreds of people to promote my own glory!" When Lena took a step toward Grof, his hands balled into fists.

Sam quickly jumped between them, holding Lena back with one hand and Grof with the other. He could feel Grof backing off, but the middle-aged woman charged forward, wanting blood. He finally had to hold her scawny shoulders with both hands. "Lena, calm down. He's not worth it!"

"What's going on here?" demanded a stern voice, and they all turned to see Captain Picard, accompanied by Ro Laren, Taurik, Jozarnay Woil, and the Romulan, Hasmek. The Romulan had a smirk on his face, as if he were amused by this internal bickering.

"She tried to attack me!" bellowed Grof, pointing at his accuser.

"I never did, but I should have!" shouted Lena, struggling to get past Sam and reach the Trill. Despite her flailing arms, he held her at bay.

"Attention!" snapped Picard in a voice which brooked no opposition. Everyone—even Grof—stood stiffly in place. "I don't care what you've been through, what you've done in the past, or how much you hate each other, on *my* ship, you will maintain order and behave like Starfleet officers."

"I'm not—" began Grof.

"Silence!" roared Picard. "Professor Grof, you will behave like a member of this crew, or you'll be held in irons. Do I make myself clear?"

Sam had never seen a Trill's spots blanch, but Grof's spots grew several shades lighter as he gulped and backed away. "Yes, sir."

The one-armed Romulan narrowed his eyes. "I suggest you do as the captain says. I have found the captain to be a formidable foe who will stop at nothing to maintain control."

The captain looked slightly contrite at his outburst, but still angry and determined. The war had even taken a toll on him, thought Sam; he couldn't imagine such an outburst coming from the Captain Picard he knew aboard the *Enterprise*. Of course, this wasn't the

Enterprise—this was a ragtag crew of desperate people in the middle of a horrendous war—a war which none of them were likely to survive.

The captain tugged on his rust-colored Bajoran tunic and motioned toward the mess hall. "Now will all of you please have a seat."

Sam stepped back, letting the others file in ahead of him. First went Lena Shonsui, the short-tempered transporter operator. Once upon a time, before the war, Lena must have been a level-headed professional, but now she was barely sane, driven over the edge by hatred and abuse. She was followed by Tamla and Enrique.

Sam looked away from them to watch Grof trying to engage Taurik in whispered conversation. The Vulcan listened politely to whatever the Trill was saying, but he had no comment as they filed into the dining hall. Jozarnay Woil followed them, and the friendly Antosian was also banged up with various superficial injuries. Taurik had done a good job of first-aid.

Hasmek, the one-armed Romulan, strolled in next, followed very closely by Ro Laren. Sam had a feeling that Ro had been assigned to be the Romulan's shadow, jailer, and bodyguard until further notice. Lucky devil.

This left Sam alone in the corridor with Captain Picard, who did not look at all pleased with his makeshift crew. "How did you keep them in line?" he asked softly.

"I told them we would escape and reach freedom," answered Sam, thinking what a crock that had been.

"Freedom is still our goal." Picard motioned to the doorway.

Sam entered the now-crowded mess hall and took a

seat at a table with Taurik and Grof. The Trill immediately leaned across the Vulcan's chest and whispered to Sam, "Did you hear him *threaten* my life? A Starfleet captain!"

Sam gritted his teeth. "Grof, the sooner you learn that this war isn't a game or a research project, the better."

"Quiet, please," sniffed Taurik.

They folded their hands in front of them and sat as attentively as schoolchildren while Captain Picard frowned in thought.

"I know none of you want to be here," he began. "We don't particularly want to be here either. We hoped to discover that the artificial wormhole was only a rumor, a myth. But it's very real, and so is our predicament.

"You know what the artificial wormhole means to the war—victory for the Dominion, the end of the Federation. You've been prisoners of the Dominion, so you can imagine such a fate for every man, woman, and child in the Federation. Not a pleasant picture, is it?"

He looked pointedly at Grof. "We all know the value of scientific progress, but that progress cannot come at the cost of a far-reaching civilization which has only sought peace and cooperation. We don't deserve to be snuffed out like a candle flame, and we won't let it happen."

The captain turned to Ro Laren. "Sometimes our search for peace has led us to make mistakes—to trust people we shouldn't have trusted, to appease those without honor. We can't undo the past, but we can save the Federation and billions of lives here and now."

The Romulan responded by pounding on the table

with mocking applause, shocking everyone with his audacity. "Nice speech, Captain, but you'll need more than words to accomplish your goal."

"That's enough," Ro warned Hasmek.

Picard held up his hand. "No, let him speak. I'll let everyone at this meeting speak his mind. I want to hear your thoughts now, before we set a course that can't be reversed."

"Thank you, Captain," replied the Romulan. "I can always speak my mind, because I don't fear for my life. By all rights, I should be dead already. I think the captain has chosen to keep me alive as an object lesson. He will stop at nothing, which is the very attitude he must have to succeed. The problem is, I think he considers me to be a more reliable crew member than some of you."

"This is too much!" roared Grof. "Now we must be lectured by Romulan spies! If the captain had a fleet of two hundred ships with him, I would be a lot more impressed. Despite his lofty ideals, I don't think he can destroy the artificial wormhole even if he *wanted* to!"

All eyes turned to Picard, expecting another explosion, but the captain leaned forward and asked, "Professor, with your vast knowledge of this machine, would it be fair to say that we don't have to destroy the entire magneton collider to render it useless? Already the Dominion has been delayed due to the lack of Corzanium to finish one small part. A machine that big must have other weaknesses, too. Could a pinpoint strike or an act of sabotage in the right place shut them down for a while?"

"Yes, I suppose it could," admitted Grof, scratching his unruly beard. "The most critical part of the collider is the magneton accelerator. If you could do enough damage to the accelerator control room, you would shut them down for quite some time."

Picard now appealed directly to the Trill. "Professor, we've already accomplished the most difficult part of the mission, getting behind enemy lines. Although we're not a fleet of ships, we are poised to make a pinpoint strike. We have all the knowledge we need among the people on this ship, and I can tell you, Professor, I have overcome difficult odds before. I'm not against science—I'm against hordes of Dominion ships pouring through an artificial wormhole. If we can delay them just long enough to turn this war around, maybe we can capture the collider intact. That would be my preference."

Now Sam saw where the captain was headed. *Brilliant.* By appealing to Grof's tremendous ego and love for his creation, he was winning him over. Given the serious look on the Trill's face, he was giving the compromise strong consideration. Theoretically, it would save both the Federation and his work.

"Captain," declared Grof, "I believe this is a plausible beginning, but it's only a beginning. I still have to put my notes about the project on an isolinear chip and make sure it gets to safety. That is my price for participation. I'm the only one who can tell you how to find the accelerator control room. You can be assured that none of the prisoners worked on it—only myself and the Vorta engineers."

Lena Shonsui rubbed her eyes. "I can't believe it— he's *bragging* about being a collaborator! What a piece of work."

"The past is over," said Picard evenly, looking in turn at everyone in the room—Hasmek, Ro, Grof, Taurik, Sam, Tamla, Enrique, Woil, and Shonsui. "Forget about everything that happened before we arrived at this place and time. We have *one* mission—to shut down that artificial wormhole before it can open. If we have to make compromises and jump through hoops, then we will.

"Professor Grof, why don't you go back to the bridge and work on your notes. You might also tell Commander La Forge about the accelerator room being our specific target. He's the best engineer in Starfleet, and I'm counting on you two for most of the planning. Meanwhile, Ro and I will consider our options and how best to get your notes back to the Federation."

"Fine," said Grof, rising to his feet. "I'm glad you've decided to see reason, Captain. See all of you later." Looking smugly satisfied, the Trill marched out of the mess hall.

Captain Picard's face did not reveal his feelings, but Sam knew exactly how he felt. He had also bent over backward to cajole and pacify Enrak Grof, and he knew what a demoralizing task it was. With his arrogance and intelligence, that pompous Trill had managed to enthrall the Dominion and hold two crews hostage. But psychologically Picard was his better. First, he had scared the hell out of him, then he had appealed directly to his monster ego. It was a combination that was apparently working; Grof was now on board with the rest of them.

"Does anybody else have anything to say?" asked Picard. He looked around the room, and his eyes settled on the quizzical Antosian. "Go ahead, Mister Woil."

"Sir, I was wondering, if we do pull this off, how are we going to get back to the Federation?"

Picard motioned to a tiny porthole. "Out there is the *Enterprise,* waiting for us to release a coded subspace beacon. They know our approximate location and will get here as quickly as they can. The *Enterprise* can outfight and outrun Dominion ships."

"Thank you, sir," said Woil with a smile. He promptly sat down.

After that reassuring if optimistic response, tension seemed to ebb from the room. Relieved laughter and whispered conversations filled the stale air. It was clear that nobody wished to continue the heated confrontations—it was time to move on.

The captain must have sensed the change, too, because he rose to his feet and smiled like the host at a party. "The food replicators are operational. Shall we have a drink and a bite to eat?"

"Yes, sir!" came a chorus of responses.

The captain strode to one of two food replicators in the mess hall, and a short line formed at the other. Sam waited patiently for his turn; he was still in shock that Picard had managed to tame this unruly crew so quickly. Maybe they really could save the Federation, and maybe the *Enterprise* would arrive in the nick of time to whisk them away to safety. They had accomplished miracles before.

"Tea, hot," said Picard to the replicator. When nothing happened, he repeated, "Tea, hot."

Still nothing happened.

"Water," he ordered with a concerned look on his face. When no glass of water materialized, he pointed to Enrique at the other food dispenser. "Try yours."

"A glass of water," ordered Enrique. Nothing happened. "Toast, dark." The receptacle remained empty, despite all the indicators being lit.

Now Ro Laren studied the replicator with concern. "It's been working fine for a week. Maybe the voice-recognition system is down." She pushed some buttons, and Enrique did the same at his slot. Even with manual input, nothing issued from either of the replicators.

Captain Picard looked more concerned than ever, leading Sam to conclude that these two replicators were their only source of food and water, two substances that had to be hard to come by in the Badlands.

Picard turned to Ro and said, "Would you please relieve Mr. La Forge and send him down here. We already have to find a way to get Grof's isolinear chip back to the Federation—perhaps we have to find food and water as well."

"We still have some fresh fruits and vegetables in the hold," said Ro, heading toward the doorway.

"I'll check on them," offered Enrique, following her out.

This incredible meeting, which had inspired so much confidence, was ending with fear as the prevalent emotion. Worse than being captured by Cardassians and Jem'Hadar was the prospect of dying of thirst and hunger. They couldn't drink reactor coolant.

It was left to the Romulan, Hasmek, to sum up the feelings of the suddenly silent gathering: "You can't fight, or do much else, on an empty stomach."

Deanna Troi haunted a corridor on Starbase 209, wondering how she had gotten talked into this. Of course, all Riker had really asked her to do was talk to Shana Winslow, but that had proven to be a much more difficult task than she had expected. Three messages for Captain Winslow had gone unanswered, and her aides were extremely protective of her. They had been downright surly to Deanna.

Somehow they must have known the real purpose of her efforts was to pry the *Enterprise* out of their grasp, and they weren't going to relinquish the pride of the fleet until they were good and ready. *It has been less than a week,* she told herself. *They aren't behind schedule . . . yet.*

More troubling was the fact that Shana Winslow seemed to be hiding from everyone but her work associates. Once she had taken Will as a companion, she ought to have enjoyed his company more than one night, especially with a war going on. The way she had ducked him since seemed odd. Still Troi wasn't ready to assault a Starfleet captain in public over a romance turned sour. Instead she was waiting to talk to the starbase's chief counselor, Dr. Arlene Bakker.

A door whooshed open, and Troi tried to appear as if she just happened to be strolling in that direction. Dr. Bakker, a tall, dark-skinned woman with a regal bearing, stepped into the corridor and nearly bumped into the Betazoid.

"Counselor Troi," she said with surprise. "How are you?"

"I'm fine, Counselor. And you?" They began to walk slowly down the corridor.

Bakker sighed. "Hectic, crazed—I feel as if I'm being pulled in ten different directions. Are you going to the conference on time management?"

"I was thinking about it. Do you mind if I tag along?"

"Not at all. I don't know how much of this will apply to us, but we can always be hopeful." The tall woman took a right in the corridor and strode toward the turbolift. Troi skipped to keep up.

"You're doing a good job here," said Troi with sincerity.

"Thanks. We all appreciate how you, Dr. Crusher, and her medical staff have been helping us out. It's been a big morale booster, I can tell you."

"Has morale been a problem?"

Bakker rolled her eyes. "You've been out at the front, so you wouldn't know. It's not easy to sit in the bleachers and watch the casualties roll in. A lot of us feel as if we should be at the front—doing more— even though we know we're needed here."

"You're not missing anything," replied Troi.

"I know." Bakker strode into the turbolift, and Troi meekly followed. "Level thirty-eight," ordered the base counselor, and the door whispered shut.

"Of course," said Troi, "people on a starbase have a lot of stress to deal with, because everyone thinks they're miracle workers."

"No kidding."

"Especially in positions such as . . . head of the repair section."

Bakker nodded sagely. "Commander Winslow has it worse than any of us. If you knew what that woman has gone through."

Troi made her face an inquisitive blank. "Like what?"

"She lost her husband, her ship, and quite a bit of her own body. She's been a line officer, so she's really torn, thinking she should still be out there. And she's expected to work more miracles than anybody on the base, all with shrinking resources."

"Does she come to see you much?"

"She used to," answered Bakker with a quizzical expression. "But not for a while. Probably no time."

The door slid open, and the taller woman led the charge out of the turbolift. Troi could see a gathering of people around a set of double doors at the end of the corridor, and she knew she wouldn't have much more time alone with Arlene Bakker.

"Counselor," she said, holding out a hand and stopping the woman in mid-stride. "I have something to ask you."

Bakker stopped, looking mildly impatient. "Yes?"

"Somebody has asked me to talk to Shana Winslow," blurted Troi. "He says she's been acting erratically."

The other woman crossed her arms and frowned. "She's *my* patient."

"I know. But she happens to be in charge of *my* ship, and she's romantically involved with *my* friend. I don't want to step on any toes, but you've admitted that she has many issues to deal with and has stopped coming to see you."

"Yeah, that's true," grumbled Arlene Bakker. "I've been meaning to call her and reschedule. And it might not be a bad idea to have some . . . telepathic assistance." Troi smiled, not bothering to correct the assumption that she was a full Betazoid.

Bakker sighed. "I'll schedule her for an appointment as soon as possible, and I'll let you sit in. But you've got to promise not to push when it comes to your ship."

"I can't promise that," answered Troi, "but I promise not to be the first one to bring it up."

"Okay. Now go on about your business. You don't have to pretend to be going to this conference anymore."

"I can always learn a thing or two about time management," said Troi with a smile. "And I don't get to talk to a colleague very often."

"Come on." Bakker grinned and guided her down the corridor.

Captain Picard sat forlornly in the mess hall of the *Orb of Peace,* watching Geordi La Forge take apart the second of two food replicators. He had sent everyone else away, because their expressions were simply too depressing. After all they had been through, they could still be horrified by the prospect of starving to death.

Fortunately, Ro had determined that they could produce water in the hardware replicator, but only small quantities. Most of the fresh fruits and vegetables in the hold were still edible, too. Picard thought he had struck a bad bargain way back at the Cardassian farming colony, trading exotic fabrics for produce. But at this point, the deal could turn out to save their lives.

La Forge picked up a singed circuit board, studied it, and shook his head. "I can't believe this. We gave the replicators a complete diagnostic before we left the *Enterprise.* They were working perfectly."

"What happened?" asked the captain.

"It could be normal wear, but on two replicators at once? The phase-transition coil chambers are shot, along with the waveguide conduits."

"Can you fix it?" asked Picard hopefully.

"I don't think so. I don't have the tools or the parts."

The captain leaned forward, not anxious to ask his next question. "If it's not a normal failure, do you think it's sabotage?"

The engineer let out a long sigh. "If you wanted to wipe out the food replicators, you couldn't pick two better subsystems to disable. On the other hand, I don't have much experience with this equipment—it might've been caused by a power surge or something."

But there could be a saboteur in our midst, thought Picard grimly. *And there's no shortage of suspects: a Romulan spy, a Dominion collaborator, a Maquis officer, and six escaped prisoners who should be under psychiatric care. And all of them had unlimited access to this room.*

"For the time being," said the captain, "let's keep these suspicions between ourselves. It may be a coincidence, and we don't want the crew members to turn on each other."

Geordi tossed the burnt circuit board onto the table and said, "Maybe one of them already has."

Chapter Four

THE *ORB OF PEACE* SLICED cautiously through a gritty kaleidoscope of pink, salmon, and mauve dust clouds. All around the transport, glimmering bursts of plasma lit the way like warning lights in a foggy tunnel. Normal space was empty and dead, while the Badlands was alive with crackling electricity, pulverized debris, and sudden death.

Seated at the conn, Ro was able to make slight course changes to avoid the worst of the storms, but her efforts were illusory. There wasn't really anything she could do if one of those errant bolts of plasma hit them—they'd be turned into just another swirl of dust and gas. "You are at the mercy of the Prophets," declared one of the platitudes above the viewscreen, and that surely was the truth.

The bridge seemed crowded, although there were

only four other people present: Captain Picard, Sam Lavelle, Taurik, and Hasmek. Grof and the others had joined Geordi in engineering, or they were taking a sleep shift.

She hated having to trust that murderous Romulan, Hasmek, but he had just spent several months in the Badlands. His knowledge was more recent than hers, a fact which he had been quite smug about. In this shifting morass, the most current data was the best.

Hasmek seemed very certain about the location of Death Valley, a fabled region of derelict ships. Ro had heard of Death Valley but had never seen it. Although it had once been a Maquis hideout, it was considered too dangerous to visit by the time she had joined. She had heard that scavengers often visited the place, looking for spare parts and salvage. If so, they might find people willing to trade water and food, or deliver an isolinear chip to the Federation.

Still, Ro didn't quite believe in Death Valley. How could a bunch of lost ships exist in this diabolical dust cloud? If they had been caught in the plasma storms, there would be nothing left of them. Something else must have destroyed them, but what? There were mysteries piled upon mysteries in the Badlands, concluded Ro.

She could have navigated them back to the OK Corral, but no one was anxious to see Shek and Rolf again. As long as Ferengi and Orion pirates were using the wrecked space station as a base, they would pick an alternate destination. She sure hoped that Hasmek knew what he was talking about.

Ro glanced back at the Romulan and noted with satisfaction that he was tugging nervously on his empty sleeve. Confident at first, he had leaned over her shoulder, suggesting course changes. Now he stared at the viewscreen, and the flashes of plasma glinted off his dark, almost frightened eyes.

Only Taurik appeared unaffected by the deadly gloom. Stationed at tactical, the Vulcan hardly took his eyes off his instruments. Occasionally he glanced at the viewscreen and regarded it as if it were an Impressionist painting. In a way, with his implacable calm, Taurik seemed the most insane of all of them.

"Ro," said Picard with concern, "this is awfully dense. Do you think we should stop and check our position?"

"No, sir," answered Ro. "We don't have much to gain by stopping here. Our chances of getting out are better if we keep moving."

"Do you think we could find a bubble?"

"No idea, sir. I suggest you ask our Romulan friend—he's the one who guided us here." Having diverted attention onto Hasmek, Ro took some time to study her readouts. Long-range scanners weren't working at all, and short-range scanners were working only intermittently. There seemed to be no end to the floating quaqmire.

The Romulan shifted uneasily under the gaze of the bridge crew. "Captain, I can assure you we are headed for the right coordinates. I came here with Shek only four weeks ago."

"Through *this?*" asked Sam Lavelle, who was seated at the science station.

The Romulan sighed with exasperation. "We approached from another angle, but that doesn't matter. It's *here!* Captain, if you think I want to be vaporized by one of these plasma bolts, you're mistaken. If we weren't out of food and water, we wouldn't have to risk—"

Something odd suddenly appeared on Ro's instruments, but Taurik spoke first. "Captain," said the Vulcan, "I am picking up a high concentration of metallic residue at a heading of two-two-eight-mark-seven-nine."

"That's it!" exclaimed Hasmek with relief.

"Are you sure it's not a false reading?" asked Picard.

"Not entirely," admitted Taurik. "The scanners have been erratic."

"I'm changing course to intercept," declared Ro, not waiting for Captain Picard to make a decision. After all, she was still captain of this vessel, and there was no point in waiting. Any destination was better than plowing endlessly through this morass, waiting for their luck to run out. A concentration of metal could be Death Valley, a Cardassian patrol, or worthless space junk. At this point, it didn't much matter.

The Romulan leaned over her shoulder and said, "The pirates had a Capellan helmsman who had a sixth sense about the plasma storms, but you aren't bad, Captain Ro."

"Anybody who can navigate through this is more lucky than good," answered the Bajoran. "We're starting to get a visual."

On the viewscreen, ghostly shapes began to emerge from the swirling layers of dust. There were sleek fins, graceful nacelles, and plump hulls, tilted at odd angles. They looked like a pod of whales captured in three-dimensional quicksand. A plasma burst illuminated the clouds from behind, and the ghostly fleet was silhouetted for a brief instant, making them look like tombstones.

Ro could see lights twinkling near the closest ship.

As she steered them closer to Death Valley, she saw that the lights were in reality crystalline clouds which glimmered like spun sugar as they floated among the somnambulant ships. When plasma bolts exploded behind them, the crystal clouds glistened with every color in the spectrum. They looked like sundogs, those halos of color that Ro had seen in snow clouds over the mountains of Bajor.

"All stop," ordered Picard.

Ro instantly obeyed the order, thinking that they should investigate before plunging deeper into this eerie cemetery. Although the ships looked fairly intact, there was the nagging question about what had disabled them. It couldn't be the plasma storms, which left nothing behind but memories. These spacecraft looked like a child's toys that had been casually discarded, then gradually engulfed in multicolored spider webs.

"Why were all these ships abandoned?" asked Picard, giving voice to the question on everyone's mind.

Hasmek shook his head. "I don't know, but it looks to me as though a great battle took place here—a long time ago."

"No," said Sam Lavelle, frowning at the bizarre scene on the viewscreen. "It looks like they came here for a meeting, a big conference, and something killed them all. The question is, what?"

"With any luck, we won't be here long enough to find out." The captain stepped forward and stood close to the conn. "Well done, Ro."

"Thank you, sir."

He looked back at the tactical station. "Mister Taurik, can you identify any of these ships?"

"Negative, Captain. The *Orb of Peace* has a limited

computer library of ship types. They are not common Federation or Cardassian vessels. I would be curious to explore one of the better-preserved crafts."

"Me, too," replied Picard with a slight smile. "Let's hope that someday we can safely return to the Badlands with a scientific team. For now, we have to find food and water. Are there any functional ships, any salvagers, in the area?"

The Vulcan shook his head. "No, sir, but the range of our scanners is extremely limited. There could be a large fleet two thousand kilometers off starboard, and they would register as metallic residue. We do, however, appear to be in a bubble, with all ship's systems functional again."

"Can we use transporters?" asked Picard.

"For short distances, perhaps," answered Taurik. "Chief Shonsui would be the expert on that."

"Right. Set the sensors to look for water in any of those vessels. Conn, ahead one-tenth impulse. Take us on a slow sightseeing tour, Ro. Stop whenever you feel our safety is threatened."

"Yes, sir." She piloted the boxy craft into the graveyard of lost ships at even less than one-tenth impulse. Up close, the clouds of crystals seemed like white carnations sprinkled upon the graves. The ships appeared fantastical and extremely advanced—uncomfortably akin to Dominion ships. They had an otherworldliness about them that wasn't due entirely to the fact that many of them listed at right angles to the others.

It was also clear that the magnificent ships had been cannibalized to a large degree. Holes were punched indiscriminately in hulls; deflector dishes, hatches, and outer equipment had been ripped off; and some nacelles, tail pieces, thrusters, and impulse engines were gone, leaving gaping wounds in the once-proud vessels.

After a somber tour through the silent graveyard, Taurik reported, "Captain, I would say the age and condition of these vessels precludes finding any fresh water or useful supplies. It will take approximately thirty hours to scan every vessel from stem to stern."

The captain scowled. "I don't suppose we could find a working replicator, or parts that we could use?"

The Vulcan raised a doubtful eyebrow. "Every vessel shows signs of being forcibly entered many times. One would have to assume that they have been successfully ransacked."

"Keep looking. I'm going to engineering." The captain wasn't entirely successful in hiding his disappointment as he strode off the bridge. It wouldn't take long for a starving crew to mutiny, especially this crew in this place.

"Captain!" called Sam Lavelle. "I've picked up something!"

"Water? Another ship?"

"No, sir—*life-signs,* four of them." Sam stared at his console, then pointed toward the viewscreen. "Yes, sir—that large gray ship on the left. It sort of looks like an old New Orleans-class starship."

"A bit," allowed Picard. "Is there life support on that ship?"

"I'll check." Sam squinted at his readouts and frowned. "That's weird—now I've lost the life-signs! I could have sworn they were there."

"Parts of that ship are shielded from sensors," added Taurik. "It is difficult to say whether this is accidental or deliberate."

"Mysteries upon mysteries," muttered Ro, gazing

at the behemoth of a wreck, silhouetted against the glittering scrim of the Badlands.

"Any gravity? Any oxygen over there?" asked Picard.

"None in the sections I can scan," answered Taurik.

"All right, Lavelle, you're with me on the away team," ordered the captain. "We'll take La Forge, too. You don't have a problem with space suits and gravity boots, do you?"

"No, sir," answered Sam, rising to his feet. "I've worn them a lot lately, working for the Dominion."

"Ro, you have the bridge," said Picard as he strode into the corridor.

Deanna Troi knew immediately why Will Riker had been attracted to Commander Shana Winslow. Not only was she an interesting, intelligent woman, but she was a study in contrasts. With her prosthetic limbs and slight limp, she was both fragile and strong. She had a pleasant face, yet a severe haircut, and Troi could see the determination in her violet eyes. After spending most of her life in space, Shana Winslow had been grounded, literally and figuratively. She seemed like an ethereal creature, a fairy with broken wings.

Dr. Arlene Bakker conducted her into her private office and motioned toward the Betazoid. "This is Deanna Troi, a colleague of mine. I hope you won't mind if Counselor Troi sits in on our session—she has unique talents and experiences."

Winslow gave her a curious look and a bemused smile. "Counselor aboard the *Enterprise,* aren't you?"

"I am," admitted Troi with a nod. "I didn't expect you to know who I was."

Winslow's face grew tighter. "I saw your name on the officer's roster, and I know you've been trying to see me. But in what capacity, counselor or bridge officer?"

"Friend of a friend," answered Troi with what she hoped was a nonthreatening smile.

Now Captain Winslow's face hardened into a mask, and she turned to the base counselor. "I don't really appreciate this, Arlene. I'd prefer to see you alone, not to be ambushed by a stranger."

"We didn't mean to ambush you," explained Dr. Bakker. "Counselor Troi might be able to help you, and she won't be on the base much longer."

"Nothing you say to me will leave this room," promised Troi. "I'm really only here to help you."

"You're not worried about your ship or Will Riker?" asked Winslow incredulously.

"I'm a realist," answered Troi. "It does no good to worry, but it often does a lot of good to talk. I'd like to know why you're so defensive about Will Riker and the *Enterprise*."

Winslow gave a sharp intake of breath, and Troi was certain that she was going to bolt from the room. Instead she stood her ground. "You're the Betazoid—you tell me."

"That's not the way I work. But I've studied your files and drawn some possible conclusions. I'd say you were charmed by Will until he got too close, until he saw you in a moment of weakness. Because of your injuries and your immense responsibilities, you're very careful not to let anyone see you as weak or helpless. But we all feel that way sometimes, especially now, in the middle of a war.

"It may be your survivor's guilt that won't allow you to enjoy any happiness, even a fleeting wartime romance. You might be suffering a post-traumatic stress disorder, which will only get worse if untreated. I don't know why you're so secretive about your work, but it could be control issues, or feelings of inadequacy. You don't want anyone to second-guess you—"

"That's enough!" snapped Winslow, her calm facade breaking apart. "I don't need some half-baked mind-reader telling me what's the matter wth me!"

"I don't read minds. And nothing's the matter with you," countered Troi. "You're normal. Everything I mentioned is perfectly normal for a person in your circumstances. It's your reaction to these issues which is abnormal."

Winslow's eyes drilled into Troi's. "Don't try to cause me problems. I have backing in high places, and my staff is loyal to *me!*"

"I couldn't make half the problems for you that you are making for yourself," Troi replied evenly. "I'll be happy to leave and say no more about this, if you'll work with Arlene."

"There's no time!" snapped Winslow. "Do you want your ship back or not? It's finally moved to the top of the heap, the parts are in, and I've put my best team on it. That's the best I can do, and all the counseling in the galaxy won't make the shortages any better. Now I've got to go." She turned to leave the room.

"Talk to Will—he might be good medicine," advised Troi, pushing her own feelings of jealousy to the bottom of her heart. *I would.*

Winslow froze for a second in the doorway, and her shoulders stiffened as she shuffled out. The door snapped shut behind her with a resounding thud.

"It's worse than I thought," muttered Dr. Bakker. "So what should we do?"

Troi sighed and shook her head. "It's your call

whether to report her to the CO—you have grounds. But I don't think causing an uproar will help her, or get the *Enterprise* repaired any faster, so I'm against it."

"I don't even know Will, but I wish she would talk to him," grumbled Arlene Bakker.

Troi sighed. "Yes, he's the right man for the job."

Sam pulled on the helmet of the Bajoran space suit, which was beige colored and much lighter weight than the industrial suit he had worn during his labors for the Dominion. Of course, this suit was designed to be used with magnetic boots for getting around a ship that had lost artificial gravity and life-support. The Dominion suits had been designed for extended spacewalking and manual labor, which were more strenuous pursuits.

He looked at Captain Picard and Geordi La Forge, both of whom were checking the controls on their sleeves. At the transporter console stood Lena Shonsui, looking once again like a calm professional, not a wild-eyed instigator. He couldn't blame her for hating Enrak Grof. Plus Lena had been the only one to know his final escape plans from the tanker, and she had kept his secret under stress. He would always respect her for that.

"Chief, any life-signs on our target?" asked Picard, his amplified voice sounding hollow in Sam's helmet.

"No, sir. The bridge reports no life-signs on that craft, but we've found a wide-open space where I can beam you down."

"I saw life-signs," insisted Sam. "Right about in the middle."

"Don't worry, Lieutenant," said Picard's calm voice, "we're not putting much stock in sensor readings taken in the Badlands. We have to start looking for supplies, and it might as well be here. Double-check your oxygen levels."

Sam, Geordi, and the captain adjusted the controls on their sleeves, and Picard stepped onto the transporter platform. Sam spent a few moments fighting an uncomfortable sense of *déjà vu,* as if he were once again joining a Dominion work gang, hounded by cruel Cardassians who would execute him for working ten seconds too slow. The more he thought about it, the more he liked getting revenge against them—even if this was a suicide mission.

Last onto the transporter, Sam had barely found his spot when Picard motioned to Shonsui and ordered, "Energize."

Sam turned to see the unfamiliar transporter room dissolve into utter darkness. A moment later, the lights on their helmets and wrists flicked on and pierced the abject gloom with narrow beams, revealing a massive chamber. Every arm movement sliced through a curtain of dust, which hung in weightless suspension. Sam was reminded of his grandpa's barn and the way dust used to float in the beams of sunlight that slipped through the old wooden slats.

As his feet began to leave the deck, the captain's voice echoed in his helmet: "Activate boots."

Sam grabbed his wrist and turned on the magnetic boots. His feet returned to the deck with a sudden impact that shuddered through his body. Lifting his feet heel to toe to deactivate the pressure plates, he learned how to walk all over again.

La Forge was already taking tricorder readings. "Captain, I'm getting what looks like the residue of a temporal phase inversion."

"Time travel?" asked Picard.

The other helmet turned slowly back and forth. "Hard to say. Maybe it's a phase shift, and not that long ago either."

"Is it localized in here?" asked Sam. His voice sounded odd, echoing in his own ears.

"It's like it's all around us," said Geordi. "Wow! I know you two just see darkness and our light beams, but I can see spots of energy and heat that shouldn't be here. It should be as empty as space, but it's not."

Sam consulted his tricorder and concentrated on finding the two things which had brought them here: life-signs and water. At the farthest range of the Bajoran tricorder, about eighty meters away, a single life-sign appeared briefly, then vanished. He put the reading into flash memory.

"I saw it again—a life-sign."

"Which way?" asked Picard.

Sam pointed into the blackness, and the captain bravely led the way. La Forge fell in behind him, but he was still gaping in every direction, seeing things in the darkness that Sam could only imagine. From his cautious crouch, it was clear that the engineer wasn't comfortable in this place, and Sam couldn't blame him. The way the life-signs kept appearing and disappearing was very spooky.

The captain walked vigorously forward, pushing off heel to toe. Without warning, he bounded upward, waving his arms to keep his balance. His voice sounded in Sam's helmet: "I've lost gravity."

La Forge let go of his tricorder, which floated in the darkness, as he reached up to grab the captain. Still several meters behind them, Sam just tried to train his light beams on the rescue, and he saw what had happened: There was a hole on the deck where a chunk of metal had broken away. That chunk of the deck was still attached to Picard's magnetic boots, broken off when he bounded upward. Essentially, he had fallen up a hole.

La Forge pulled the captain back down to a sturdy part of the deck, and it took them a few seconds to reestablish artificial gravity. While Geordi retrieved his tricorder, Sam checked his again. To his utter amazement and delight, he began picking up the other object of their search—water!

"Commander La Forge," he said excitedly. "Do you see water on the deck above us, at about sixty meters?"

Geordi quickly checked his tricorder, then nodded his helmet forcefully. "Yes, only it wasn't there a little while ago."

"That is a problem," admitted Sam.

"How do we get up there?" asked Picard, craning his helmet back and gazing at the ceiling.

Sam shined his light at the distant surface and spotted a hatch where one shouldn't be. "I think that's the deck above us, and we're walking on the ceiling," he said. "This ship is upside-down."

"Or we're upside-down," replied Geordi. "Take your pick."

"This place reminds me of a funhouse I used to visit at the Pier in Jersey," added Sam.

"All right," ordered Picard, "bend your legs and get ready to push off. Then turn off your boots and jump upward. We should be able to get enough momentum to float to the deck above us."

With his recent experience, Sam gave the best push and was the first one to reach the distant deck. Still weightless, he worked his way along the surface with his hands until he reached the hatch, which proved to be open already. Hanging on to it, he extended his hand and pulled the captain and Geordi to the anchor. After positioning their feet on the deck, they reactivated their boots and were soon walking again. Sam pulled the hatch open all the way, and the trio slowly climbed down to the lower level.

Standing in a dark, nondescript corridor, Sam and Geordi took more readings and determined that the water must have collected in a conduit about forty meters away. Captain Picard again took the lead, but he was now very careful about where he put his feet.

After several moments of cautious travel, they reached a part of the corridor that appeared to be blown inward, as if with a careless grenade. *Some people can't be bothered to look for hatches,* thought Sam. They had to crawl along the bulkhead to avoid the rubble around the hole, but they finally squeezed past. Sam shot a beam of light into the cavity and saw the remains of tables and equipment, most of which was reduced to wires snaking from the bulkheads.

About ten meters from their goal, La Forge gave a startled cry. Sam caught up with him and found him staring at his tricorder. "It's gone! The water is gone."

"Impossible," said Picard, "it was just here in this conduit." He shuffled forward in his magnetic boots and bulky suit until he reached a sturdy conduit embedded in the bulkhead.

From a distance, the conduit appeared to be intact, but when Sam and Geordi reached the spot, they saw that it had gaping holes, ringed with ancient corrosion. *That conduit hadn't held water for a thousand years,* thought Sam, despite the false alarms on their tricorders.

"I don't get it," muttered Geordi. "It clearly registered water. It's like small sections of this ship go in and out of phase, on sort of a random basis. I think this ship is too dangerous to explore."

"I'm inclined to agree," said Sam.

"Take down these coordinates," ordered Picard. "If water shows up here again, I want to retrieve it . . . in however few seconds it exists."

"Yes, sir," responded Geordi, entering data into his tricorder.

Something possessed Sam to look up, and he did just in time to see a white-suited figure at the far end of the corridor. "Captain!" he croaked, pointing toward the apparition.

Picard and La Forge looked up just as the mysterious figure turned and disappeared into an open cabin door. At least that's what *appeared* to happen.

"Did you see him?" asked Sam eagerly.

"I'm reading a life-sign," said Geordi, his voice sounding none too confident as he studied his tricorder.

"I saw *something,*" agreed Picard. "A glimpse of light, a wisp of fabric—"

A loud chirp in their helmets made them all jump, and Sam could barely hear the captain's voice over his pounding heart. "Away team," snapped Picard.

"Captain, this is the bridge," said Ro's voice. "Another ship has shown up, and they're hailing us."

"Who are they?"

"Talavians, in a freighter. I think they were hiding on the outskirts of Death Valley, watching us. I've told them that our captain is on his way to the bridge."

Picard looked reluctantly down the dark corridor,

where the white apparition had vanished. Sam could tell that he didn't want to leave this haunted derelict with so many questions unanswered, but he had his priorities.

"Away team to transporter room," ordered Picard. "Three to beam back."

Chapter Five

JUDGING BY THE FIGURE on the viewscreen and glimpses of crew in the background, the Talavians were a scrawny, yellow-skinned race with prolific amounts of wiry red hair sprouting from unlikely parts of their bodies, such as ankles, knees, elbows, and shoulders. Yet the captain's head was bald and covered with tiny purple veins. He wore a tight leather vest and knee-length pants, which showed off his exuberant hair. Picard wondered if the hair had evolved to protect their bony joints and keep them warm.

The Talavians hardly looked like saviors—neither did their beat-up freighter—but Picard and the crew of the *Orb of Peace* were in no position to question help from any quarter.

"Hello," said the captain with his most magnanimous smile. "I am Captain Boothby, and this is a joint Romulan-Bajoran scientific mission. We are very glad to have your company."

The skinny Talavian guffawed. "Scientific mission? Oh, come now. Nobody would take the risks necessary to get to this place unless they were desperate. Or hiding. And what kind of name is Boothby for a Bajoran."

"It's a nickname," muttered Picard.

"Why are you really here?" asked the Talavian.

"Food and water. We have problems with our replicators."

"You won't find anything here, unless you are very brave." The transmission was momentarily scattered by streaks of interference and dithered pixels.

"Can we talk in person?" asked Picard. "On my ship?"

"I couldn't possibly join you on your ship without entertaining one of your crew here," answered the Talavian with a sly smile. *He's requesting a hostage,* thought Picard. Given the way they were treated by Rolf and Shek on their last trip to the Badlands, Picard could appreciate this precaution.

"Perhaps your first officer, with whom I spoke." The Talavian seemed to leer at Ro.

"How about *two* of my crew?" asked Picard. "And you can bring an aide with you."

"But no Romulans," said the Talavian nervously. "They provoke uneasiness in my crew." He was clearly referring to Hasmek, who stiffened his spine and stuck out his chin.

"In five minutes, we'll do a mutual exchange," said Picard. "We look forward to meeting you." He nodded to Taurik, who ended the transmission.

"You can't trust them, Captain," hissed Hasmek. "At best, they're smugglers, and they'd cut all of our throats for a strip of latinum. We ran them out of the Romulan Star Empire."

"I used to see them on Bajor and Terek Nor," said Ro. "I mean, Deep Space Nine. That was before the Federation came. They're a client world of the Ferengi, and they have about the same scruples. I remember that some Talavians have strong religious beliefs, but that doesn't keep them from cheating you."

Picard looked around the room, and his eyes settled on Sam Lavelle. The handsome lieutenant rose to his feet and smiled gamely. "Am I about to volunteer for hazardous duty again?"

"I'm afraid so. You and Ro report to the transporter room. Go unarmed, but keep an extra communicator badge hidden on you. Be careful what you eat and drink."

"It will be hard to turn down food," said Sam, rubbing his concave stomach.

Five minutes later, Captain Picard stood in the small but tasteful transporter room of the *Orb of Peace*. Ro and Lavelle stood on two of the transporter pads, and the other four were empty, awaiting their guests. Outside in the corridor, Woil and Maserelli stood by with phasers in their belts, just in case.

The captain wasn't planning on doing anything that might disturb his guests, unless they were disturbed by requests for food. Hasmek and Taurik would stay on the bridge with Geordi, so as not to cause the visitors undo concern about Romulans.

"Signal received," reported Lena Shonsui.

"Lower shields and energize." With some trepidation, the captain watched the departure of two of the few people he trusted on this starcrossed vessel. After they disappeared altogether, two thinner, taller figures materialized on the opposite transporter pads. The captain mustered his most charming smile as the hirsute, yellow-skinned Talavians came aboard.

"Welcome to the *Orb of Peace.*"

The one to whom he had spoken on the viewscreen stepped down first, followed by his obsequious aide. "Ah, Captain Boothby, I am Captain Fraznulen of the *Star Redeemer.* This is my scribe, Leztarlen."

Fraznulen looked around at the subdued appointments of the Bajoran ship and smiled. Then his ruby eyes rested upon Lena Shonsui at the controls. "Captain, you have a human on board. This is not wise in this sector, at these times."

"We are a scientific vessel with a crew composed of many races, and we have proper clearances," Picard assured him.

"Then why don't you leave here and seek help from the Dominion?" asked the Talavian snidely. With the unusual tufts of hair on elbows, knees, and shoulders, he looked like a preening rooster.

"It's taken us some time and trouble to get to the center of the Badlands," answered Picard. "We know there's a war going on, and we don't want to get caught in it. Mainly we don't want to lose time by going out and trying to come back in. Do you have working replicators?"

Fraznulen bent his scrawny neck forward. "Do you want to buy a replicator?"

"That would be the best arrangement," answered Picard, "although I don't know about your prices. Out here, you don't have much competition."

The Talavian laughed. "I like you, Boothby. Do you

have someplace we can sit down? I know you're woefully short of supplies, so I have taken the liberty to bring some Rigelian ale." He snapped his languorous fingers, and his assistant hurried forward with a clay bottle.

"Thank you," replied Picard. As he led his visitors toward the door, he heard scuffling sounds in the corridor, and he rushed forward to see Enrak Grof, trying to push his way past Woil and Maserelli. "Grof!" he snapped. "What's the meaning of this?"

"I had to see him! I had to see our visitor," insisted the Trill. "Can he take my notes back for us?"

Picard moved forward, grabbed the burly humanoid by the shoulders, and ushered him down the corridor. With a smile plastered to his face, he whispered, "Professor, if I need you, I'll call you. Right now, I need you in engineering."

"With La Forge on the bridge, I suppose you do. All right, I'll go, Captain—but don't forget to ask him."

"I won't." Picard took a deep breath to calm himself, then he returned to his guests. "I'm sorry. A captain's job is never done."

"Oh, I know, one crisis after another." Fraznulen spied the mess hall and hurried in ahead of the captain. He was studying the stripped-down replicators as Picard and the other Talavian caught up with him.

"Yes, this is most unfortunate," agreed their guest. "What could have disabled your food dispensers and left the rest of the ship intact?"

"I wish we knew," answered Picard. "Can you help us?"

"First, the ale." He uncorked the clay bottle and took a swig from the open neck, without the benefit of a glass. Then he passed the bottle to Picard, who lifted it to his mouth. He recognized the ale's distinctive bouquet, so he screwed up his courage and took a swig. Relieved that the ale tasted as expected, he handed the bottle back to Fraznulen. The scribe, Leztarlen, was not offered a drink, nor were any members of Picard's crew, who watched curiously from the corridor. This wasn't exactly the opulent welcome Picard had received aboard the pirate ship, but he hoped the results would be better.

Fraznulen sunk into one of the hard chairs and put his skinny legs up on the table. Red hair popped from his knees, looking like tassels of Indian corn. "All right, Boothby, I believe you are what you say you are, which means you probably have nothing to trade."

"Can we appeal to your altruistic nature?" asked Picard, holding out his hands.

The Talavian guffawed loudly. "Do you think we have come all this way for nothing? Oh, no, Captain, I can assure you we have a goal. There are treasures here, if you know where to look for them. We can't cover all these ships by ourselves, and we need help."

Picard frowned. "We only searched one vessel, but we found it very dangerous . . . and strange."

"Oh, yes, the Valley of Death is haunted." The Talavian nodded sagely and stared at Picard. "Sightings have been getting more numerous in the last few seasons, driving most visitors away. You can't get a Cardassian to come here anymore, and they used to be our primary diggers."

He quickly added, "We revere ghosts, and this is a place of legend for us. These ghosts are very special, because they leave gifts for the living."

"Gifts?" asked Picard doubtfully.

"Yes, they bring gifts from the spirit world. I've seen them." He narrowed his eyes at Picard. "And so have you. I can always tell when someone has been blessed by the ghosts."

"We took some inexplicable readings," said Picard guardedly. "Since you know what we want, we should find out what *you* want. We must have something to offer in trade."

Fraznulen pointed to the open doorway and the gawkers in the corridor. "Can we have some privacy?"

"Yes." Picard slapped the wall panel, and the door slid shut.

The Talavian leaned forward and craned his bald head downward. "Captain, we revere the objects which the ghosts transport from the spirit world, and we collect them . . . reverently. If we could find a ship's plaque, officer's insignia, or some such, it would pay for this entire trip."

The captain scowled. "You are talking about objects which—to us—appear to be coming from an unknown phase shift. And they don't stay here long. It could be very dangerous."

"I didn't say it wouldn't be," answered Fraznulen frankly. "We have come here for the gifts from the dead, nothing else. If this work is unacceptable to you, then we have nothing to talk about."

"We only need a few days' worth of food and water," insisted Picard. "If you could look in our cargo bay, or in our hardware replicator, maybe you could find—"

The Talavian cut him off with a sneer. "Bajoran technology offers us nothing we don't already have. If you want food and water from us, you will do precisely what I ask of you."

"You'd leave us here, without food or water?" asked Picard with disgust.

Fraznulen grinned and motioned into space. "The

benevolent Dominion is all around you, and I'm sure they would be happy to help you, if you need charity. *Food for work* is what I offer, with no questions asked. Every time you retrieve something, we'll give you commensurate food and water. If you find something really valuable, we'll give you a new food replicator."

Captain Picard sighed heavily, not wanting to risk his crew on a salvage operation. But what choice did he have? Without food and water, the mission was over, and they faced either capture, mutiny, or slow death. Time was running out, and this was the best offer they were likely to get.

"We need a down-payment to start," said the captain.

The Talavian gave him a predatory grin, then rose to his feet. "This is just the accord I was hoping to reach with you, Captain. You have chosen to search a worthy vessel—we call it the *Ancestor*. You may have a knack for this work after all. We shall be nearby, searching the *Soul Maker*."

The gangly alien took a swig of ale from the clay bottle and offered it to Picard. The captain had searched archaeological sites before, but this was different. This was plunder. He had never imagined he would be pushed to such extremes, but then these were extreme circumstances. With a scowl, the captain took the bottle and sealed the deal.

"There's one more thing that has to be part of the arrangement," said Picard. "We have Professor Grof's isolinear chip, which needs to be delivered to the Federation. It contains scientific notes."

"Scientific notes?" Fraznulen laughed and pried the bottle from Picard's hand. He took a long drink, then wiped his thick lips on his hairy shoulder. "I can't tell if you are a ghost-hunter yet, Boothby, but you are certainly a gambler."

Ro Laren paced the confines of their gilded cage like a neurotic lioness. Although it was a luxurious boudoir with a sumptuous bed, silk pillows, a plush loveseat, and a coffee table covered with luscious-looking food, it was also a cage. Ro understood that the Talavians were holding them as insurance for their captain's speedy return, but she didn't like to be confined. From the moment she had realized that the outer door was locked, she had complained.

It didn't help that Sam Lavelle was imprisoned with her. He had listened with sympathy to her tirade, but he looked annoyingly comfortable, stretched out on the bed, nibbling from a plate of sliced meats and pungent cheeses.

"I thought the captain told us not to eat anything," she snapped at him.

"Neither one of us needs to go on a diet," replied Sam with an insolent grin. "One thing I've learned in this war—you eat good food when you have the chance. It may not be there tomorrow, or *you* may not be there tomorrow."

Ro scowled and continued pacing. "You still look too comfortable."

"I've had more practice being a prisoner than you have . . . at least recently. Maybe the captain knew what he was doing when he sent us over here. I think he was giving us a break."

"This is hardly my idea of relaxation," muttered Ro, pacing anew.

"I would say that the Talavians are a bit at a loss. They didn't know what to do with us, so they put us in here. It's the best cell I've been in lately, and the chow beats Cardassian prison cuisine by a parsec."

With a disgruntled look on her face, Ro sank into the loveseat and grabbed a roll from a basket full of elegant pastries. She munched on it hungrily, but with a scowl on her face.

Sam sat up and crawled across the mattress toward her. Lolling on the edge of the bed, he wiped his mouth with a silk napkin. "Relax, I doubt the captain's meeting is going to last very long. He just wants to get what he came for, and get out of here. We'll probably be back on the ship in a few minutes."

She grunted. "Sorry, but I don't like being told what to do. It's a problem I have with authority."

"You must have been a natural candidate for Starfleet," said Sam with some amusement.

Ro smiled in spite of herself. "Let's say I was taken with the ships, the adventure, the grand ideals, and the chance to get out of the squalor I was living in. It took me a while to realize that Starfleet played politics, too, and I was always going to have a problem with authority. In the end, you have to answer to yourself and no one else. I can do that now."

Sam nodded sagely. "I know what you mean. Until this war—and my capture—I was like Grof. It was always *my* career, *my* promotion, my chance to kill Cardassians. I was selfish. After I was captured, I began to think about about other people and how I could help them. My happiness doesn't depend on career advancement and recommendations anymore."

He laughed and looked at the chunk of cheese in his hand. "Food and clean underwear are enough."

Ro chuckled. "Well, we have one of those items on board the *Orb of Peace*."

"So, how did you become captain of that noble vessel?"

Ro grimaced, remembering Derek and all the friends she had lost when the Dominion cracked down on the Maquis colonies, and she couldn't bear to answer his question. "It's a long story, and not a happy one. Like you, I thought I was escaping from the war—but I wasn't."

"I'm sorry," said Sam with genuine concern. "You've got to go some distance to get away from this war."

He looked frankly at her, and what he was thinking was very transparent. Sam was very appealing, now that he had gotten some cynicism to go with his good looks. A wartime romance might ease the pain for a few minutes here and there, but she could feel herself withdrawing emotionally, isolating herself from the threat of more pain. If Sam's motto was "Live for today, for tomorrow we may die," hers was "Live like a hermit, for tomorrow we may die."

She rose from the loveseat and began to pace again, sorry that she had to hurt Sam's feelings. It was flattering that he wanted her . . . and so human.

The door banged open with a sudden thud, causing her to reach for a phaser pistol she didn't possess. Two gangly Talavians stood in the corridor, looking sheepishly at them. It wasn't that Ro felt unwelcome or unworthy; it was the opposite. Their hosts seemed to be embarrassed to be in their presence, as if *they* were unworthy. Ro wondered whether the Talavians might have a rigid caste system, with few members of the crew who were actually entrusted to talk to them.

"Wait here. Going home. Good-bye." The taller of the Talavians bowed respectfully.

When Sam began to fill his pockets with tasty

morsels of food, Ro couldn't help but smile. A moment later, she felt the familiar tingle as a transporter beam rearranged her molecules.

She and Sam materialized in the transporter room of the *Orb of Peace,* where a grim-faced Captain Picard stood waiting to greet them. As Ro stepped off the transporter platform, a crate of food packets appeared behind her.

"We're getting some food," said Picard, "but it has come at quite a price. I've called a meeting in the mess hall to explain what we have to do to earn it."

Will Riker sat at lunch with Jack Torrance, Beverly Crusher, and two other marooned officers who were waiting for their ships to be repaired. Their tactical meeting had been abruptly canceled, and the brass had all left the starbase suddenly. So Captain Torrance, commanding officer of the base, had taken them to the officers' lounge for a previously delayed welcome lunch.

The tastefully appointed dining room was empty, except for two tables filled with young ensigns, who kept glancing nervously their way. They also kept looking at the chronometer on the wall, as if they were about to ship out any moment.

"So what's up?" asked Dalivar, captain of the *Earhart,* after an elderly Saurian had taken their orders. "Where is everybody going?"

"There must be something cooking," agreed Beverly. "A big offensive?"

"Nothing official," said Jack Torrance with a helpless shrug. "All of you would have gotten orders to ship out, too, if your ships weren't banged up."

"Speaking of which," said Riker, clearing his throat

uncomfortably, "we need to talk about getting our ships out of the shop."

"Quit being such a worry-wart," said Torrance with a reassuring smile. "I've seen the progress reports, and they're almost on schedule."

Almost on schedule, Riker muttered to himself. *That could mean anything!*

"Never mind that," said Dalivar, leaning forward. "What's going on? Are we finally going to retake Deep Space Nine?"

Torrance shrugged noncommittally. "Like I say, I can't say."

"You might as well tell us," grumbled Riker. "It's not like we're going to go anywhere."

"Secrets must be kept," said Torrance, the smile fading from his youthful face. "For example, Commander Riker, you can't tell us anything about the secret mission that Captain Picard is on."

"Trust me, you wouldn't like to hear about it," said Beverly with a bittersweet smile.

Although Riker wanted to complain loudly and often about the *Enterprise* being held up, he knew this wasn't the time or the place. He still didn't want to lodge an official complaint against Shana Winslow, but his gut feeling told him that he had to do *something.* Deanna hadn't told him anything about her meeting with Shana, but he could read Deanna fairly well. The look on the Betazoid's face had announced that she considered the meeting unsuccessful. And nothing had changed.

He had sent an intermediary, and it hadn't worked out, which made him feel even lousier. Things were happening all around them, and they were sitting on their rumps. Will felt like asking if they had a spare ship he could borrow, but he already knew the answer: they didn't.

He managed a smile. "So . . . we can't talk about the war, and we can't complain about our ships being docked. What *can* we talk about?"

"Who's going to win the Solar Cup this year?" asked Jack Torrance. "I like Luna's chances."

"Are they still having the games?" asked Beverly.

"Last I heard," answered Torrance. "Have to keep the morale up back home."

Riker heard other voices, and he turned to see a few more officers enter the vast dining hall. He caught sight of a gray-haired, blue-skinned Andorian standing in the doorway, as if scanning the room for people he knew. When the Andorian didn't see anyone he recognized, he headed on his way, but Riker had recognized *him*. He was one of the technicians who worked for Shana Winslow—in fact, he had written up the *Enterprise*'s work orders the first day.

With nervous energy pulsing through his veins, Riker rose to his feet. "Excuse me, I'll be back soon. There's something I've got to do."

"Go ahead," said Beverly with an encouraging smile. "I'll hold up our end of the conversation."

The other men looked a bit surprised by Riker's abrupt exit, but none of them said anything. This was wartime, and everyone was entitled to be moody.

Will dashed out of the officer's lounge into a busy corridor. He spotted the Andorian immediately, thanks to his height and long antennae; he was striding down the corridor, making good speed on his long legs. He turned left into another hallway, and Will charged after him before he vanished completely.

Thankfully, this side corridor was not as crowded

as the first one, and Riker was able to catch the taller alien. He wished that he didn't have to ambush the man in the hall like this, but he had tried every regular channel, except for going over Shana's head. The Andorian was going to regret his little stroll through the base.

"Lieutenant!" called Will, recognizing the Andorian's rank by his collar pips.

He turned to look down at Riker with implacable blue eyes. "Yes, Commander?"

"I'll be blunt—what's taking you people so long fixing the *Enterprise?*"

The Andorian scowled, turned, and walked away. Riker chased after him, feeling like a little dog nipping at the heels of his much bigger playmate. "I can order you to talk to me."

"Yes, you can," answered the Andorian, not slowing down. "But that doesn't mean I will. Go through channels."

"I've tried all the channels," insisted Riker. "I'm being stonewalled."

The Andorian stopped and stared down at him. "Everyone wants their ship, and everyone wants it now. But we know where these ships are going after they leave our shop—back to the front—back to a mismatch against Dominion warships. *Your* life depends on the job *we're* doing now, just as surely as if we served on your bridge crew."

"Look, I don't need a lecture," snapped Will. "I just want my ship back, so I can rescue my crew behind enemy lines."

The Andorian snorted. "Don't you understand, Commander, that if it hadn't been for *us,* you would be shipping out *today,* going in the opposite direction. You actually have a guardian angel looking out for you, and you don't even appreciate it. That is all I will say."

Riker gazed thoughtfully at the Andorian, who turned and walked away. This time, he let him go. If what he hinted at was even remotely true, then Shana Winslow was purposely delaying repairs in order to keep from sending people out to die. This attitude could permeate her whole staff, who were in a unique position to play God. Juggling their limited resources, they could give thousands of officers a few extra days before they faced combat again.

Perhaps she had done him a favor by making sure the *Enterprise* wasn't caught up in the big push, but she had also broken numerous regulations. On the other hand, it would be difficult to prove she was doing anything but her job, given the circumstances.

With a start, Riker realized that he was more concerned about Shana than he was the *Enterprise*. If all he wanted was his ship, he would just go over her head and let the chips fall where they may. A court-martial wouldn't be out of the question.

But he couldn't do that to her, not without trying to help her first. *She has to see me!* He tapped his combadge and announced, "This is Commander William Riker to Commander Shana Winslow, Repair Division."

A male voice answered. "This is Ensign O'Reilly, Repair Division. I'm taking all nonessential calls for Commander Winslow."

Riker sighed, thinking that he had been called worse than "nonessential." Politely he said, "It's really urgent that I speak with her."

"I'll relay the message, sir."

"Isn't there any way you can put me through to her?"

"No, sir. I'll relay the message: Commander Riker wishes to speak to Commander Winslow."

"What about the status of the *Enterprise?*" Riker cut in.

"I'll relay the message," answered her aide. "Repair Division out."

Will grumbled under his breath, thinking that no admiral in Starfleet was as insulated as Commander Shana Winslow. *So I can't reach her, and I won't go over her head—but maybe I can go* under *it.*

Five minutes later, Riker strode onto the operations center of Starbase 209 and sat down at an empty auxiliary console, of which there were at least a dozen. The regular operations crew gave him a few glances, but they didn't question him. With satisfaction, Riker realized that they knew who he was—the mystique of the *Enterprise* extended deeply into Starfleet.

"Computer," he said, "patch me into the Library Computer Access and Retrieval System of the *U.S.S. Enterprise-E* in dock nine. Command authorization: Riker delta-two-six-one-eight." While the ship was tethered to the starbase, starbase computers had control of it. Maybe Shana's people could dodge him, but he had the authorization to query the ship directly. Everything was stored in the central data base, if one knew where to look for it.

"Access granted," reported the base computer.

Will inserted an isolinear chip into the slot on the console and waited until the computer popped the data back at him on the screen. It was the manifest of parts which needed replacement or repair, as generated during their initial consultation with the base technicians.

"Computer," he continued, "compare the items on

this manifest with the list of parts which have been requisitioned and received by Repair Division for the *Enterprise-E*. Compare both of those lists to the parts which have actually been installed in the *Enterprise-E* during the last ninety-six hours. Report discrepancies."

After a few moments, the computer's feminine voice reported, "There are twelve discrepancies between the manifest and requisitioned parts list, all involving gel packs that are not in inventory. A substitute has been ordered. There are 2,679 discrepancies between the manifest and the parts which have been installed."

They've got the parts, but they're way behind putting them in, concluded Riker. "Assemble a report with these comparisons," he told the computer, "and send it to Commander Shana Winslow, compliments of Commander William Riker."

"Yes, sir," answered the computer noncommittally.

On the derelict starship, named *Ancestor* by the Talavians, Sam Lavelle activated his magnetic boots and slammed feet-first onto the deck. All around him, five space-suited figures gradually found their footing, as they probed the darkness with their narrow beams of light.

Most of them unfolded tricorders, while La Forge set an object shaped like a pyramid on the deck. He pushed a button, and brilliant lights bathed the cavernous chamber, chasing the shadows to the most remote corners. With ease, Ro Laren lifted a weightless phaser rifle and used her laser-beam scope to scan the room.

To Sam, the room appeared to be a cargo hold, or perhaps a shuttlebay. If there had once been shuttlecraft or supplies stored here, they were long gone, replaced by drifting debris and broken ceiling panels. And dust—the dust of ages seemed to hang all around them.

Four of them, Sam, Geordi, Taurik, and Enrak Grof scanned the ship with tricorders, while Ro and Tamla Horik stood guard with phaser rifles.

"Commander La Forge," said Sam, his voice echoing in his own helmet. "Do you see any of those anomalies you saw before?"

"Do I!" exclaimed Geordi. "It's like there are ghosts made of air and heat—and power fluctuations. They last a while, too. I should start timing them—that data might come in handy."

"Does anyone see any of those artifacts we're looking for?" asked Ro.

"No," came several disappointed responses.

"All right," ordered Ro, "Lavelle and Taurik, you're with me. We're going to make our way to the bridge. Geordi, you and the others stay here and take readings. Remember, if you find an artifact, slap a combadge on it, activate it, and step away. The transporter chief will beam it into the stasis field."

"I wish we had someone competent at that post," muttered Enrak Grof.

"We want to keep this channel open for crucial data, not idle conversation." Ro glanced at Taurik, and the Vulcan pointed to a distant doorway that had been blasted open. The two of them were off immediately, and Sam shuffled behind them, checking his tricorder for phantom readings.

They were soon plunged back into eerie darkness, broken only by the lights on their helmets and wrists. Sam could feel a thin layer of sweat inside his suit, and his breathing pounded in his ears. It wasn't exertion or the clumsy boots that caused his heart to race, it was the pervading gloom, broken only by bizarre readouts on his tricorder. Even Taurik was speechless as he stared at his hand-held device.

"What are you seeing?" demanded Ro. Sam glanced down, letting Taurik reply.

"There are indications of unusual substances and energy sources," reported the Vulcan, "including life-signs of unknown origin. There are so many, in fact, that it is difficult to say where we should begin."

"Pick one," said Ro, gripping her phaser with her heavily gloved hands. "The nearest—or the most recent."

Taurik chose a direction and plunged down the dark corridor. Sam purposely hung back and let the Vulcan and the Bajoran lead the way. He had already seen the ghosts on his previous visit with Picard, and they hadn't. So they got the honor.

His path illuminated only by the wavering beams of light, Taurik found a low hatch that was hanging open on one cracked hinge. Without a moment's hesitation, he ducked into the hidden quarters beyond. To Sam, it looked like a cave in there, and he glanced down at his readings to see a mixture of gases: carbon dioxide, nitrogen, and oxygen, in barely breathable amounts. There was *air* in that room, where there shouldn't have been any atmosphere.

Sam followed Ro through the hatch. He heard her gasp, and he peered over her shoulder to see Taurik aiming his light beam at a corner of the room. When Ro added her beam, they could clearly see a pocket of air—it was quivering like a giant soap bubble. Inside this apparition, there were shining fixtures rising from an elegant slab—faucets, sinks, beakers, and burn-ers—which existed nowhere else in the stripped room. It was as if they were watching a window into the past, a ghostly peepshow.

With extraordinary presence of mind, Taurik reached into the pouch on his belt, pulled out a spare combadge, and squeezed it. Holding the badge firmly, his hand reached through the air bubble and affixed it to the nearest unattached object, a purple beaker with a yellow thong around its elegant neck.

While Sam watched this supernatural encounter, he didn't see the sudden pulses on his tricorder. When a hand reached out from the ether and grabbed his shoulder, he yelled and pitched forward, practically crashing into Ro. Taurik was coming fast from the other direction, trying to get away before the transporter kicked in, and they almost bumped into each other. Fortunately, the magnetic boots kept them upright, but weightless momentum turned them into rag dolls.

"Watch it!" growled Ro.

"Behind us!" While Sam grappled with Ro's encumbered body, he tried to twist around to find the intruder. A chubby beige creature bounded into the room.

Sam's gasp was wiped out by amplified laughter, which boomed in his ears. "Oh, did I startle you?" asked Grof with undisguised mirth.

"Why didn't you tell us you were coming?" snapped Ro.

"Oh, I didn't know if it was *crucial* enough for me to use the comm channel," sneered Grof.

"Why did you leave La Forge?"

He shrugged. "I thought we were proceeding quite well with the search of that large room, but La Forge and I disagreed about something or other. So I went off in search of you."

"Were you trying to take over?" asked Sam.

"Well, of course I made a few suggestions," answered the Trill huffily.

Sam could hear Ro take a sharp breath, but before she could unload on Grof, a scratchy voice cut in: "Transporter room to away team. Looks like you've got something there and it's stable."

"Congratulations!" exclaimed Grof. "I've got a power reading down the corridor here. I'll check it out."

With lumbering footsteps, the Trill disappeared into the darkness. Taurik shouldered past them in pursuit, leaving Ro and Sam alone in the darkened room. He shined a light in the direction of the gases, but the elegant fixtures and marble-like counter were gone. The dust that hung all about them was the only testimony to the former splendor of the laboratory.

Through her mask, Ro glared at him, as if to say "Nice move."

Sam could only point to his tricorder and the four life-signs about twenty meters straight overhead. Ro shined her light across the ceiling and found an access tube in the corner that was missing its hatch.

"This is Ro to the away team," she announced. "We seem to have split up into three groups now. I'm with Lavelle, going up one level. Grof and Taurik have kept going down the central corridor. Geordi, you and Horik are still at base, right?"

"Yes, sir," answered the engineer. "You know, Ro, doesn't this remind you of that time when you and I—"

"Yes," she admitted, knowing exactly what he was talking about. Once, when a cloaked Romulan spy had gotten loose on the *Enterprise,* she and Geordi had been out of phase and unable to interact with anyone, except one another. On this ship, it was like everything was out of phase—long dead, yet long-lived.

"Everyone, keep your eyes open, and stay in contact," ordered Ro. "At no time is anyone to be alone. Do I make myself clear?"

"Yes, sir," came the subdued responses.

Feeling rather embarrassed over his jumpiness, Sam took the point. He walked up a vertical bulkhead in his magnetic boots and stopped outside the access tube. Unlike a Jeffries tube, this one was wide enough for only one person at a time to climb, and his boots were going to be a hindrance on the narrow ladder. He turned them off and let his legs float free.

"Ro," he said, "I turned off my boots, and I'm just going to use my arms. It'll be faster."

"Okay," she said. "I'm right behind you." He felt a gloved hand brush his heavily insulated calf.

A moment later, Sam was pulling himself upward with ease through a narrow shaft of darkness. He tried to tell himself that he was actually safer in here, because nothing could leap out and grab him, although that was only a theory. Sam had to push away some unraveled wires and broken circuits at the next hatchway, but he hoisted his weightless body onto the upper level without any problem.

Although Sam would have preferred to float around weightlessly, he activated his boots, anchored himself on the deck, and took more readings. Four life-signs were straight ahead of them, in what appeared to be private quarters. From the remains of tables and chairs, this room could have been a recreation lounge, or perhaps a classroom.

He waited until Ro emerged from the access tube and got her feet under her again. He showed her his tricorder and motioned toward the open doorway. There was a slight glimmering of light within that gloom, and it shouldn't have been there either.

Sam tried to take the point, but Ro insisted—and she was the one with the phaser rifle. He was right behind her, armed with nothing but a tricorder and several extra combadges. When they entered the quarters, they both gasped in unison. Seated at a table, apparently enjoying a meal, were four thin creatures with heads that reminded Sam of refracted crystals. The elegant candles on the table sparkled in their multifaceted faces, and the utensils and glasses gleamed.

The look of horror in the diners' faces was unmistakable. They bolted to their feet and shrunk back in terror from the intruders. One of them ran to a far bulkhead and opened a wall panel, but both he and the panel were on the edge of the phase shift. Gradually he faded away, like the glow on an antique television set.

The others cowered or ran to places outside the range of the ghostly window, and they too disappeared. Ro lowered her phaser rifle, and grumbled, "Remember the mission."

"Right," muttered Sam.

He reached into his pouch and pulled out a Bajoran combadge, which he activated and placed on one of the crystalline candelabras. He had barely pulled his hand back before the candelabra vanished in a sparkling swirl of molecules. A few seconds later, the entire scene began to fade away, but the ghosts hovered in the background with accusing looks on their jewel-like faces.

Aghast, Sam turned to look at Ro, and the air

escaped his lungs in a burst. "Something tells me this isn't right . . . or safe . . . or legal."

"I know what you mean," answered Ro. "Let's just explore and not tag anything else." She looked at the controls on her wrist and added, "We've only got another twenty minutes."

He motioned to the door. "After you."

Geordi was drawn to a ghostly object which few people could have seen, let alone identify. It suddenly appeared like a beacon over the double doors at the far end of the large hold. He had concluded that their base was a cargo hold, but he had no idea what that object over the doors was. It appeared to be a hologram, which looked very distinctive to him, although sighted people were completely fooled by them. At least it had all the signatures of a hologram; perhaps it was a holographic work of art.

To Tamla Horik, it was nothing at all. La Forge could tell, because the Deltan had looked right at the disk without any indication of seeing it. To her, it was just an empty space over the door. The tricorder didn't find the apparition very impressive either— just a weak energy reading.

"I'm going to go look at something," he told Horik.

She lifted her phaser rifle. "Do you need help?"

"I don't think so," answered La Forge, smiling through the faceplate of his helmet. "It's just one of those irregularities that only I can see. I won't leave the room—you stay and keep an eye on our equipment."

"Yes, sir," she answered in a deep, mellifluous voice.

Geordi hurried across the room as quickly as the

clumsy boots would allow. He didn't know how long this holographic image would remain, but he wanted to get a good look before it vanished.

When he was within about ten meters, he perceived it clearly enough to assume that a person with normal sight could see it now. Even then, he didn't think it would look very impressive—a small disk, perhaps a shield, with a shifting holographic design on it.

Wait a minute, thought Geordi, *could this be one of those ship's plaques that the captain had mentioned?* The seal did look official. Then again, perhaps it was a sign saying "Stay out."

He stepped closer, knowing that he should be getting out a combadge to mark it for transport. He had a feeling that this was a self-contained unit, a low-power hologram with a light source small enough to hold in his hand.

Focusing on his infrared vision, Geordi was able to isolate the source of the light in the center of the plaque. Hesitantly, he reached a gloved hand toward the small cube, almost unwilling to disturb it. Clearly this was a work of art, exquisite in its subtlety and detail. The images on the disk depicted an outdoor celebration in which throngs of gaily colored merrymakers danced. He wondered whether they were in costume or actually had crystalline heads of every hue in the spectrum.

As his hand moved closer, he realized that he would not be able to touch it without either climbing or floating half a meter higher. If he were going to go to that much trouble, he might as well tag it for collection. After all, it could mean a new food replicator for them.

Then he paused. *This piece of art may or may not belong here, but it sure doesn't belong on a Talavian freighter.* Geordi wanted to keep his find secret, which he could, but they had to secure supplies as quickly as possible and get back to the mission. This was no time to be overly analytical.

With reluctance, La Forge reached into his pouch for a combadge. The door under the disk was so beaten and bent that he doubted if he could walk vertically on it. Using the controls on his sleeve, he turned off the magnetic boots and bounded ever so slightly upward. After activating the combadge, Geordi waited patiently for momentum to bring his hand closer to the prize. He held out the extra combadge and prepared to puncture the illusion.

As his hand zoomed in, it struck an invisible wall—a force-field—and a potent blast of electrical shock ripped into his body. As he tumbled away, Geordi had the presence of mind to scream before everything went dark.

Chapter Six

"Horik to Ro!" shouted the Deltan. "La Forge is injured!"

"What kind of injury?" Ro shot back.

"He's just floating—looks unconscious! I haven't reached him yet."

Ro reacted immediately. "Away team to bridge. We've got an injured man—La Forge. Request emergency transport."

"Is he bad?" asked Picard.

"We don't know."

"Acknowledged. Boothby out." The channel crackled with static, which was not reassuring to the Bajoran.

"Away team, assemble back at the base," she ordered. "Repeat—break off search and return to base."

"But we're on the trail of a beautiful silver goblet," protested Grof."

"Okay, Grof, we're going to leave you here alone—"

"No, wait. I'll go!"

"Good. Now move it." Ro began to clomp back to the access tube, and Sam followed closely behind. By his body language, he looked eager to get out of this ghost ship, and she couldn't blame him. They deactivated their boots and used their hands to descend head-first to the lower level. It seemed like a good idea to hurry.

Picard knelt on the transporter platform and pulled Geordi's helmet off his head. The engineer was out cold, and Picard snapped his fingers at his assistant, Hasmek, the one-armed Romulan.

"Hypospray of lectrazine!" ordered Picard. "The red one."

Fumbling a little, the Romulan pulled the correct device from the box and handed it to Picard. "I recognize this one."

Picard wasted no time in administering the hypospray to Geordi's neck. He didn't even know if his trusted officer was dead or alive—this was the only recourse he had, so he might as well use it.

"Unnh!" moaned Geordi, a moment before he doubled over and started to cough violently. Picard sat him up and rubbed his back. "Just stay calm— you're alive."

"Get the others back!" he croaked, grabbing Picard's collar. "Get them back! Too dangerous—"

The captain stood up and pressed his combadge. "Away team, assemble and account for everyone. We'll beam you back to the ship in two minutes."

"Yes, sir," answered Ro.

"I've got to talk to our employer," said Picard with a scowl.

Fraznulen, the Talavian captain, looked lustfully upon the objects assembled before him—a jewel-encrusted candelabra, a purple glass beaker, and an exquisite porcelain cup. The tufts of red hair on his ears seemed to twitch with excitement. "You have done well! I knew you would have an affinity for this work, Boothby."

He reached for the sparkling candelabra, which seemed to be studded with rubies, but his hand hit an invisible force-field, which gave him a slight shock. "Ow!" he yelped, recoiling. "What is the purpose of this security? I *own* that object, pre-paid!"

"I rigged that up," answered La Forge, folding his arms. "Something over on the *Ancestor* nearly killed me by delivering a much bigger shock. There are risks you didn't tell us about."

"We also encountered sentient beings," added Ro. "And they didn't seem at all happy about being robbed."

But Fraznulen was ignoring her as he stared at Geordi. "You encountered security devices? What was the object you were pursuing?"

The engineer held his hands apart. "It was a disk about this wide—a hologram, a piece of art."

The Talavian clapped his bony hands together. "This is too great to hope! That *is* a ship's plaque. Can you describe what is on it?"

"No, he can't," answered Picard, cutting in. "We're done with this business, and we just want to leave. If you want these objects, just give us another batch of food and water, and we'll be on our way."

"Oh, no, Boothby, you can't do that!" groaned the scrawny Talavian, wringing his hands. "We can all be *rich* if we secure that plaque. I will trade you *two* food replicators if you will help us get it."

He motioned regally toward La Forge. "I don't know what gifts he possesses—this one with the strange eyes—but if you will loan him to me, I will split the proceeds with you."

Ro could see the captain barely contain his disgust. "Captain Fraznulen, we will not do this anymore. It's unethical and extremely dangerous. It's insane to be mucking about these ships, with parts of them coming and going out of phase."

"Just help me get that plaque, and I'll do anything you want!" promised Fraznulen. "I'll even get that message of yours to the Federation, which is a service you won't find easily in Dominion space. We'll send over the food replicator right now and install it. What do you say, Boothby?"

Picard's lips thinned, and Ro knew he had a tough decision to make. She didn't envy him. "Have you got a way to send our isolinear chip right now?" asked the captain.

"Yes, we have shuttlecraft—*fast* shuttlecraft! I'll send my best pilot with the chip this instant." Fraznulen turned to La Forge. "Just answer me one question, I beg you. What was on this holographic image that you saw?"

He shrugged. "It looked like a festival, a celebration. People were whirling around, dancing, I think."

Fraznulen sighed with rapture. "Yes, yes! It couldn't be better! The *Ancestor* was the mothership, we're almost certain of that."

"Why did they come here?" asked Picard. "And what happened to them?"

The Talavian shook his bulbous head sadly. "There are many theories, but none that pleases everyone. My favorite theory is that they are hiding from someone. Whenever I see people in the Badlands, I assume they are hiding. Why come here otherwise? Maybe an enemy is chasing them—someone from another dimension." He shrugged his hairy shoulders.

"As you say, this a strange place, and perhaps they don't know they have been dead for thousands of years. The ghost worshipers I told you about are sincere—they believe that the ghosts are sending these objects back to the living, because they want us to learn their history. The faithful collect them, and they have instruments that can authenticate these finds of yours."

He shrugged apologetically. "Of course, few of these devout worshipers have actually been to the Valley of Death. They don't know what it's like to go aboard these wrecks. I have to pay exorbitant prices to get anyone to do this work, especially with a war on and the plasma storms closing in. I sense that we haven't got much time left to consort with the ghosts."

"Whether you call it religion or thievery, you know we're stealing from those people," said Ro.

"I don't have to justify our religion to you," answered the Talavian. "When you think of it, our beliefs are not much different than Bajoran beliefs. Don't you worship gods who live in a wormhole? And don't they give you gifts? Your ship is named after one of them."

Ro squirmed at this comparison, because it was uncomfortably close to Bajoran beliefs. She stopped herself from saying more, because the captain had to speak for them.

From a vest pocket, Captain Picard produced a rectangular, jewel-like circuit board, containing the collected wisdom of Enrak Grof. "Here's the cargo; call your shuttlecraft. After you take this away and install the replicator, Mister La Forge will show you where that special artifact is located. No one can predict when it will reappear, but you can be ready when it does."

The Talavian rubbed his hands gleefully. "I can assure you, we will be ready. Thank you, Captain, thank you."

Will Riker walked down the main concourse of Starbase 209. The broad thoroughfare was lined with passenger loading ramps and duty-free shops, all of which were crowded with officers about to ship out. They looked so young, most of them fresh from the Academy on an accelerated program. Were they ready for combat? That was hard to say; no one was truly ready for battle until they experienced it. He was certain that none of them were ready to die, and many of them would.

Will was in no hurry as he strolled the concourse. Unlike the young officers, he had no place to go. His ship was still in space-dock, and its repair status was still a mystery, at least to him. He had hoped that the report he had sent to Shana, documenting that she had been stalling repairs on the *Enterprise,* would force a confrontation with her. It hadn't so far. Now he was resolved to wait until the week was up and the promised deadline was past, then he would have to make an official inquiry.

Overwhelmed by all the people, Riker slipped into an alcove off the thoroughfare and found himself looking at a display case of travel accessories, such as adapters, guide books, and universal translators. These objects seemed to be from a distant era, when people could travel for pleasure and exploration, rather than war. He wondered if life would ever get back to normal . . . or what passed for normal.

"Thinking of taking a trip?" asked a feminine voice.

Will turned to see a slender brunette. Although Shana Winslow was a petite woman, her physical presence was commanding. He hadn't realized until that moment how much he had missed her, even with that daunting scowl on her pretty face.

"Yes, I feel like taking a trip," he answered, "but I'm having a little trouble with my vehicle."

Shana crossed her arms. "I saw that report you sent me. What was the point of that?"

"Just to let you know that I *know.*"

"Know what?"

He lowered his voice as a cadre of young officers walked past. "I know that you've been stalling repairs on the *Enterprise,* and probably other ships as well."

"Why would I do that?" she asked with an angry glint in her eye.

"To keep us from going back into combat."

"That's preposterous!" snapped Shana, speaking so loudly that heads turned in their direction.

Will gently took her real arm and piloted her into the travel store. They took refuge between tall racks of luggage; when a salesclerk approached, Will waved him off.

"You'd have an awfully hard time proving that accusation," muttered Shana.

"I don't want to prove it . . . except to you." He shook his head in amazement. "You don't even know you're doing it, do you?"

"What I'm doing is my *job* . . . with no resources. My staff should be two hundred percent bigger, according to our workload. They're all pulling double shifts, making repairs they're not even qualified to make. And even when we do have the parts, we don't have the *people*. Do you know how hard it is to keep good staff, when they know the war is out *there?*" She pointed accusingly toward space.

Riker gritted his teeth and tried to keep calm. "I've been doing my homework. The *Gettysburg* was in and out of here in three days, with worse damage than ours. The *Targ* was two days, because her Klingon captain made complaints about you right away. Captain Torrance is petrified that you'll leave, because you *are* getting the job done . . . somehow. He can go ahead and pretend that everything is okay with you, but I know differently. This is all part of the nightmares, the chills, all the other symptoms you've been—"

"You've been talking too much to your friend," countered Shana. "I've been doing some homework on you, too, and you're . . . a real Don Juan, aren't you?"

"Don't change the subject," Riker whispered. He glanced around and saw that the salesclerk was busy with customers at the canteen display.

"You want your bloody ship?" asked Shana, her eyes glinting, "I'll give you your bloody ship!" She turned and limped away at such speed that Riker had to run to catch her.

He grabbed her gently by the waist. "Shana, wait—"

"Take your hands off me!" she hissed, pulling away from him.

Now everyone in the store was looking at them, and they were about to drag this quarrel into the crowded concourse. She kept moving toward the door, and he called after, "It's not about my ship—it's about *you."*

Her back stiffened for a moment, then Commander Winslow lowered her head and joined the cheerful surge of young Starfleet officers, headed off to war.

A beat-up, khaki-colored shuttlecraft with red stripes on its hull pulled slowly away from the blackened ships of Death Valley. Almost reluctantly, it left the relative safety of the bubble to disappear into the dense clouds of the Badlands. Distant plasma storms sparkled in the murky heavens, as if welcoming the small craft as an offering.

Picard turned away from the viewscreen and looked pointedly at Enrak Grof. "There goes your precious information, Professor. We have risked our lives and allied ourselves with some unsavory characters for this. Now that we've sent your data to safety, I expect you to cooperate with us fully."

Grof snorted derisively. "Do you really think you can trust the Talavians? What's to keep them from turning around and giving that chip to the Ferengi, or even the Dominion?"

Picard frowned. "We put encryption on it, and we sent it the only way we had. I wish I could guarantee people's honesty, but I can't."

"All right," muttered Grof, "I appreciate the effort.

Yes, I guess you have fulfilled your part of the bargain. As soon as possible, I'll draw a map of the artificial wormhole and the location of the accelerator room. It'll be from memory, but my memory is fairly accurate."

"Make it so," said Picard. "As soon as we conclude our business with the Talavians, we'll finalize our plans."

Taurik at the tactical station cut in. "Captain, it's Fraznulen. He's ready to begin the operation."

"Shall I get suited up?" asked Grof.

"No," answered Picard. "You're too valuable to risk on this. We're sending the minimum number of people to the *Ancestor,* just Ro and La Forge."

"You know, they say that not all the ships that disappear in the Badlands get hit by plasma." Ro Laren looked pointedly at Geordi La Forge and pulled her helmet over her head. She tucked her collar into the suit, zipped it up, and took a step toward the transporter platform. She hated the bulky magnetic boots.

"Where do they go?" asked Geordi.

"Other dimensions, maybe the other side of the galaxy—or so they say."

"I'd believe it," agreed the engineer. "What I can't believe is that the Maquis used to hide out in here."

"This has always been a good place from which to launch an attack against the Cardassians," said Ro. "They're scared of it."

"They have reason to be," countered Geordi. He pulled his helmet onto his head and adjusted the faceplate.

From the transporter console, Lena Shonsui cut in,

"Interference is picking up, and I may not be able to keep the transporter lock much longer. Plus the Talavians have already beamed over and have asked about you."

Ro glanced back at the diminutive transporter chief, who was about her favorite of the rescued prisoners. Shonsui took no guff from anybody and told people exactly what she thought. The Bajoran could imagine herself turning into such a grizzled veteran, if she had stayed in Starfleet long enough, or if she were to live long enough.

"We're ready," said Ro with a resolute nod. She and La Forge stepped onto the transporter platform, and Shonsui worked her console.

"Energize," said Ro, hearing her own voice reverberate in her helmet. She braced herself and gripped the handle of her phaser, without drawing it.

This time, when they materialized in the cargo hold of the *Ancestor*, it was already lit like a grand ballroom by racks of lights. They were surrounded by a score of Talavian technicians in orange environmental suits. Weapons and equipment hung on their backs, and another dozen were armed with weapons already drawn. The amount of equipment and containment pods assembled here was impressive, but it looked to Ro as if they were hunting big game rather than ghostly artifacts.

Geordi looked at her; even partly obscured by his helmet, his expressive face showed his reservations. They activated their magnetic boots before they drifted too far off the deck.

From the assemblage of Talavians, a towering figure stomped toward them, and Ro recognized Fraznulen. He grinned exuberantly behind his faceplate and mouthed something Ro couldn't hear. She adjusted the controls on her sleeve in order to pick up his frequency, and Fraznulen waited for her to finish.

"I said, we're about to make history today!" crowed the Talavian captain. "Have your expert show us the place where the ship's plaque is hanging. We'll take a few readings, and then your job will be over."

Ro wanted to ask why they needed so many armed guards to collect one piece of art, but she didn't want to delay their departure a second longer than needed. She nodded to Geordi. "Tell him where it is."

"All right." The engineer turned slowly to get his bearings in the vast cargo hold, then he pointed to a distant wall. "It's over those double doors."

Waving his hand, La Forge led the way; a contingent of armed Talavians fell in behind him, with Fraznulen urging them along. They were followed by technicians bearing machines and containers of various sizes. Ro was soon forgotten by the entourage, and she trailed cautiously behind them.

Geordi stopped about ten meters away from the doors, which were worn and broken when seen at close range. It looked as if a good shove would rip them from their frames. He pointed to an empty place over the doors. "It was up there."

Instantly, he was surrounded by gangly technicians armed with hand-held devices and strange containers. The Talavians scoured the area, checking and re-checking their instruments, but Ro noted that they never got any closer than a few meters to the spot Geordi had indicated. They were afraid, too.

She moved closer to Fraznulen. "Captain, can we leave now? Our job is done."

He waved impatiently at her, never taking his eyes

off the busy workers. "Let's finish our investigation . . . and make sure you're telling the truth."

"We have no reason to lie," said Ro, bridling at his insinuation.

"Oh, yes, you do. You've told us in no uncertain terms that you don't approve of us collecting these objects, so you could be protecting them. It will only take us a few moments to verify your claims. Excuse me——"

He walked over to his workers, and they conferred on a frequency which Ro couldn't hear. Geordi motioned to her and said, "He won't let us go?"

"Not yet. It seems they have to make some tests."

"It was over that door," insisted La Forge, pointing to the spot. "But it's not there now—no trace."

Ro and La Forge watched the technicians huddling around Fraznulen. Every so often, one of them glanced at Geordi, but Ro had a feeling that they hadn't made a decision yet. She thought about contacting Captain Picard, but what could she tell him? He already knew they were in danger from many different sources. If they had to run for it, they might elude the Talavian freighter in the Badlands, but they couldn't outfight or outrun them.

Plus, they had struck an honest if onerous deal, and Ro wanted to conclude it honorably.

After a lengthy time, Fraznulen clomped over to her in his crimson space suit, and he motioned toward the door. "The evidence is inconclusive, I'm afraid. Some of our people think your man may be, how shall I put it . . . mistaken."

Ro fought down her impulse to chew out this gangly popinjay. "We don't know enough about these matters to fool you, and we have nothing to gain. You know how unusual these sightings are, by their very nature—"

He held up his gloved hand. "There is one test we haven't done. Actually it is more than a test. We have a tachyon beam inverter which can force a small area to appear for a few moments . . . under ideal circumstances."

"I advise against that," said La Forge, shaking his beige helmet vigorously. "They've got to be crazy to shoot tachyons into a temporal flux—inside a ship—and this isn't a dead ship. Plus they're bringing back an energy source, along with whatever else. Personally, I'm leaving before they do this."

"You two are not going anywhere," insisted the Talavian with a sinister tone to his voice. He didn't motion to his armed entourage, but they all leveled their weapons and took a step forward. "You don't want to endanger your ship also, do you? We can throw a tractor beam on it at a moment's notice."

He spread his lanky arms, looking like some kind of nightmarish bird in his scarlet suit. "There's nothing to fear. We've done this process in the past, and we're not planning to capture the plaque, just make sure we have the right place. For us, this test will be definitive, and our agreement with you will be concluded."

Ro glanced at Geordi, and he muttered, "Like I said, I've always wanted to see someone shoot inverted tachyons into a roomful of temporal fluxes and phase shifts."

"Can we stand back?" asked Ro, noting that the technicians were already assembling an ominous metal barrel about ten meters long.

"Certainly," replied Fraznulen. "I will even send a cadre of my guards to protect you."

Ro and La Forge backed away from the frenetic scene as Fraznulen assembled a team of four armed underlings to "protect" them. Now it really was time to contact the ship. "Ro to *Orb of Peace,*" she said.

"Boothby here," came a prompt response riddled with static. "Can we transport you back?"

"Not yet, but be ready to transport us at the first sign of trouble. They're about to try a very dangerous experiment."

"Understood," said the captain. "I'll alert the transporter room. Please exercise caution."

"It's a little late for that now," she replied, "but it's a good thought. You might look out for a tractor beam from the Talavians."

"We'll take precautions. Boothby out."

Ro sighed and looked back at the huddled workers as they assembled a metallic cannon which evidently concentrated the inverted tachyons at a specific area. The look of horror on Geordi's face told her everything she needed to know about the device.

"They're insane," he said. "It will give them a glimpse into a random number of time-lines, but they had better not try to enter the tachyon stream. I would also say that the Badlands has got to be the worst place in the galaxy to try this."

"Would these ships exist anywhere else?" asked Ro. She had felt so near to death lately that the prospect of dying trying to make contact with a long-dead race didn't seem as bizarre as it should have. Bajorans were a fatalistic people, and she had been taught that death could come immediately or haunt them from either the past or the future.

When she looked up from her reverie, the Talavians were aiming their tachyon cannon at the spot on the bulkhead above the door. Fraznulen motioned grandly, and the technicians hunkered down at their posts. Several of the guards backed away, but the massive hold was suddenly very small—there was nowhere to run. Along with everyone else in the room, Ro was forced to watch, with her own rapid breathing echoing in her ears.

A dull purple streak shot from the mouth of the cannon, illuminating a circular area above the door. Some of the guards cowered in fear. The spot glowed like a miniature sun a moment before it morphed into a holographic disk, much as Geordi had described. Ro was too far away to see any detail, but the technicians were beside themselves with joy at this sight.

When they shut off the beam a moment later, Ro let out her breath. Perhaps their benefactors knew what they were doing after all. Now they could let the *Orb of Peace* go.

Geordi looked at her and sighed. "I don't care if they do this every day for a living, I don't like it."

"Let's tell them good-bye." Ro began to walk toward Fraznulen, who was conferring with his excited technicians. Before she had taken two steps in her cumbersome boots, the area over the door began to glow all by itself. Ro stopped and stared at the strange apparition.

"Captain Fraznulen," she said, but the Talavians had seen the metamorphosis, too. They turned and pointed with excitement, and some of them rushed to fetch equipment and containers. Ro gaped with awe at the sparkling image—even from a distance, the disk was exquisite.

Grinning, Geordi stepped up beside her. "Call me a liar, will they."

Ro started to alert the ship to beam them up, when

the disk changed in hue to blazing white, like a miniature nova. Without warning, white beams shot from its depths and penetrated the first row of Talavian technicians. Four of them erupted in fiery explosions.

Geordi gripped her arm, and both of them ducked as a blazing beam streaked from the now deadly disk. It missed them, but turned two guards into smoldering bits of fabric.

Rolling onto her back, Ro barked into the communicator in her helmet. "Two to beam up! Now!"

She flinched as a Talavian fell on top of her, a look of horror in his dazed eyes. A moment later, she saw why, as a pallet stacked with supplies came into sharp focus right beside them. The hold began to fill with ordinary supplies and goods, and elongated tubes of light materialized in the ceiling, making it as bright as daylight. Most disconcerting of all, Ro could feel gravity holding her to the deck.

The ship is coming alive!

"La Forge to bridge!" yelled a familiar voice in her ear. "Two to beam up!" She tried to look for Geordi, but the sudden appearance of stacks of supplies had cut off her vision.

"Bridge to tranporter room!" echoed another voice, sounding distant and shot with static. "Bridge to transporter room—come in!"

That voice faded out, and Fraznulen's frantic voice boomed in her ears: "Implement rescue plan! Prepare to retreat!"

Ro could make out nothing else in the strangled grunts which followed. All around her it was chaos, as some of the Talavians fired at the security disk, and others ran for their lives. The cargo hold was reeling—supplies and equipment rose from the deck like a lost civilization emerging from the ocean.

She struggled to sit up in her bulky suit, while she kept looking for Geordi. Finally all she could do was gape as the mighty derelict reverted to its ancient splendor.

Chapter Seven

ON THE BRIDGE of the *Orb of Peace,* Captain Picard gripped the back of the conn chair as his ship was jolted by a tractor beam. He wanted to put up the modified shields, but then they couldn't beam La Forge and Ro aboard. And they had to escape before the old wreck in front of them finished its startling metamorphosis into a gleaming warship.

Since he had dispatched Sam Lavelle to the transporter room to see why Chief Shonsui wasn't responding, the conn was empty. Reluctantly, the captain took the seat and told himself, *steady as she goes.*

He motioned to Jozarnay Woil on tactical. "Hail them. Demand that they release the tractor beam. Don't they see what's going on?"

"Yes, sir," replied the Antosian. His forehead tightened, pulling his bun of dark hair downward. "I'm hailing them, but they don't respond."

"Keep trying," ordered Picard, scarcely able to take his eyes off the spectacle unfolding on the viewscreen. One by one, the enormous metal hulks were glimmering to life as if awakening from a deep slumber. The crystalline halos of light which had danced around the derelicts were suddenly gone, as if they had been absorbed into the ancient wrecks.

His combadge chirped, and he answered it. "Bridge."

"Captain," said Sam Lavelle, "I'm in the transporter room, and Shonsui is unconscious—she looks bad. I'll get the first-aid kit."

"Get on the transporter," ordered Picard. "Lock onto Ro and La Forge and keep trying to get them back. I'll get someone in engineering to do first-aid."

"Yes, sir."

"Any sign of what happened to the chief?"

"No, sir."

"Get them back. Out." Picard tapped his combadge again. "Bridge to engineering."

"Taurik here," came the calm voice of the Vulcan.

"Send somebody with a first-aid kit to the transporter room."

"Yes, sir," responded Taurik. "Have we gotten La Forge and Ro back?"

"Not yet. Stand by, and be ready to give me maximum impulse power—we may have to break a tractor beam."

"Yes, sir."

His jaw clenched, Picard leaned forward and stared at a massive warship that was listing vertically—he watched as it slowly righted itself. All along its sleek hull, green lights beamed on and began to pulse.

"We're being scanned," said Woil in a quavering voice.

"By the Talavians?"

"No. By the *Ancestor*."

Picard tapped his combadge. "Bridge to transporter room. Have you got them, Lavelle?"

"Not yet, sir. There's a lot of electronic interference that wasn't there before. What's going on?"

"Cut through it, and find them. Without delay."

"Yes, sir."

"Sir!" barked Woil urgently. "The Talavians have dropped the tractor beam—I think they're retreating."

"Ready shields." Picard leaned forward and gaped at a fleet of magnificent warships which had been resurrected from the grave. Even the plasma storms in the distant heavens seemed to pale in comparison.

Ro crawled on her belly across the deck of the cargo hold, trying to avoid the deadly crossfire that streaked over her head, ripping up stacks of supplies. From one torn box, tiny pellets rained down on her. Since her communicator still was not working, Ro took a chance and pulled her helmet off. She wasn't sure she would find breathable air, but she did.

"Geordi!" she yelled. "Geordi!"

She had to find him, because they weren't being transported out. With all that was happening, the ship must have lost their transporter signal. If she and Geordi were together, their combadges and life-signs might make it easier to find them and lock on. In this bizarre chaos, there wasn't much else she could do.

Ro crawled to the intersection between two aisles, and she saw a pair of beige-garbed legs. With relief, she looked up, and her mouth hung open in shock.

Above her was one of the residents of the *Ancestor*, a gangly alien with a multifaceted, jewel-like head. He held a long thin hose toward her, and his intentions looked hostile.

Ro spun around and knocked his legs out from under him; he tumbled into a broken box of pellets. As she scrambled away, she drew her phaser and made sure it was set to stun, but the alien didn't pursue her down another aisle.

"Geordi!" she yelled. "Geordi!"

You are thieves, said a voice in her head. *Demons, sent to torment us.* Ro hurriedly pulled her helmet over her head, thinking that she was imagining the voice, or it was part of the melee. As she crawled over a dying Talavian, the voice returned: *The Ancient Enemy has sent you.*

"No!" shouted Ro, scrambling to get away from the voice and the destruction. "Ro to Geordi! Can you hear me?"

He has found our hiding place, insisted the cultured voice in her head. *We thought it would last forever.*

"Ro to bridge!" she barked, trying to cling to her sanity. "Ro to the *Orb of Peace!*"

When no one else responded, she finally decided to talk to the entity in her head. "We don't know anything about an Ancient Enemy—we thought these ships were deserted."

Thieves, concluded the voice. *Nothing is left. Begin destruct sequence.*

Ro pulled off her helmet once again and shouted, "Geordi!"

"Over here!" came a muffled response.

"I'm coming!" she yelled while she crawled toward the sound, her helmet in one hand and phaser in the other.

"Ro!" he called back. "Here!"

When one door closes, another opens, said the voice in her head.

"Bridge to transporter room," asked Captain Picard, keeping his voice calm. "What is your status?"

"This is Grof," cut in a garrulous voice. "Sam is busy with the transporter, and I'm trying to revive Lena. It doesn't look good, though. I'm not a medical doctor, but I'd say she's dead."

Picard gritted his teeth. "Keep trying. Bridge out."

He looked up at the viewscreen just in time to see the Talavian freighter turn on its thrusters and try to escape. At once, a white bolt from the massive *Ancestor* shot across space, engulfed the freighter, and blasted it into rainbow confetti. Picard looked on in horror, certain that the bolt was similar to the brilliant plasma bursts that lit the murky clouds. It had happened so quickly, now he was uncertain what had destroyed them—a weapon or a storm.

Picard slowly took his hands off the controls, thinking that he wasn't going to move from here any time soon. The emerging ships looked fully armed and operational, but they seemed to be on auto-pilot, reacting to stimuli instead of creating it. For the moment, he was doing nothing to provoke them.

"Transporter room to bridge," came the breathless voice of Sam Lavelle. "We've got them! When they touched helmets, the signal was just strong enough to lock on."

"Good work. Stay at that post."

"Yes, sir. Uh, you heard about Lena Shonsui?"

"We'll deal with that later. Bridge out." Picard pointed to the Antosian. "Shields up."

"Yes, sir. Shields at full power," answered Woil.

Could we absorb one of those blasts, wondered Picard, *and survive?*

Probably not. The captain studied the positions of the strange fleet in relation to his own. A mad dash to the Badlands seemed to be the most direct approach, but it was suicidal. In retrospect, it had taken the *Ancestor* a second or so to react. There were so many other craft nearby—would they risk firing that dreadful weapon at their own ships?

"Captain," said a concerned voice. He turned to see Ro Laren stride onto the bridge, looking wide-eyed and disheveled. "We've got to get out of here! I think they were talking to me telepathically. They said something about a destruct sequence—at least that's what I understood."

Then she saw the reality of the awakened fleet on the viewscreen, and her mouth hung open. Ro finally gulped back her fear and stood at attention.

"The Talavian freighter tried to escape and was destroyed by a powerful weapon that looked like a bolt of plasma." Picard stood and offered her his seat at the conn. "I have an idea, but I need a good pilot."

"Yes, sir," answered Ro, taking the conn.

"Do you know what awakened them?" asked Picard. "Was it that experiment?"

"It all happened so fast—we thought the experiment was a success." Ro shook her head. "I think they're hiding, but I don't know from what."

"Sir!" cut in Woil at the tactical station. "I'm getting huge power increases from the ships. They could be powering up to leave."

"Or self-destruct," warned Ro.

The captain leaned over her, and they stared at the majestic fleet, which seemed to be caught in a blinking web of its own making. These ships and the

Badlands were all part of the same mysterious fabric, thought Picard. All along their sleek hulls, green and blue lights were darkening into a violet hue, and he knew that their time was running out.

"They're in a tight formation," he told Ro. "Can you get close enough to one of the other ships—in a split-second—so that the *Ancestor* can't fire at us?"

"If we go to full impulse, we can, but we'll be going awfully fast—we might hit one of them. But if I go in reverse, I'll have the strongest thrusters at the back to stop us."

"Now they're scanning us again," said Woil urgently.

"Auxiliary power to forward shields," Picard told him.

"Yes, sir."

The captain slid into an empty seat and nodded to Ro. "Proceed when ready."

She plied the controls, and he felt his body surge forward with their sudden acceleration to the rear. The *Orb of Peace* jagged sharply to starboard at the same instant that the *Ancestor* fired a charged bolt. The streak grazed their shields, shaking the transport, but they were still in one piece as they swerved behind another ship.

Picard was tossed back into his seat when Ro activated rear thrusters to slow their progress. They were so close to the second ship that they could see the rivets in its hull.

He leaned forward to say, "Continue evasive maneuvers, but get us out of here."

"Yes, sir." Ro gave up finesse as she piloted the boxy transport through the awakened fleet, zigging and zagging between the massive hulks, using them for cover. From his console, Picard put a split image on the viewscreen, half of it showing the foreboding dust cloud ahead of them and the other half showing the eerie scene they had left behind.

As they entered the thick cloud, the other half of the viewscreen erupted in a blinding blaze of light. Like a horrible chain-reaction, each one of the newly resurrected ships lit up for an instant and exploded, forming an immense circle of fire that seemed to burn the heart of the Badlands. Picard held his breath, thinking that a shock wave was bound to overwhelm their ship, but the horrible devastation faded as quickly and mysteriously as it had begun.

Ro let out a loud sigh and gazed at her controls. "I'm slowing down to one-fourth impulse."

"Come to a full stop," ordered Picard, astounded by what he was now seeing on the viewscreen. "Come about . . . quickly!"

He adjusted the scene on the viewscreen, compensating for a sudden rash of interference. Soon all three of them gaped at a sight which boggled the mind.

There before them, floating at obscene angles like toppled tombstones, were the dead, gray hulks of ships that hadn't flown in thousands of years. It was the same eerie sight that had greeted them almost twenty-four hours earlier.

"That can't be!" exclaimed Woil. "We saw them *explode.*"

"Full stop," ordered Picard softly. "Don't get any closer than this."

"Yes, sir," rasped Ro.

"They self-destructed," insisted the Antosian, staring blankly at the screen. "We *saw* it."

Picard answered, "Perhaps in this time-line, in this

dimension, they are always like this—rotting dere-licts. Everybody who comes here will see them this way. In the other phases where they exist, who knows?"

"Taking gifts from the ghosts will be more difficult now," said Ro.

"At least we got our replicator," murmured Woil.

"But at what cost?" Picard shook his head. "One ship destroyed with all aboard, and our transporter chief dead—all to collect a few trinkets. Ro, you have the bridge. Keep a steady course for the artificial wormhole, but stay in the Badlands."

"Yes, sir."

"I'll send a relief crew up here to man some of these stations. Well done, Ro."

"Thank you," she said quietly.

Feeling both lucky and cursed, the captain walked off the bridge and descended the spiral staircase to the lower level. He wasn't surprised to find a crowd gathered outside the doorway of the transporter room, but he was surprised to find Hasmek holding a hand phaser.

"What are you doing?" Picard asked the Romulan. He motioned to the weapon and held out his hand.

"I heard there had been a murder." Hasmek handed the phaser to the captain. "You can't be too careful."

"Did you see anything to confirm that?"

"No, Captain. I was asleep when all the commotion started."

"Lucky you." The captain shouldered his way past Maserelli and Horik. "Get back to your posts."

"Yes, sir," they answered in unison. Whispering to each other, the Deltan and the human scurried away.

When Picard entered the transporter room, he found Grof and La Forge bent over Lena Shonsui's lifeless body, grimly trying to revive her. Sam Lavelle stood at the transporter console as ordered, and he looked stunned over the death of his shipmate.

The captain walked slowly toward the prostrate figure and the two men who were working on her, with no chance of success.

"It looks futile," said Picard.

"That's what the tricorder says." Geordi shook his head and sat back on his haunches. "And there's not a mark on her—no sign of what happened to her."

"The tricorder doesn't tell you anything?"

"No, sir. And we don't have the equipment or personnel to do an autopsy."

"Maybe it was her heart, all the excitement," suggested Grof. "I often thought she wasn't a well woman."

"You hated her," muttered Lavelle.

"No, I thought she was incompetent, which is not the same thing. She did, however, hate *me.*"

"Belay that," ordered Picard through clenched teeth. "Hasmek was talking about this being a murder. I want to know what gave him that idea."

"Maybe it was the suspicious timing of it," said Sam. "Just when we were about to get La Forge and Ro on board—and finally get out of here—our transporter operator dies."

"Well if somebody had listened to me," muttered Grof, "she wouldn't have been transporter operator!"

"Don't you have any feelings?" asked Sam angrily.

"I did everything I could to save her!" growled the Trill.

"That's enough," ordered Picard. "Since she was in

this room alone, we can't say what happened to her. None of us have a medical background, and we don't have anything but a first-aid kit. For the time being, we'll have to attribute her death to unknown causes. Unless someone can furnish proof, I don't want to hear any more talk about murder."

"A lot of us were physically weakened by captivity," admitted Sam, looking somewhat chastened. "Grof, I'm sorry—you did try to save her."

"Of course I did," muttered the Trill. "With this pathetic crew, we can't afford to lose anybody."

Picard sighed deeply, glad that the two men had concluded their argument without his intervention. Unfortunately, Sam was correct that the circumstances and timing of Shonsui's death were suspicious. He didn't want to believe there was a murderer in their midst, but then he hadn't wanted to believe there was a saboteur either. He couldn't ignore facts: The unexplained failure of the food replicators had cost them time, effort, and Lena Shonsui's life. On top of that, he had almost lost his two most trusted crew members.

Picard glanced at Geordi, and the stricken look on the engineer's face showed that he was thinking the worst, too. Talk of murder and the bad blood between Shonsui and Grof was sure to spread through the tiny ship. They still had a dangerous mission ahead of them, and Picard had to keep this crew together . . . somehow.

One thing was certain, they couldn't survive any more incidents like this one.

"La Forge and Lavelle," said the captain, "I'd like to put a two-person guard on our new food replicator. Would you take the first shift?"

La Forge didn't look surprised, but Lavelle blinked

at him. "Do you think somebody sabotaged the other replicators?"

"I'm taking no chances," answered Picard. "I'll also revise the schedule, so that nobody is left alone."

The Trill shook his head with disbelief. "There was no privacy on this ship before, and now there will be even less!"

Geordi motioned to Sam. "Come on, let's get to our post. I could use a few peaceful moments."

As La Forge and Lavelle filed out of the room, Lavelle stole a suspicious look at Grof. That look worried the captain.

"Grof," he said, "from now on, you're with me."

The Trill scowled. "You don't trust me either, do you?"

"Just the opposite. If somebody is trying to sabotage our mission, then you would be the most logical target. If we lose you, we don't stand a chance."

Grof smiled smugly at the compliment, then his smile twisted into a grimace. "Do you think somebody will really try to kill me?"

"Only if somebody in this group wants to sabotage our mission," answered Picard. "Maybe it was, as you say, poor health that killed her." He didn't add that if the saboteur turned out to be Grof, Picard was going to keep him under tight and personal surveillance.

"I bet it's that Romulan," said Grof with a knowing nod. "Or maybe Ro Laren—somebody told me she was a Maquis."

"Let's not speculate," replied Picard, thinking most of the speculation would focus on Grof. He bent over Lena Shonsui's body. "If we get stopped and searched again, I don't want to have her body on board. Help me get her ready for the funeral."

* * *

Will Riker was awakened from a sound sleep by the chirping of his combadge. He rolled over in the narrow bed and looked around the unfamiliar quarters. "Lights," he said, and the lights came on.

He grabbed his badge from the nightstand. "Riker here."

There was nothing but silence in the guest cabin, which was a utilitarian room hardly five meters wide. "Riker here," he said again.

A raspy, hesitant voice answered him, "It's me."

"Shana!" exclaimed Will, sitting up in bed. "Are you all right?"

"No," she admitted with a nervous laugh. "I had another nightmare again . . . worse than all the others. This time, it was *me* going up in a ship with shoddy repairs and bad parts. It was my fault that *I* was going to die!"

Will threw back the covers. "Are you in your quarters? I'll be right there."

"No, Will, no—" she pleaded. "I can handle this . . . I just wanted to talk."

"We'll talk in person," Riker said soothingly. "Stay there."

A few minutes later, he stood at her doorstep. When his first chime wasn't answered for several seconds, he wondered if Shana would again try to avoid him. "Come on, Shana," he muttered to himself as he rang once more.

The door slid open, and she stood before him, fully dressed in her uniform, as was he. Even in the midst of personal crisis, they were still Starfleet officers. She slumped gratefully into his arms, and he held her up, thinking she felt as light as a person in moon gravity.

When the slender brunette gazed into his eyes, he

could tell she had been crying. "I'm here now," he assured her. "Whatever you need, I'll get it for you."

She sniffed and gave him a brave smile. "You won't be here for long—your ship is almost done. Be ready to take her on a test spin in about six hours."

"My ship is silicon and deuterium—it can always be fixed. What about *you?*" Will held her by the shoulders, and he could feel her body tremble under the crisp fabric of her uniform.

"You'll be gone, and so will I," answered Shana. "I'm resigning."

She pulled away from him and moved resolutely into the dining area of her quarters. Riker followed her, and he spotted a padd on the table; on its screen was the beginning paragraph of a letter.

"What happened?"

She snorted a rueful laugh. *"You.* I read those reports you sent me, and I went back and reviewed all of our records since the war began. You were right! Subconsciously, I was taking longer to schedule ships when I knew their commanders, or their crew had been in a lot of combat. You were right—I wasn't in any hurry to send you back to the front, even after you started to make my life miserable. I was protecting those crews, and it was easy, because there were always plenty of rush jobs to delay them."

She shook her head with disbelief. "Some of my own subordinates saw it, but they didn't *say* anything! In wartime, the absurd becomes the norm. I mean, somebody was going to have to wait—why shouldn't it be crews we liked? It made crazy sense. Most of the crews didn't complain about a few extra days of shore leave, I can tell you."

Her hands flopped to her sides. "That's why I have

to resign, Will. I can't be trusted to do this job properly."

"I was really hoping you could avoid this," said Riker. "Before you do anything rash, check in with your base counselor. Maybe you can take a leave of absence instead."

"I was coping all right until this damn war started," grumbled Shana, pounding a fist on the table. "It's like I could see what was going to happen to them—since I went through it myself! I guess I couldn't send them back to the front."

He put his arm around her shoulders, feeling limbs that were fragile, yet sinewy and strong. "What's the name of your base counselor?"

"Arlene Bakker."

He tapped his combadge. "Commander Riker of the *Enterprise* to Counselor Arlene Bakker."

"This is Bakker," answered an alert, if rushed, voice. Riker had the feeling that he had caught her at work, not rest.

Will gazed fondly at Shana as he answered, "I'm with Commander Shana Winslow, and she would like to place herself under your care. Also she wants to take a medical leave of absence."

Bakker paused as the seriousness of his request apparently sunk in. "I'll meet you down at the psychiatric wing right away. I believe you know where it is."

"Yes. Riker out." He looked at Shana and mustered his most encouraging smile.

She stared right past him. "So I'm crazy because I won't send people off to die."

Riker frowned. "You're not crazy, Shana. This war is. You've done your duty. Come on, let's get you some help."

He touched the panel to open the door, and they

stepped into a quiet corridor. This odd couple—a strapping, bearded man and a fragile, dark-haired woman—walked slowly toward the turbolift.

Wrapped in a water-resistant fabric, Lena Shonsui's body looked even more slight and inconsequential than it had before. Captain Picard was reminded of the dozen bodies they had piled on the *Orb of Peace* transporter platform only a few days ago. All of the deaths seemed so senseless, although it wouldn't have been any better to see them die by enemy fire or consumed in a plasma storm. Death was part of war, and part of exploring space—but that never made it any easier.

Picard heard footsteps and looked up to see the rest of the crew filing in, two by two. He had paired Lavelle with La Forge, Hasmek and Taurik, himself with Grof, and had kept the established pairing of Tamla Horik and Enrique Maserelli. Ro Laren and Jozarnay Woil remained on duty on the bridge, with Ro cautiously steering them through the deadly muck of the Badlands.

Is one of them a murderer? he asked himself as he studied the earnest, frightened, and arrogant faces. The Romulan was already known to be a killer, but he was also Picard's personal reclamation project. *Would he risk his life to stop this mission? Why?*

He glanced at Grof, whom he had picked to be the new transporter operator, a fitting punishment for complaining so much about Shonsui. Transporting her lifeless body into space would be good practice for him.

The Trill studied the transporter console and nodded smugly. "Ready when you are, Captain."

Picard gazed at the ragtag crew standing before

him, and he wished he had more confidence in them. Of course, there were La Forge, Lavelle, and the Vulcan, Taurik, whose implacable expression brought an air of normality to the proceedings, but the others were strangers. They studied the body on the transporter platform with a mixture of fear, grief, and curiosity.

"Thank you for coming," began the captain. "I've given far too many eulogies lately, so I'll be brief. Although I didn't know Chief Shonsui very well, her conduct under adverse circumstances demonstrated her training and dedication. She was a veteran Starfleet officer, so she must have led many lives, performed many duties. All of the thousands of officers who served with her can be proud. I don't know anything about her family and friends, but I feel certain she will be missed."

He took a deep breath. "I know there's been a lot of speculation about her death, but we have no proof that it was anything but a natural cause. However, we are now taking precautions we weren't taking before, because we are so close to fulfilling our mission."

He balled his hand into a fist. "I know it will be difficult to destroy the artificial wormhole, but we have the knowledge and the resolve to do it. We will soon have the opportunity. For all the brave men and women who have died, for all those who will die if we aren't successful, we must submerge our fears and complete this mission. If we fail, there will be no one to deliver a eulogy for the Federation."

With tight lips, he looked at the body. "May her beliefs in the afterlife be fulfilled. Energize, Mister Grof."

"Yes, sir."

The Trill plied the controls, and the small bundle on the transporter platform disappeared in a sparkling blur.

Sam Lavelle rubbed his eyes. "Anyone want to join us in the mess hall for a toast?"

"Certainly," said Taurik, glancing at the Romulan. "That is, if you have no objection."

Hasmek motioned to the door with his remaining arm. "Lead the way."

Geordi looked at the lieutenant and sighed. "Sam we've got to get back on watch."

"I want to give everyone a break," said Picard, "in shifts. Maserelli and Horik, you return to engineering. Grof and I will relieve the bridge crew."

"But the transporter—" protested Grof.

"Is unneeded at the moment. Let's go." Picard strode purposefully out the door, making it clear that they were all still on duty.

Sam sat at a table with La Forge, and across from them sat Taurik and Hasmek, who looked uncomfortably like cousins. He didn't trust Hasmek, he didn't trust Grof, and he wasn't too sure about some of the others. It was clear from the awkward silence that the others had their suspicions, too.

Geordi looked at him. "You said something about a toast?"

"Oh, yes." Sam lifted his glass of apple juice and mustered a smile. "To our fallen crew member, Lena Shonsui."

Taurik and Geordi politely lifted their glasses, mumbled their regards, and drank. The Romulan looked quizzically at his protein drink, then at them, and asked, "What is the purpose of this ceremony?"

"Just to show our respect," answered Sam.

"To whom? She is a dead body floating in the Badlands—how can she understand this gesture?"

Sam felt himself getting short-tempered with the Romulan, when Taurik broke in, "To humans, death brings great suffering to the survivors. They console each other with gestures such as this."

"Oh," said Hasmek, nodding. "They're a very emotional race—I forget."

"I've seen Romulans get emotional, too," countered Geordi. "You aren't exactly Vulcans yourselves."

Hasmek smiled wistfully. "I'm afraid we are Vulcans, even though we're trained differently."

"On what criteria do you base that theory?" asked Taurik.

"On the theory that I'm married to a Vulcan," answered Hasmek, staring off into the distance. "I went through the Koon-ut-la, Pon farr, the Koon-ut-kal-if-fee, the whole thing . . . and I could never love anyone but my wife. She's burned into my soul."

"That is very unusual," said Taurik in a classic of understatement. "Where is your wife now?"

"I wish I knew." Hasmek rose to his feet, looking tired and disgruntled. "I've had enough of these funeral ceremonies. So, my Vulcan cousin, why don't we relieve the happy couple in engineering?"

Taurik efficiently finished his drink. "Yes, I am refreshed. Thank you, Sam."

Lavelle waved to his old friend. "Look out for yourself, Taurik."

"I will take every possible precaution." The Vulcan stood and strode swiftly from the room, with Hasmek shuffling after him.

Geordi watched them go, then shook his head. "I'm

sure the captain knows what he's doing, but that Romulan makes me nervous."

"The captain is looking at the big picture," said Sam. "If the Romulans ally themselves with the Dominion, the Dominion won't need to bring reinforcements from the Gamma Quadrant. We've got to make it clear to the whole galaxy—right now—that we're going to win this war."

Geordi smiled and lifted his glass. "I'll drink to that."

Chapter Eight

ON THE VIEWSCREEN of the *Orb of Peace* was an amazing sight, which Ro hadn't seen in what felt like an eternity. It was pure, unadulterated space, with nothing but stars and nebulae glimmering as far as the viewscreen could scan. After days of negotiating the murky clouds of the Badlands, she felt as if she could pilot regular space with her eyes closed. Unfortunately, there was a war raging in that beautiful starscape, so they were stopped on the outer edge of the Badlands, deciding how best to proceed.

"Captain," said Enrak Grof, "from this point onward, I believe your plans are rather sketchy."

"First we need to collect information," declared the captain, undaunted by the obstacles facing them. He turned to the assembled group, which consisted of Grof, Ro, Hasmek, and Sam Lavelle. "We need an observation point, from where we can keep an eye on the collider. We need to find out how close they are to making the artificial wormhole operational. Some of you have been there—do you know of such a place?"

"Working on the collider, we only saw what we could see with the naked eye," answered Sam. "And our course to the black hole was closely monitored."

"I never paid much attention to where we were," admitted Grof.

When no one else commented, it was left to the Romulan to step forward. "My previous ship made a pass very near the collider, and we noticed that one of the planets in that grid has a large outer ring. You might be able to hide a small ship like this one in that ring, and you could track them from there with your sensors."

Picard crossed to the science station and brought up a chart of the sector on the viewscreen. "Can you locate this planet?"

"I think so." The Romulan stepped in front of the viewscreen and pointed to a black cloud in the center. "Okay, here are the Badlands." He moved his finger slowly to the left and asked, "Can you enlarge that region?"

Picard consented to the request, and they soon focused on the likely location of the magneton collider. While they were doing that, Ro checked the ship's data banks from the conn, and she found confirmation of what the Romulan was telling them.

"Captain," she cut in, "the ship's computer shows a planet matching that description in solar system SU-395. It has a fairly large ring system."

Hasmek smiled smugly. "I haven't steered you wrong yet, have I, Captain?"

"But how do we get there?" asked Sam. "Without the Dominion swarming all over us."

"It's a pity that you don't have a Romulan cloaking device," said Hasmek.

Captain Picard gestured thoughtfully at the Romulan. "I've considered this problem. Every time we cut straight across space, the Dominion picks us up on their long-range sensors and sends a ship to investigate. The problem is that we stick out when we're all alone. But there must be other merchant traffic in this sector. What if we were to follow closely behind another merchant ship, maybe even a convoy?"

Hasmek smiled. "That's an excellent idea—to piggyback on another ship and disguise ourselves. You're thinking like a Romulan, Captain."

"I'll take that as a compliment," replied Picard. "Activate long-range and short-range scanners. Check the computer for known shipping lanes around here."

As his orders were being carried out, the captain stepped closer to the conn. "Ro, you've been on duty now for twelve hours straight—why don't you take a break and get some food. You too, Mister Lavelle. We've got enough people here to monitor the shipping lanes. When we need you, we'll call. When you see La Forge in the mess hall send him back to engineering."

"Yes, sir," answered Ro. She rose from her seat, surprised at how stiff her legs and back felt. She really did need a short break, and Sam would be good company.

They wound their way down the spiral staircase and strolled into the mess hall, where they found Geordi La Forge staring curiously at a plate of very rare meat, surrounded by a ring of puffed pastry.

He looked up at them as they entered. "Hello. Taking a break?"

"Under Captain's orders," answered Sam. "What is that you're eating?"

"That's a good question," answered Geordi doubtfully. "I asked the replicator for a hamburger, and this is what I got."

"Talavian cuisine is not quite what we're used to," said Ro distastefully.

"But it's not bad," added Sam, never taking his eyes off the food. "If you don't want it, I'll take it."

Geordi shook his head. "You're a better man than I, Gunga Din. If you're going to stay here in the mess hall, I can go back to engineering."

"That's the plan," said Ro.

La Forge jumped to his feet and strode out the door. "If you don't get sick, Lavelle, maybe I'll try it next time."

Sam immediately sat down in the chair vacated by La Forge and tore into his Talavian hamburger.

With amusement, Ro asked, "Are you planning to eat your way through this war?"

"In a word, yes," mumbled Sam, his cheeks bulging with food. He swallowed, then gazed at her. "When the war is over, I plan on being a restaurant reviewer on Pacifica, and I'll weigh about two hundred kilos. What are *you* going to do?"

"I haven't thought that far," answered Ro, trying not to think how unlikely it was that any of them would survive. She finally got a glass of water from the new food replicator and sat down next to him.

"What were you planning to do *before* the war?" asked Sam.

Ro snorted a derisive laugh. "I was planning on being a farmer and raising a bunch of half-human, half-Bajoran kids. Silly, huh?"

He frowned at her. "No, it's not silly at all. I could see you doing that."

"It's too late for some things," said Ro somberly, "and that's one of them. Even if we drive out the Dominion, I'll probably spend several years in a Starfleet brig."

"How could they do that to you, after all the help you've been?"

"Well, let's see—I deserted from Starfleet, then waged war against them as part of an outlawed organization. If we had run across anybody but Captain Picard and the *Enterprise,* I would probably already be in the brig."

"Even though you and the Maquis were proven right," grumbled Sam, "and we really couldn't trust the Cardassians."

"That's little comfort to me now."

Sam leaned forward and looked at her with sympathetic brown eyes. "You lost somebody very dear, didn't you?"

Ro shook her head. "I was foolish to think I had gotten away from war and killing; it was just beginning. And you—you've never lost anyone special?"

"I've never had anyone special to lose," answered Sam wistfully. "Oh, there have been women—and friends, like Sito—but I've never had time to think about marriage and raising a family. I can tell you, I'm a different man than the one who charged head-first into this war . . . it seems like a hundred years ago. When I get out of this, I'm going to take time to enjoy life. Maybe I'd even like to be a farmer. Is it hard?"

Ro smiled and nodded slowly. "Hardest and most

138

rewarding thing I've ever done. After a life spent among nothing but death, it's nice to give life to something."

For several moments, they sat quietly in each other's company, just two people caught up in a whirlwind, unable to escape until the wind died down. The longer they sat there, the more introspective Sam grew; the lines on his handsome face furrowed deeply in the austere lighting.

"What's worrying you so much?" asked Ro.

He leaned forward and whispered, "What do you think happened to the transporter chief?"

"She died. Of what, we don't know." The Bajoran had her suspicions, but she wouldn't say any more than that.

"And here we are, guarding the food replicator," muttered Sam, shaking his head. "Who are we guarding it from? It must be one of *us.*"

Ro could feel her neck muscles tightening, and she craned her head back to stretch them. "If I had an explanation, I'd tell you. All we can do is proceed with the mission and take extra precautions, as the captain is doing. Besides, replicators can break down, especially in surplus craft like this, and the chief's death could have been a coincidence. Like you say, being imprisoned by Cardassians causes a lot of stress."

"I know," muttered Sam. "There wasn't a mark on her, and I looked. Something else bugs me—why kill Shonsui and leave the transporter operational?"

"Unless you needed the transporter," answered Ro.

Sam didn't respond, long enough that Ro began to wonder if he'd heard her comment about the transporter. Then an odd smile broke out on his face.

"Ro," he said softly, "if you go to the brig, I'm going, too. I want to look after you, and make sure no more harm comes to you."

Ro looked deep into Sam's eyes, and saw sincerity and a kind of affection she thought was long gone from her life. Did she feel the same way? She didn't know. "I'll think about it," she said. "I don't want to make any promises I can't keep."

Sam looked at her wistfully. "That's not your nice way of saying 'let's just be friends,' is it?"

Ro leaned across the table, put her arm around Sam's shoulder, and pulled him toward her in a forceful embrace. Then she kissed him squarely on the lips, an action to which he gratefully and passionately responded.

Ro finally let go of the breathless man. "Sam," she said in his ear, "does that answer your question?"

Sam blinked at Ro, took a deep breath, and said, "Yes, I guess it does."

Ro said nothing, unsure of exactly what to say next. She was rescued from the awkward silence by the beep of her combadge. She tapped the badge and answered, "Ro here."

"This is the bridge," came Picard's voice. "We found a merchant ship within range, and we need you and Lavelle on the bridge immediately. I'll send someone else down there."

"Yes, sir. On our way." Ro bolted to her feet, but Sam caught her hand.

"That was nice," he added.

"Yes, it was," Ro said. She hurried out, with the human right on her tail.

Captain Picard beamed broadly at the face of a solemn Patonite in the center of the viewscreen.

Beside him stood Hasmek, Ro sat at the conn, and Taurik manned tactical. Lavelle crouched in a dark corner of the dimly lit bridge, manning an auxiliary console and a phaser pistol aimed at the Romulan.

"Thank you for giving us the protection of your noble vessel," said Picard with a friendly bow.

"Peaceful travels," said the Patonite, "and may you avoid the conflict."

"If it is the wish of the Prophets," replied Picard, glancing at a similar sentiment on the frame of the viewscreen.

"Defeat to the Federation," added the Patonite.

"Defeat to the Federation," seconded the captain, his smile now stretched to the breaking point.

The transmission ended, and the screen returned to a view of the sparkling starscape, oblivious to their ruses and machinations. Picard slumped his shoulders and released the rictus grin from his face. Everyone breathed a sigh of relief, and the captain motioned to Ro. "Set course for the ringed planet. Does it have a name?"

"Not in our records," answered Ro, her fingers moving swiftly over her console. "Course laid in. ETA: five minutes at maximum warp."

"Engage."

Once again, the stars reverted to a blur—mere streaks of light in the black firmament. This was a crucial moment—the last five minutes of their run, when they would be naked to Dominion sensors. But Picard hoped that the sensor sweeps weren't that constant—the Dominion had a lot of space to watch.

"Weren't you once enemies of the Patonites?" asked Hasmek, making small talk.

Picard took a breath, glad to be distracted. He

rummaged through the historical data in his mind and answered, "We had a serious disagreement. That was about a hundred years ago, and they still hold it against us."

"What does that tell you?" asked Hasmek smugly.

"That doing good isn't always good," answered Picard. "We've always known that, which is why we've strengthened the First Contact protocols. Would it have been better to simply conquer the Patonites?"

"By now," said Hasmek, "a hundred years later, they would no doubt be loyal vassals, willing to fight for you, rather than trade with the enemy and root for your demise."

"We win some, and we lose some." Picard looked pointedly at the Romulan. "But we're going to *win* this one."

"I believe you might," replied the one-armed Romulan with amusement.

"Taurik, any sign of pursuers?"

"No, Captain," answered the Vulcan from the tactical station.

"I can put the planet on screen," said Ro, sounding satisfied with their progress.

Picard nodded, and the screen was taken over by a blurry image of a banded, oblate spheroid. As the image cleared, they saw a cloudy, blue-gray planet encircled with black and yellow rings. The captain couldn't help but be reminded of Saturn in his home solar system, despite differences in coloration of the clouds. As they drew closer and saw more detail, plus a squadron moons, it was clear that the planet was a giant.

"Class-A planet," said Taurik. "Failed star. Planetary surface may be tenuous; atmosphere of methane, ammonia, hydrogen, helium—unsupportive of life. The planet has thirteen moons. The rings have a thickness of one to two kilometers, and they consist mostly of unconnected particles of silicate and ice."

"How big are the particles?" asked Picard.

"They are small in size, mostly between ten and a hundred centimeters in diameter. We should be safe with our shields up."

"And well hidden," said Hasmek with approval.

We'll be safe from Dominion patrols, thought Picard, *but will we be safe from each other?* He couldn't shake the nagging fear that one of their number was trying to terminate the mission.

"Entering the rings in thirty seconds," reported Ro.

Picard turned to see thick tan and black bands cutting across the pale, gaseous surface of the planet. As they drew closer, he could see the granular consistency of the rings, which looked like a strip of beach suspended in space.

"Juno," said Picard with a smile.

"Pardon me, Captain?" asked Ro.

"This planet reminds me of one in my home solar system, Saturn. It was named after an ancient god, and I'd like to call this planet Juno, who was Saturn's daughter."

"That's easier to remember than 'seventh planet in SU-395,'" replied Ro. "Entering the rings of Juno in five seconds."

"Slow to one-fourth impulse."

"Yes, sir."

Soon they were engulfed in sand-colored particles, which were so thick that Picard found himself squinting at the viewscreen. "Shield status?" he asked.

"Shields holding at ninety-four percent," answered Taurik. "Damage is minimal, but a prolonged stay of several days would compound the damage and seriously degrade shields."

"I plan to be here no more than forty-eight hours," replied Picard.

They suddenly entered a field of particles which were entirely black, like lumps of coal or obsidian. *This must be one of the black bands,* Picard decided.

"I'm trying to find the collider," said Lavelle from the rear of the bridge, "but a heavy concentration of magentic particles is affecting the sensors."

The captain stepped behind Ro. "Conn, get us back into the light-colored particles, and come to a stop."

"Yes, sir."

A moment later, the crate-like transport floated in a thick morass of sand, rocks, and ice cubes.

"That's better," said Sam.

Picard walked between the stations. "I want everyone to look for that artificial wormhole. Use the coordinates we stored before."

"There is a gravitational drift," added Taurik. "If we don't compensate, we will be on the other side of the planet in seventeen-point-six hours."

"Can we use a synchronous orbit?" asked Picard.

"Inadvisable, sir. We would have to be on the inner rings."

"I can compensate," said Ro, "and keep our relative position, even though the ring is moving."

"Sir, I found it!" called Sam Lavelle. Picard took two quick steps toward the rear of the bridge and hovered over the lieutenant's shoulder.

"It's about an hour from here," he explained, gazing at his readouts. "Our scanners have gotten a very strong signal, which matches your earlier sighting."

"Begin recording and monitoring," ordered Picard, "energy readings, magnetons, comm signals, whatever emissions are coming from that thing. Can you put it on the viewer, Lieutenant?"

"Yes, sir."

A moment later, a silvery, skeletal tube appeared on the screen, floating in the blackness of space. It was hard to realize how immense the collider was until Sam fine-tuned the image to show the ships surrounding it. Some darted through its coils like fish on a tropical reef; others cruised the outside of the structure like flies on the carcass of a giant beast. *Ten kilometers long and two kilometers wide,* Picard reminded himself, and every centimeter of it looked impregnable. Their entire ship would fit inside one of the joints connecting the supports at the gaping mouth.

He tapped his combadge and said, "Bridge to Grof."

"Grof here," answered the Trill.

"The collider is in scanner and viewer range," said Picard. "If you would, Professor, come up to the bridge and start analyzing the data."

"Are we in a safe place?"

"Relatively," answered Picard. "We're in the rings of a planet that I've code-named Juno. It doesn't seem we've been detected."

"On my way, Captain," said the Trill excitedly.

"Why do you need him?" asked Hasmek with curiosity. "It's clear that most of your crew doesn't trust him."

"They don't trust you either," whispered Picard, "but you continue to prove your worth."

"Touché," replied the Romulan with a sly smile.

When Enrak Grof stomped onto the bridge a moment later, Hasmek was careful to retreat toward the rear, standing beside Taurik and Lavelle.

Suddenly the bridge was crowded again, with people staring at the tubular structure on the viewscreen. It looked like what it was—a tunnel through the stars. Despite the crowded conditions, Picard didn't have the nerve to send any of them away. It was clear that Grof reveled in seeing his handiwork again, while Sam grimaced as though he were going to be sick to his stomach.

"Do we really have to destroy it?" begged Grof. "It's so *magnificent!*"

"The accelerator room," Picard reminded him gently. "Remember, you said that if we destroyed that control room, it would set them back a long time."

"Sir, I've been thinking," Sam cut in, taking a step forward, "we might be able to start a chain reaction that would damage the collider along its entire length."

"You just want to destroy it, don't you?" hissed Grof angrily.

"Yes, I do!" snapped Sam. "That thing's an *abomination,* built on the blood and bones of innocent people!"

"Mister Lavelle, you're dismissed." Picard spoke firmly but not without some measure of sympathy. He had been depending a great deal on Sam Lavelle, pushing him hard, when his mental state was less than ideal.

"I'm sorry, sir," muttered Sam, lowering his head. He rose from his station and backed toward the door.

"Mister Hasmek, go with him," ordered the captain. "The two of you are a new pairing in our buddy system. I think you could both use some rest."

Sam paused in the doorway. "We really could take it all out."

"We'll have a strategy meeting later," promised Picard. "Keep your idea in mind."

"Some of us have *earned* your trust," said Hasmek as he followed Sam off the bridge. With a parting glance at Grof, he added, "Others just demand it."

The captain gritted his teeth and said nothing. He hated siding with Grof, but the professor hadn't exaggerated when he said that he was the most important member of this party. None of the rest of them possessed one-tenth of his knowledge of the massive magneton collider and its potential weaknesses.

"What insolence," muttered the Trill, gazing angrily after the the human and the Romulan. "I'm afraid Sam has become partly deranged by his experiences. I don't see why we need him for anything else. Why not confine him to quarters for the duration? And the Romulan, too."

"Until we have devised a plan, we don't know whose talents we need." Captain Picard pointed to the console vacated by Lavelle. "Have a seat, Professor. There's a lot of data coming in, and we need to know what stage they're in. If you can tell us what to look for—"

"No," grumbled the Trill, "it's simpler to do it myself than to try to educate everyone. Just keep people from interrupting me."

Picard cleared his throat. "Very well."

* * *

An hour later, the same crew remained on bridge duty: Ro on conn, Taurik on tactical, Grof on the auxiliary station, and Picard in charge of pacing. He was doing an excellent job of buffing the deck with his soft-soled Bajoran boots, but he wished the bridge of the *Orb of Peace* were a few meters longer.

Grof finally leaned back in his chair, folded his arms, and clucked. "I'm sorry, Captain, but this doesn't look good."

The captain loomed over him. "What doesn't look good?"

The Trill pointed to overlapping windows of data streaming across his screen. "The neutrino readings show that they've been testing it, although not on a large scale. The residual magneton readings are higher than I would have liked—if I were still there working on it—but they're within acceptable levels. I only see a handful of workers and a lot of support vessels."

"What is your conclusion?" asked Picard.

The burly Trill frowned. "It seems to me, Captain, that it's already operational. I would say they're in the latter stages of testing—still doing some tweaking, though."

Picard gritted his teeth and asked, "How soon before they can bring through reinforcements from the Gamma Quadrant?"

"The post-construction plan was to bring through a lone Jem'Hadar ship as the final test," answered Grof. "I would say they are close to running that test. If it's successful, the floodgates will open twelve hours later. That's how long it will take to assemble the fleet."

Picard looked deeply into the bearded, spotted face

of the Trill, wondering if this information were entirely truthful. Even if Grof were honest, was he accurate? All of their plans, their lives, and the future of the Federation depended on Grof's analysis, and he knew it. If he really wanted to protect his creation from harm, all he had to do was feed them false information.

Unfortunately, Picard had little choice but to trust the Trill. Lavelle and Taurik knew a few details, but only Grof knew the layout.

"Mister Taurik," he asked, "do you concur with the professor's analysis?"

The Vulcan nodded. "Yes, sir. Given the emissions, it would seem that tests have commenced. Certainly, the number of workers has been greatly reduced from when we left."

"What's it been, a week, a week-and-a-half?" asked Grof.

"Eight-point-three days," answered Taurik, cocking his head.

"At least they don't seem to be operating with undo haste," said Grof, gazing at his readouts. "They're sticking to the regular timetable."

Picard straightened up and felt an unpleasant stiffness in his back. "All right, we know we haven't got much time. They could start bringing through ships any moment, so we have to act quickly. Grof, I need you with me; I'll have La Forge join us."

"Fine, Captain, I'd like to get this meeting over with." Grof stood and rubbed his hands importantly.

Picard turned to the conn and gave his trusted pilot a smile. "Ro, I need you to stay on the bridge."

"Yes, sir," she replied. "I'll keep making the necessary course corrections."

The captain nodded. "Taurik, you stay here, too,

and monitor the collider. Let us know immediately if there are any developments."

"Yes, sir."

Picard took one last look at the skeletal tunnel stretching through the cosmos, and he shook his head. Such control of time and space was unheard of—it was both a remarkable achievement and a monstrous threat. If only the Dominion could have created this artificial wormhole in a time of peace, in a spirt of peace. But so many inventions came during war, when desperation, fear, and hatred fueled the imagination and the will.

Chapter Nine

SAM PACED ANXIOUSLY in the narrow confines of his cabin, which was nothing but a converted storage room. It was made even more cramped by the lean Romulan stretched out on the sofa he had borrowed from the rec room, which left Sam a flimsy cot. They were both supposed to be sleeping, but Sam couldn't, not after having embarrassed himself with his outburst on the bridge.

Of course, he told himself, *Captain Picard has to defer to Enrak Grof. I did the same thing when I was Grof's captain. There's no way around that selfish Trill, even though he is a collaborator and a traitor!*

"Will you stop grinding your teeth," muttered Hasmek, keeping his eyes purposefully closed. "We might as well admit it, we're all part of Grof's Follies.

He just wants to keep everything revolving around him. You never know what he'll tell the captain next, but it's always something that will keep him in the spotlight."

"He's valuable for his knowledge, not his personality," answered Sam.

"And does he know half as much as he claims to know?" scoffed the Romulan. "Thus far, Ro and I have piloted this craft, and the captain has kept us focused on the mission. What has Grof contributed, except to cause dissension? What an egomaniac—the way he got his notes delivered to the Federation. I'll bet that scurrilous courier is sitting around some tavern."

Sam stopped his mindless pacing and stared at the Romulan. "You'd kidnap Grof in a flash and take him home with you, if you could. We all want to know what he knows, and what he's going to do with his knowledge."

"I'll tell you one thing," countered Hasmek, "he's *not* going to destroy his precious invention. It was good that you challenged him on that point, because it showed him for the liar he is."

"Yeah," answered Sam absently. He was thinking about Ro Laren and how unlikely it was that he would be given a chance to spend any time with her— alone—until this was all over. He tried not to think about how it would probably end.

"And now you and I have been dismissed from the bridge," grumbled Hasmek, "although we've done more than anybody for the success of this mission. We brought the captain all the intelligence he has. Without us, he'd be totally lost! Not that he has much of an idea of what he's doing, as it is."

"That's enough," said Sam, flopping onto his bed. "At least we're alive. That's more than billions of people in this war can say. I remember when you were telling us how grateful you were just to be alive."

"It's true," admitted Hasmek. "For that, I owe Picard my allegiance and respect." He laughed at Sam's startled expression. "Oh, you thought I didn't know who he was? A bogus name and that dreadful earring are not going to hide the best officer in Starfleet. But you're a fool if you think Jean-Luc Picard can protect us from death. Death stalks this ship like a pack of hounds."

Sam screwed his eyes shut and tried not to think about the Romulan's dire words. Still, it was hard to rest when his life was in the hands of a man he didn't trust and didn't like—Grof.

Captain Picard folded his hands in front of him and concentrated on the animated conversation between Enrak Grof and Geordi La Forge, two men who could bat around technical terms with the best of them. They were sitting in the captain's quarters, which had recently served as brig on the *Orb of Peace*. Now, with the addition of a table and chairs, it served as a ready room.

Picard understood most of the concepts and hypothetical possibilities under discussion. He certainly understood their goals and desired results, but Grof and La Forge had yet to touch on the most difficult part of their task.

"Let's forget the collateral damage and the amount of explosives for a moment," said the captain, slicing a hand through the air. "We've got to figure out how to get *in* there, deliver the charge to the right place, and get *out*. Grof, I'm certain you'll know how to find the control room and where to put—"

"Me?" blurted Grof. He laughed nervously. "I'm not going in there, or anywhere near the collider. Do you know what they would *do* to me if they caught me? This is a suicide mission, and I never agreed to that. No, sir." He folded his arms and gazed obstinately at Picard.

The captain's lips thinned. "I don't intend to lose a single person on this operation. I intend to get in there and get *out*. Every step will be planned in advance, including the escape route. Believe me, Professor, if we don't do this correctly, all of our lives will be in danger."

The captain opened up his padd and took out a stylus. "The first step is to get within transporter range of the collider. We'll list all the options for doing that, even if they're bad."

Geordi shrugged. "Well, we could fight our way in—that's the most direct and worst idea. We could hijack a Dominion ship—"

"Bah," grumbled Grof. "Why don't we just go up to them and ask politely, 'May we please bomb your collider?' This is pointless. It's a suicide mission, no matter how you look at it!"

Picard frowned at the Trill, fighting down an impulse to slap a hand over his mouth. "Are you saying that nothing ever comes close to this giant structure, floating in the middle of space? What about meteoroids and space debris? How does their security handle near-collisions and pass-bys?"

"Of course, there is a normal amount of debris," conceded Grof, "especially with all the construction and traffic. The collider has shields, but they draw a lot of power. They're really intended to be used only during a full-scale attack. The wormhole can't operate with shields up. Normally sensors probe the passing objects, chart their course, and pass the information to the computer. Then robotic phasers shoot down any objects that look as if they'll hit the collider."

"So a certain amount of debris just drifts by," said Picard, "and is allowed to go on its merry way."

The Trill looked at him, his dark eyes widening in excitement. "Yes, yes, that is true! I believe the tolerance is two hundred kilometers."

"Well within transporter range," said Geordi with a smile.

"So we could float an unmanned bomb disguised as space debris close to the collider," said Grof, "but what then?"

"It wouldn't necessarily be unmanned," replied Picard, thinking on his feet. "If we could disguise our space debris well enough, we could station two or three people inside—and beam the charge over to the target. If necessary, we could send a team over there, too."

"If the decoy is small enough, we can jam their sensors, no problem," said Geordi. "You know, we already have the perfect shell to build this thing around."

Picard smiled. "The escape pod. Of course, that's our last pod, and when it's gone, there's no way off the *Orb of Peace.*"

Grof gulped. "These people who go over to plant the bomb—do you think you could beam them back?"

"That would be the plan," answered Picard. "Although we might need a diversion. It's also possible that we won't need to beam anyone over. We might be able to accomplish this entirely with the transporter."

Grof nodded thoughtfully. "This plan is still mostly suicidal, but not completely. I'm impressed."

"We're also good at what we do," said Geordi, rising from the table. "I've got to scrounge together a portable transporter, because the escape pod doesn't have one. I may have to disable the main transporter. Is that all right, Captain?"

"Wait a minute, Geordi. I want to discuss other matters with you." The captain turned to the Trill, who was making notes on his padd. "Professor, I hope you're working on a schematic of the collider, especially the accelerator room and surrounding corridors."

"I was listing the subsystems we need to take out," replied Grof. "I'm going to hate to destroy the accelerator room, but it can be rebuilt, given time."

"Why don't you go back to the bridge and start drawing those schematics. I understand you're working from memory, but be as accurate as you can."

"Count on me, Captain." Gripping his padd, the burly Trill jumped to his feet and charged out the door.

Geordi watched him go, then smiled. "I'm glad he's on our side . . . finally."

"He had better be," said Picard, thin-lipped. "You've got a lot to do. Realistically, how long do you think it will take to prepare our decoy?"

The engineer shrugged. "We'll need time for construction and testing—let's say, twenty-four hours."

"I hope we have that long," answered Picard grimly. "Before we get distracted, I think we should manually program the subspace beacon and ready it for launch. We don't know how long it will take for the *Enterprise* to get here."

Geordi nodded. "Yes, sir. Do you know what message you want to encode?"

"Just these coordinates, the coordinates of the collider, and a deadline in twenty-four hours." Picard led the way out of the room.

The engineer followed his captain into the bowels of the ship—the little-used third level. In the aft part of the underbelly were pipes and tubes for life-support systems; they squeezed through there and entered a long, narrow room with rails on the deck and ceiling. This was the torpedo room, a lonesome place since they had spent all but one torpedo early in their journey.

According to the green light, their single remaining torpedo rested in chute one, aimed fore; the aft chutes were all empty, as were the racks which normally held spare torpedoes. However, a long silver cabinet rested under the racks—it looked like a large toolbox with a lighted membrane panel for a lock. Geordi bent over the tiny instrument panel and studied it with his implants.

"I was thinking," he said, while entering key-strokes, "we could use the hydrogen scoop to gather particles to camouflage the meteoroid."

"I'll assign someone to that," promised Picard.

Geordi frowned at the box. "Why isn't this thing working? Let me try the alternate code. . . . Ah, there it is." He stepped back.

With a slight whir, robotic arms gently lifted the

cabinet and set it on the tracks. The upper covers of the box lifted automatically and folded neatly aside, revealing a small beacon the size and shape of a fireplug. An amber light blinked soothingly on its tip.

Geordi still looked troubled. "It's not supposed to come up, armed like that. I haven't done anything to this beacon. Have you, sir?"

"No," answered Picard, not liking the tone of his companion's voice. "Who's had access?"

"We haven't sent anyone down here since we rescued Lavelle and his crew." The engineer lifted the cover and put it carefully back into place over the beacon. "Although we haven't restricted access down here either."

The captain scowled, realizing that he had made a grave mistake in not protecting the torpedo room. But he only had a skeleton crew, and it wasn't possible to guard every square centimeter of this ship, especially from someone on board.

Geordi yanked open an access panel on the side of the beacon, revealing an array of miniature circuits and wires. He also opened an instrument panel located on the rear fin of the beacon. Checking the readouts as he manipulated the inner circuits, his expression grew more and more concerned. Picard could tell that the prognosis was not good.

Finally La Forge sat back on his haunches and shook his head. "We were lucky they didn't know exactly what they were doing, or I wouldn't have noticed that they miscalibrated the guidance system and disabled the subspace relay. We would have launched this thing, thinking all was well, and it would have crashed in silence."

Picard's eyes narrowed. "There can't be any doubt it was sabotage?"

"No doubt. When they got into it, they accidentally reset the defaults, which is why my access code didn't work, and why it came up in ready mode."

"How much knowledge did someone need to do this?"

"A passing acquaintance with Starfleet codes and beacons is all they'd need. In fact, this could've been done days ago."

The engineer looked around the cramped under-belly and scowled. "And no video logs down here . . . or anywhere else on board. I've been on the *Enterprise* too long. I forgot that security isn't built in on every ship."

"Is the beacon fixable?" asked Picard.

"Yes, but not if I'm devoting all my attention to making a fake meteoroid, a bomb, a jamming device, and a portable transporter."

"The mission comes first," said the captain gravely. "At least now we know for sure that the enemy is on board. You'd better check all of your equipment."

Geordi looked stricken. "The explosives and fuses!"

He ran down the long deck, between the torpedo rails, then squeezed under the pipes. With a dagger twisting in his stomach, Picard trailed after him, certain that they were at least one step behind their tormentor, probably more. What had been an unpleasant possibility was now a terrible reality. They had a traitor within their midst, and he would have to deal directly with the threat.

Under normal circumstances, the captain would

turn back, abort the mission. But these were not normal circumstances. No one else knew about the artificial wormhole—no one else was in a position to stop it. As happened so often to Picard, the job was his or no one's.

The saboteur hadn't wanted to reveal himself just yet, but they knew. Could they use this to their advantage—hunt the traitor down before he, or she, knew they were on the trail? On this tiny ship, with everyone already in each other's pockets, could they even keep this a secret? So far, the only ones who knew were him, Geordi, and their foe.

No, thought Picard, *he had to be rooted out and chased to ground. We cannot be distracted from our mission.*

With a number of decisions weighing heavily on him, the captain followed La Forge to a locked storage room off the main cargo hold. The smell of rotting fruit was rather pungent down here, and Picard made a mental note to have the crates removed. At the moment, food seemed to be the least of their concerns.

He stood stoically as the engineer unlocked the door to the storage room. The walls were partly mesh. Although they looked intact, they looked uncomfortably flimsy, too. The transporter didn't have vaults or force-fields, so it was difficult to say what precautions they could have taken.

The crestfallen look on Geordi's face told the captain all he needed to know. The engineer held up a plasma pack which had been roasted black—it looked like a bag of old coffee grounds.

"Our friend has been here," growled Geordi. "If I had a tricorder, I could tell you how bad it is, but all of the stores look ruined—fuses, plastic explosives, plasma packs, everything."

"Haven't you got anything else that will do the job?"

Geordi smiled grimly. "Well, there's that old standby—a phaser on overload. But that's highly inaccurate, and we don't even have Starfleet phasers."

Picard felt his shoulders slump, and he quickly straightened them. "What about the hardware replicators?"

"They're in engineering, right under everyone's noses." The engineer quickly tapped his combadge. "La Forge to engineering."

"Woil here," came the pleasant voice of the Antosian.

"Yes, uh . . . listen, I planned to run a level-three diagnostic on the hardware replicators, but I forgot. Have they been operating?"

"Yes, sir, I think so. We replicated some magnesium couplers about half-an-hour ago. Want me to run that diagnostic for you?"

"No, no, that's all right. Get all the systems up to date, because we have a lot of work ahead of us."

"I heard, sir, and I think it's a good idea to float the bomb in there as space debris!"

Geordi looked stunned. "Who told you that?"

"I think Grof started the rumor, but it is correct, isn't it?"

"Keep your mind on your job," ordered the engineer. "And keep an eye on those replicators. La Forge out." He shook his head with disgust. "Blabbermouth!"

"Let's remember, Grof is a civilian."

Geordi scowled. "What a fix. We haven't got enough people to guard every system on this ship, and we don't know if we can trust the people we've got!"

"Leave that to me," ordered the captain. "You go ahead and turn that escape pod into a meteoroid. Use as many of the crew as you need. In fact, it will be good to keep people working in a group—make sure they're involved."

"Yes, sir," replied Geordi. "And I ought to be able to re-create some of the lost explosives with the hardware replicators. It will be hard to work with these people and look at them, and not wonder who it is. *Who could it be?*"

"Right now, I'm only ruling out you and me."

"You suspect Ro?" whispered La Forge.

Picard rubbed his chin. "Let's say I can hear Will Riker in my mind, telling me that she's an avowed enemy of the Federation. We've been counting on a lot of leopards turning their spots—maybe too many."

"Still, it's hard to believe . . . we have to find them." La Forge slammed a fist into his palm.

"Geordi, you have to forget about the spy, the beacon, and everything else, and concentrate on building the meteoroid."

"Yes, sir," said Geordi with resolve. "I'll be sleeping in a hammock in the escape pod until further notice. Nobody gets in or out, without *my* permission. Security will be my job, too."

As Geordi stepped carefully through the underbelly of the transport ship, Picard called after him. "Let's keep this between ourselves until I tell you otherwise."

"I'm in no hurry to tell anyone, Captain," Geordi

assured him. He headed up the ladder and disappeared into the second deck.

Picard tugged on his Bajoran earring, knowing that he would have to eliminate his shipmates from suspicion—one by one—until he found the enemy in their midst.

Chapter Ten

RO LAREN THOUGHT she would go mad if she had to listen to any more of Grof's cackling and gleeful muttering to himself. He was quite pleased with his genius, but she wished he would take it elsewhere, away from the bridge of the *Orb of Peace* while she was on duty.

"This is really good!" he complimented himself as he worked. "Yes, it was exactly like that."

She turned to look at the obnoxious Trill and caught the eye of the Vulcan, Taurik, on tactical. He raised an eyebrow and resumed monitoring his read-outs. Ro sighed loudly, and turned back to the conn. She wasn't due to make another correction for three minutes, and floating in a sand pile was getting a bit boring. She had to admit that some of her resentment with Grof stemmed from the fact that he was privy to the captain's plans and she wasn't, although the Trill hadn't tried very hard to keep them secret.

From his exuberance, she assumed that the plan to float a bomb, disguised as space debris, close to the collider was a good one. At least the opinionated Grof was satisfied. In his zeal and creative flourish, she could see why he had succeeded so well in his profession, undoubtedly at the expense of anyone who got in his way.

The Bajoran was startled from her reverie by the sound of footsteps, and she glanced back to see Captain Picard enter the bridge, followed by Tamla Horik and Enrique Maserelli. Suddenly it was crowded again.

"Status, Mister Taurik?" asked the captain.

"No change, sir, although a few more work parties are active."

"Last minute tweaks," suggested Grof, barely looking up from his work. "I'd bet they're going to make another test soon. You'll be happy to know, Captain, that my work is progressing well."

Picard gave him a forced smile. "Thank you, Professor. Ro and Taurik, please come with me."

The Bajoran breathed a sigh of relief. *Finally I'll hear what's going on from the captain, not Grof.* She rose from her chair just as Tamla Horik sauntered toward her.

"You've got a correction to make every four and a half minutes," Ro began. "It's along this gradient—"

"I know," said Tamla Horik. "The captain told me about it, and I studied your log. I don't foresee any problems." She plunked herself into the vacated seat.

"Great," muttered Ro. With relief, she turned to the captain and was surprised to find him looking stern and tight-lipped. She had the uncomfortable feeling that she was about to be chewed out rather than taken into his confidence.

"Keep working, Grof," said the captain.

"Aye, sir!"

With a wave, Picard led the Vulcan and the Bajoran off the bridge. They headed down the spiral staircase to the lower level, and into the captain's quarters.

Picard sat at the table, still looking grave and preoccupied. Ro took a seat across from him, and she tried to appear as unconcerned as the Vulcan beside her. Nevertheless, the captain's stern visage was disconcerting. They both folded their hands and waited patiently for him to brief them.

With his brow knit into a double-stitch, Picard's gaze shifted between Ro and Taurik. "I must take the two of you into my confidence, and I'm ordering you not to tell anyone else what we discuss in here."

"Yes, sir," answered Ro, wondering why he hadn't told Grof the same thing.

"Yes, sir," replied Taurik.

Picard's jaw clenched in anger as he spoke, "Have either one of you been in the torpedo room in the last few days?"

Now Ro didn't even try to hide her puzzlement. "No, sir. There was no reason."

"No, sir," answered Taurik.

"How about the cargo hold?"

"I was down there once or twice to get vegetables," said Ro, "and to put away the supplies the Talavians gave us."

"And I as well," answered Taurik.

"Did you see anyone else in the storage room at the time, the one with mesh walls?"

Ro frowned puzzledly, trying to remember what had been stored in there. "No, sir—"

"Is something wrong with the cache of explosives?" asked Taurik bluntly.

"Yes," answered Picard, never taking his eyes off the Bajoran. "We have to determine who has been performing acts of sabotage against this ship and her mission. Ro, would you consent to have Taurik do a mind-meld on you?"

Ro sat straight in her chair and bristled at the implications. "Is this a loyalty test, Captain?"

"No, this is a survival test. I have to find a traitor in our midst, and logic suggests I start with you."

"I was never a traitor," said Ro softly. "Call me an early-adopter of the 'Cardassians-can't-be-trusted' rule, but I'm not a traitor."

"Then let Taurik mind-meld with you."

Ro glanced at the stoic Vulcan, who raised an eyebrow, as if the prospect of melding with her might prove enlightening.

She fought down every angry, distrustful nerve in her being, and there were a lot of them. Maybe she had earned the title of "Most Likely to Be a Traitor," but she had also earned some respect, including the right not to have her mind and inner thoughts probed.

"This is unworthy of you, Captain," she said through clenched teeth.

His eyes narrowed. "I have a war to fight, and a fleet of Jem'Hadar warships could come pouring through that tunnel any minute. I haven't got time to spare anyone's feelings. I have to find out who is working against us. If you were in my position, you would do the same thing."

Ro sat back, blasted by the famous Picard forthrightness. "You're right," she said, "I'd do the same thing. All right, Taurik can go tip-toeing through my mind, but he'd better wear his knee-high boots."

Picard's stern visage finally cracked, and he gave her an anguished smile. "I'm sorry I had to be so insistent. We won't do the mind-meld—I just wanted to know if you would allow it."

Ro grinned with relief and slumped back in her chair. "Some other time, Taurik."

"I would have obeyed orders," said the Vulcan, "but I caution you, Captain, that I am unable to perform a number of mind-melds in a short period of time. Each one would be extremely draining, both on myself and the subject, necessitating several hours of recovery time."

"That's all right, Taurik," said Picard, "I don't intend for you to perform a mind-meld on anyone, but it's the only threat I have. I believe a willingness to go through with it shows some innocence. If anyone steadfastly refuses to allow it, we may have to take other measures."

"Who's next on your list?" asked Ro. "Grof?"

"No. We have to leave the professor alone to do his job. Besides, he doesn't have to resort to subterfuge to throw us off, he only has to give us false information, which he can do any time he wants. Like it or not, the mission depends on Grof. And La Forge, too. We have to leave both of them alone."

Picard looked at the Vulcan. "You present a problem, but I believe your willingness to perform the mind-meld exonerates you. None of this proves anything, of course, but it's a starting place. I want to see how everyone reacts to the threat of discovery.

"The next time we go through this process, it will be with Lavelle and Hasmek, but I wanted to try it first with the two of you. I assumed if anyone was likely to refuse on principle, it would be Ro." He flashed the Bajoran a brief smile.

"If there's a spy on board, we need to be extremely careful," cautioned Ro. "You need back-up, security—"

"I agree," said Picard, "but we have to proceed in parallel with our mission. I don't want to disrupt our teamwork, now that we're finally in position and have a good plan. Ro, I'd like you to report to La Forge in the escape pod and help him all you can. Leave the investigation up to me. I'll call you as I need you."

Ro stood and rapped on the table. "You're taking a big gamble, Captain."

"I know," he replied gravely. "But it would be worse to disrupt our mission to have a divisive witch-hunt—that would be playing into their hands. Do your jobs. This investigation is *my* responsibility."

Hasmek groaned and sat up on the sofa in Sam's makeshift quarters. "When are we getting out of here?"

Sam set down his padd, upon which he had been writing a letter to his sister in New Jersey. He had no idea how he was going to get it delivered, but it made him feel better. It made him feel connected.

"Relax," he said, "they'll get around to us when they need something. It's not that big of a crew, and the others will have to sleep sometime."

"Do you ever think about getting out of here?" asked Hasmek, staring absently at the ceiling. "I don't mean this room, but the war, the insanity. You're a smart fellow, Sam, you must think about getting out."

"That wouldn't be smart," answered Sam. "There's nowhere to go, and no way to get there."

The Romulan turned and looked earnestly at him. "You could help *me* get home."

"The captain's already promised to get you home," answered Sam uneasily.

"But we both know that's not a high priority to him. Picard is much more likely to get us all killed rather than get us home. If you helped *me,* I could make sure that neither the Federation nor the Dominion could ever harm you again."

Sam burst out laughing. "If you could promise that, you'd be a miracle worker, not a one-armed Romulan who's awfully far from home."

"When things start to go wrong," said the Romulan, "just stick with me."

"Okay," said Sam, still mildly amused. Everyone in this war thought they had a recipe for survival, a plan, when all they had was a tenuous grasp on reality and old-fashioned luck, or lack of it.

He picked up his padd and finished the letter to his sister: "So, Joanne, I hope this war is treating you better than it's treating me. I know it's affecting everyone, wherever they are. You always had a more fatalistic view of life than me, so you're probably coping all right. I keep thinking I can change it—do something to have an impact. I'm trying, but I don't know if anything can be done. I hope it will come to a head soon, one way or another. Love, your Sammy."

With his eyes getting damp, Sam turned off the padd and closed the lid, just as a knock sounded on the door.

"Come in!" called Hasmek, sounding downright cheerful.

The door opened, and Captain Picard walked in, followed by Taurik. Sam jumped up and greeted his Vulcan friend. "Hi, Taurik."

The Vulcan looked more stoic than usual as he gave Sam only a slight nod.

"To what do we owe this pleasure?" asked Hasmek, rising to his feet and bowing. "Are we about to be released?"

"That depends," answered Picard. "I have a few questions to ask both of you, and I don't want our conversation to leave this room."

"This sounds serious," replied Hasmek.

"It is. Have either one of you been in the torpedo room recently?"

"No, sir." Sam glanced quizzically at Hasmek, who smiled.

"What's in the torpedo room?" asked the Romulan.

"Please answer my question," insisted Picard.

"No."

"Have either one of you been in the cargo hold, other than to handle food?"

"What's in the cargo hold?" asked Hasmek with amusement.

"No, sir," answered Sam.

"Are either one of you performing acts of sabotage against this vessel?" The captain's stern gaze traveled from one man to another.

"No, sir," answered Sam resentfully.

"I stopped doing that when you blew off my arm," said Hasmek with a mirthless grin.

"Will you submit to a mind-meld to prove it?" asked Picard.

The Romulan burst out laughing. "Oh, go right ahead, but it won't prove a thing."

"What do you mean?" asked the captain.

"I mean, I'm married to a Vulcan, and she's an adept instructor in mind-melding. In fact, she was a child prodigy. I've been exposed to lots of melds, and

171

I've learned the techniques to resist them, which I will not hesitate to use."

The captain frowned and glanced at Taurik.

"This is possible," answered the Vulcan. "Hasmek has mentioned before that he is married to a Vulcan, and we know that Romulans have considerable interest in the procedure."

The Romulan lifted his chin with pride. "In fact, that's the reason I was chosen for this delicate assignment—my resistance to the Vulcan mind-meld."

"You would submit, if I asked you?" said Picard.

With a sneer, the Romulan pointed to his empty sleeve. "I'm in no condition to fight you, so I would submit. But I guarantee that you won't learn any more about me than you already know."

The smug smile vanished from the Romulan's face. "Besides, Captain, it's obvious that your nemesis is Grof. He's the one who stands the most to gain and the least to lose. He already runs the ship."

The captain sniffed disdainfully at the barb. "And you, Mister Lavelle, would you submit to a mind-meld?"

"Yes, sir." Sam came to attention, but he couldn't hide the fear on his face as he thought about having an unknown enemy on board. "Sir, you really should look closely at Grof."

"Or that Maquis officer," said Hasmek. "Once a traitor, always a traitor."

"It's not Ro!" snapped Sam. "You can just forget that idea."

"A little protective of the Bajoran, are we?" asked Hasmek with amusement.

"That's enough," ordered Picard. "If you accuse somebody of these very serious charges, you had better present some proof. Do either one of you have any proof?"

"His words, his own actions," insisted Sam.

"I could say the same about Ro Laren," answered Picard, "if we are going by past experience. I've tried to give everyone on this vessel a new start, but someone has reverted to type. I'll find them."

"You'd better," said Hasmek grimly, "or this crew will mutiny."

Picard's eyes narrowed at his former foe. "We're in a desperate situation, and I won't hesitate to take desperate measures. Do I make myself clear?"

"Yes, sir!" piped Sam, although his confidence was waning.

"We finally have a workable plan to take out the collider," said the captain, "and we have a lot of work to do. I'm expecting both of you to do your share."

Hasmek gaped at him. "Won't that be rather difficult, with someone on the ship trying to stop us? Isn't this the same person who tried to *starve* us to death?"

Picard ignored him. "I want the two of you to relieve Woil in engineering. Tell him to get some sleep. He lost his buddy when we lost Shonsui, but we'll find him a new one. Keep each other in sight at all times, and be prepared to assist La Forge from engineering."

"It's time to pray to the war gods," declared Hasmek, "because we are in deep trouble."

"Keep that opinion to yourself," ordered Picard, "and don't tell anyone what we discussed in this room. We're going to depend on the buddy system. Now go to your station."

"Yes, sir," answered Sam, squeezing past them to get out the door. He was glad to be going back on duty, but he couldn't shake the feeling that he was headed downhill in an old red wagon with the wheels falling off.

Ro Laren followed Captain Picard and Taurik onto the bridge of the *Orb of Peace*. Grof sat at the auxiliary console, looking self-satisfied and self-absorbed, Tamla Horik was on the conn, and Enrique Maserelli was on tactical. The viewscreen showed a split view of the magneton collider in one half and the perpetual sandstorm of Juno's rings in the other.

"Hello, Captain," said Grof cheerfully, "I was just about to show you the first draft of the floor plan. I believe it's very close, although there may be some things I've forgotten."

Picard gave him a polite smile. "That's excellent, Professor. I need to devote full attention to that, so let me dispose of a few other matters first. Why don't you report to Mr. La Forge at the escape pod. He has a few questions for you."

Ro smiled inwardly. She had been with the captain when he had warned Geordi that he would be sending Grof down, and that he should keep him busy.

"Of course," answered Grof, bounding to his feet, the picture of cooperation and confidence. "Is there anything else you would like me to convey to Commander La Forge?"

"Only that the three of us will meet later." With a nod of his head, Picard dismissed the scientist and turned his attention toward Maserelli and Horik. As Grof stomped down the stairs, Enrique squirmed under Picard's baleful gaze, while the Deltan kept her attention on her console, and her back to the captain.

Taurik stepped toward the tactical station, and

Enrique realized that he was being relieved. Ro moved quickly behind Tamla Horik at the conn.

"Status?" asked Picard.

"Maintaining position," answered Horik.

Enrique looked down at his readouts and reported, "Almost no work crews are present at the moment, and most of the support vessels have backed off. Grof thinks they're about to do another test, but then, he's been saying that for hours."

Picard nodded gravely. "I have to speak with both of you. Taurik, take tactical. Ro, on the conn."

Enrique looked curious as he stepped away from the tactical station. Tamla Horik relinquished the conn to Ro. She and Enrique stood at attention, respectful and alert, probably thinking they were about to be briefed on the plan to take out the collider.

"What I'm about to tell you is to be kept in confidence, and not to leave this bridge," began the captain. "Have either one of you been to the torpedo room recently?"

Enrique shook his head. "No, sir, I've never been there."

"Me neither," answered Tamla. "Is something wrong with our last torpedo?"

"No, but we have had two incidents of attempted sabotage, along with the earlier episode with the food replicators."

"What does that mean?" muttered Enrique nervously.

"It means we are taking measured precautions to root out the traitor on board, without disrupting our mission. Neither one of you is under any particular suspicion, but we have to make sure. Therefore, I'm going to ask you to submit to a Vulcan mind-meld."

Tamla gave Taurik a nervous smile. "I suppose that wouldn't be a problem."

Picard turned to Enrique. "And you?"

"I don't . . . I don't know, sir," said the handsome human with the dark beard. "I've always been scared of mind-melds—I mean, you could go crazy, or die!"

"Highly unlikely," replied Taurik. "However, reactions do vary from subject to subject."

"I'm afraid you don't have much choice," said Picard. "It's an order."

Enrique gulped, straightened his shoulders, and stared straight ahead. "Okay, sir. Can I . . . can I hold Tamla's hand?"

A smile slipped from Picard's taut face. "That's unnecessary. We won't perform the mind-meld at this time, but I'm grateful that both of you consented."

"Yes, sir," breathed Enrique, his shoulders slumping with relief.

"Return to your stations. Ro and Taurik, you're with me."

The captain strode off the bridge, and the Vulcan and the Bajoran jumped to their feet and hurried after him. He paused at the top of the spiral staircase, glanced around, and whispered, "Our last subject is Jozarnay Woil, who ought to be asleep in the dorms. I'm not sure if I should be disappointed or pleased with our progress so far, because everyone seems innocent."

"There is logic in this course of action," said Taurik, "although the findings may not be conclusive."

"I know." Picard tugged thoughtfully on his earring. "Thus far, no one seems unduly concerned about going through a mind-meld, which is interesting to me."

"Perhaps it's not as fearsome a procedure as Hasmek believes," observed Taurik dryly.

"It should be fearsome, to the wrong person."

With a wave, Captain Picard led them down the spiral staircase and along the corridor. A moment later, they stopped outside the large dormitory, where so many of their original crew had been murdered. No one deigned to sleep there now, except for the monkish Antosian, who preferred open spaces to tiny cabins and corners.

Picard tapped a wall panel, and the door opened. He led the way into the darkened room, which reminded Ro of a low-ceilinged gymnasium. Rows of hammocks, which had once hung like moss from the ceiling, were now gone, taken by people to furnish their new quarters. Geordi slept in one of the hammocks aboard the escape pod.

Loud snoring led them to the sleeping Antosian, who was curled up in the center of the room in a morass of sofa pillows, taken from the empty rec rooms. Ro regretted that they had to wake him up—in fact, he looked so blissful that she wanted to curl up beside him and go to sleep.

"Lights!" barked Picard, and a ceiling full of tubes glimmered on, bathing the room with artificial sun.

"Huh?" muttered Woil, cringing and swiping a hand at the offending light. He tried to burrow into his cushions.

"Wake up, Mister Woil," said the captain. "That's an order."

Recognizing the voice, he rolled over, blinked at Picard, and staggered to his feet. The Antosian's usually neat bun of black hair looked disheveled and ratty, with wisps sticking out at odd angles. He looked weary, half asleep, and Ro's sympathy went out to him. She hoped he wouldn't resist the order, necessitating the mind-meld. Although she didn't exactly love this ragtag crew, she didn't want to discover that one of them was a traitor and murderer.

"Am I on duty, sir?" asked Woil with sleepy confusion.

"At ease," said Picard. "We need information. Have you been in the torpedo room since your arrival on this ship?"

"No, sir," answered the Antosian, frowning in thought. "I don't think so."

"What about the cargo hold?"

"No, sir, I've mainly been in engineering, with a little bridge duty. Wait a minute, I believe I went into the hold once to check a stasis field."

"Did you ever enter the storage area at the back, the one with mesh walls?"

"No, sir." The tall Antosian rubbed his eyes, trying to wake up. "May I ask why, sir?"

"There have been two more possible acts of sabotage against this ship and her mission. Are you responsible for any of them?"

Woil blinked at him, then smiled. When he realized the captain was deadly serious, the smile slid off his pudgy face. He looked uncertainly from the captain to Taurik and finally to Ro. Her stomach started churning, because she had a premonition that the Antosian was not going to submit.

"Why do you suspect me?" asked Woil.

"We suspect everyone," replied Picard. "Will you answer my question?"

"No, it wasn't me. I didn't commit any acts of sabotage!" He sounded both pleading and indignant, reactions which Ro could easily understand.

"Will you submit to a Vulcan mind-meld?"

Woil narrowed his eyes and looked suspiciously at Taurik. "No, sir, I won't. That's against the beliefs and laws of my people."

"I should make myself clear," said Picard. "This is an order."

"I respectfully decline, sir." The Antosian lifted his chin and stared straight ahead. "We are taught that such intrusions into the mind are the same as violating a person's body."

Ro's stomach twisted into a bigger knot, and her hand inched toward her phaser. She could see Picard's shoulders rise and fall as he decided how to deal with this insubordination.

"I know Antosian teachings," said Picard with sympathy, "and this isn't the same as the techniques that were forbidden on your planet. There will be no lasting harm, no intrusion, other than to review the few days since you arrived on this vessel. Ro, did I ask the same of you, despite your objections?"

"Yes, sir," she answered.

"I still refuse," declared the Antosian. "I doubt if you'll be able to bring court-martial charges against me for refusing."

Picard's lips thinned. "Mister Taurik, can you perform the procedure on a person who is stunned?"

"Yes, sir," answered the Vulcan, surveying Jozarnay Woil with interest.

"Ro, draw your phaser and set it to light stun."

"Yes, sir." Anticipating that order, she had the weapon halfway out of its holster before the captain finished his sentence. She double-checked the setting on the Bajoran phaser to make sure it was set to stun.

"Wait a minute!" growled the Antosian, dropping into a defensive crouch and backing away from them. "This is sacrilege!"

179

"I'm giving you one last chance," warned the captain. "Nobody gets out of this test."

"What about the Trill and the Romulan?" protested Woil. "Are you saying *they* checked out clean?"

"Everyone I've asked so far had agreed to the mind-meld," answered Picard truthfully. "You're the only one who hasn't."

The Antosian grimaced at the difficulty of his decision. Ro felt sorry for him, because she knew how difficult it was to forsake long-held beliefs for a greater good.

"Submit to it," she begged him.

"No!"

Reluctantly, Picard ordered, "Fire."

The big Antosian ducked and tried to scramble away, but Ro drilled him in the shoulder with a phaser beam. He took one more step and sprawled on his stomach across the barren deck.

She lowered her weapon, regretting the stunning that would lead to a forced mind-meld. Unfortunately, Woil hadn't given them any choice. She could tell from the captain's troubled expression that he wasn't happy over their actions either. Anyone who thought a commanding officer had to like every order he gave didn't know much about command.

Picard turned distastefully to Taurik and said, "Proceed." The Vulcan closed his eyes, put his hands together, and seemed to meditate.

"Isn't there any other way?" asked Ro.

"We have to know for sure," said Picard grimly.

After a moment, the Vulcan opened his eyes and moved to the unconscious body. He turned Woil over and positioned his head and neck. Just as he spread the fingers of his right hand and placed them on the

Antosian's cheekbone and chin, Picard's combadge chirped.

"Picard here," he said impatiently.

"Captain!" came Enrique's breathless voice. "The magneton and neutrino readings from the collider are going off the scale. We think they're operating the artificial wormhole!"

"Alert Grof, and have him meet me on the bridge," ordered Picard, rushing for the door. He pointed back at Ro and Taurik. "Go ahead with the mind-meld, while he's still out."

"Yes, sir." Ro still felt reluctant, but a direct order was a direct order. She holstered her phaser and turned back to Taurik. "Go on."

He looked down at the body stretched out before him and said, "There is a possibility that he may come back to consciousness. Perhaps I can control him, perhaps not. Would you please give me the phaser, so that I can use it if necessary."

"Sure." She handed the Vulcan her phaser weapon and was surprised a moment later when he turned it on her.

"Put your hands up," he ordered. "Away from your combadge."

She gaped at him. "Is this some kind of joke?"

"It is no joke, I can assure you." Something chilling in his voice warned her that he wasn't lying, as if Vulcans could lie. She lifted her hands over her head.

Taurik took a step closer, and he stared intently at her, as if he were trying to memorize every line of her face. His own face began to shimmer and flatten, as if it were turning into a pool of water. For a moment, his face morphed into a mirror with her own image staring back at her! Ro watched in horror as his outstretched arm turned the color and consistency of liquid mercury.

A changeling! Ro reached for her combadge, as his hand extended into a gleaming tentacle and ripped the device off her chest. She whirled to escape, but another tentacle wrapped around her legs like a steel cable and yanked hard, dumping her face-first onto the deck. Ro barely had time to roll over before the creature's phaser spit a red streak into her chest, then all was peace and darkness.

Chapter Eleven

THE MAGNETON COLLIDER lit up along its entire length with a brilliant blue light, like a giant coil of gas flames. A red light pulsed down the center of the massive tube, going faster and faster until it became a blur. Picard squinted at the blazing sight on the viewscreen, but he couldn't look away; he was intent upon seeing what emerged from the glowing tunnel, even if it signaled the end of the Federation.

He heard running footsteps and a gasp, and he turned to see Enrak Grof stagger onto the bridge. He gaped at the viewscreen and murmured, "It's started— a full test—maybe the whole fleet coming through. By heavens, it's magnificent!"

Picard scowled and turned to Maserelli. "Are the levels still rising?"

Enrique gazed from his console to the screen, a look

of shock on his face. "It should be torn apart," he answered.

"Oh, no," insisted Grof with pride, "that's why we used the grid and the Corzanium—to withstand the pressure. Wait until you see it blossom—any second now!"

Picard wished that Grof could have been a little less gleeful about seeing his artificial wormhole in its full glory, but he couldn't deny that it was magnificent. If only death and destruction weren't waiting on the other side.

With the rush of a wave crashing onto the shore, a blue and white cloud opened from the mouth of the collider like the petals of a flower caught in fast photography. A golden light filled the center of the tube and shined outward like a gigantic phaser beam. From this mass of blinding light and swirling clouds, a small ship was flung into the blackness of space.

As quickly as it had begun, the petals of the wormhole collapsed onto themselves, and the kaleidoscope of lights disappeared. The massive collider went dark, except for a few errant sparks rippling along its metallic skeleton. The only difference was that a small Jem'Hadar attack ship drifted in the void of space, having traveled across the galaxy in the blink of an eye.

"I would like to know whether the Jem'Hadar on that ship are dead or alive," said Grof.

"What difference does it make?" asked Horik at the conn.

"A great deal," answered the Trill. "If they're dead, we may have a couple of days' grace. If they're alive, we have exactly twelve hours until the real fleet comes through."

Picard tapped his combadge and said, "Bridge to La Forge."

"La Forge here," came the engineer. "Thanks for sending me all the help—we're on schedule."

"No, we're not," answered the captain, "because the schedule has been moved up. The Dominion has just completed a test on the wormhole where they brought through an attack ship. We have twelve hours until it's fully operational and a fleet comes through."

Geordi gave a low whistle. "Wow. I guess we'd better get back to work."

"Double-time," answered the captain. "Bridge out."

He tapped his combadge again. "Bridge to Ro."

"Ro here," came the familiar, businesslike voice.

"Was the procedure successful?" With Grof standing nearby, Picard was forced to be circumspect. He didn't want to alarm the professor until they had gotten complete schematics from him.

"Yes," answered Ro, "in that it came out negative."

Picard frowned, being both pleased that Woil was in the clear yet mystified at the same time. *If it wasn't him, then who was it?* Given the shortage of time, he would have to rethink his methods.

"Did Taurik have any problem?" asked Picard.

"Not that I could tell. Both he and Woil are now resting."

"Stay with them," ordered Picard, "then all three of you report to La Forge. I'm afraid the Dominion just performed a successful test on the artificial wormhole. According to Grof, we only have twelve hours."

"That's unfortunate," replied Ro with extreme understatement.

"Bridge out," concluded Picard. He glanced around

at the assembled crew, all of whom were stunned, except for Grof.

"There's one good thing," said the Trill.

"What?" asked Picard doubtfully.

"Now that I've seen it work, I can destroy it with a clear conscience."

The captain nodded, wishing that he could get back to business-as-usual as easily as Grof. He tried to put the inner threat out of his mind, knowing that if they didn't stop the artificial wormhole, it wouldn't matter what their intruder did. He had made sure that everyone was under some sort of scrutiny, and that was the best he could do at the moment.

"Keep that attack ship under observation," ordered Picard. "Grof, I believe it's time to go over your schematics, and finalize our own plans."

"I would concur," said Grof, heading for the exit. "Time is of the essence."

Picard took one last look around the Bajoran bridge before he accompanied Grof to the captain's quarters. Both Horik and Maserelli looked spooked, but they manned their stations like the well-trained officers they were, falling back on routine to ward off fear. Deep in Dominion space, about to confront a Dominion fleet, and with a saboteur on board, only a madman could be completely calm.

Who was it? Picard tried to review just the facts—no suppositions or unfounded suspicions. Someone had destroyed their food replicators, delaying them, possibly forcing them into the open. If Lena Shonsui's death was connected—and he wasn't sure it was—then someone had tried to maroon Ro and Geordi. Disabling the subspace beacon was an obvious ploy—their nemesis didn't want anyone coming to their aid.

Destroying the explosives was equally transparent—they feared the mission would be successful.

"Captain Picard," snapped an impatient Trill voice, "we haven't got all day." Grof waved his padd from the top of the spiral staircase.

If Grof is the one, thought the captain, *then he's a brilliant actor. I'll keep an eye on him personally.*

"Lead the way, Professor."

Sam Lavelle straightened up, weary from leaning over the waist-high table which showed the master systems. He looked around the dreary engineering room, thinking it had none of the Bajoran charm of the rest of the ship. It was utilitarian and spartan, with few upgrades or niceties, as if engineering was a somber pursuit not given to pleasant aesthetics.

Hasmek, who couldn't sleep when stretched out on the sofa in Sam's quarters, was fast asleep at the duty console, his head cradled in his remaining arm. *So much for the buddy system.* Sam realized that if Hasmek were the saboteur, he could do a lot of damage to the *Orb of Peace* in his position. But he wasn't the bad apple—he was just an unlucky slob.

He didn't know exactly why, but his gut instincts told him that it wasn't Hasmek. Maybe that was because both of them were convinced it was Grof.

Sam looked around at the gray walls and beeping monitors, tracking warp cores and propulsion systems that hadn't changed for several hours. Thrusters were handling the occasional course correction without drawing from main power. The warp core itself was in a shielded shaft in the tail of the ship, so there wasn't much to see.

They may have been on duty, but they weren't part

of the action, and Sam knew it. He resented being segregated with the Romulan, but in truth he didn't mind the solitude. Sam didn't feel like being sociable with a group of edgy, sleep-deprived people, one of whom might be trying to kill them all.

I might make an exception for Ro or Taurik, but only them.

He got up and made the rounds of all the stations, even though he could get most of the same readouts from the master display. He almost wished this were a Starfleet vessel, so he could reassign a console to become the conn, tactical, transporter, any station on board—just to see what was going on.

Sam heard the door whisper open, and he turned around to see Ro stride into the room and lean her slim body over the display table. His first instinct was to wake up Hasmek—to keep him from getting into trouble—but it was too late for that. She glanced at the Romulan and shook her short-cropped fringe of hair.

He stepped sheepishly from behind the bank of monitors and saw Ro gazing at the master display. She glanced at him, then at the sleeping Romulan. "Things not too exciting around here?"

"I'm sorry," said Sam. "Shall we wake him up?"

"No, let him sleep. There should be somebody well rested when the action starts. Besides, I really came to see *you.*" Ro fixed him with her deep brown eyes and leaned casually against the table.

Sam stepped closer to her. "Are you here to relieve me?"

"No, just to talk to you. So much is going on around here—I need to be able to trust somebody." Ro looked away from him, as if embarrassed, and for a moment, she seemed vulnerable, approachable.

Sam took another step closer. "What's worrying you?" He cringed at his ridiculous question, thinking there were plenty of things for a sane person to worry about.

She sauntered toward him as if she had just discovered how to walk in that sexy body. "If we fail, I don't want to be alone. I want to know I can depend on somebody to be there, even if it's just to hold my hand as we go down in flames. I don't want to be alone. Does that make sense to you?"

"Sure," answered Sam, not anxious to be alone ever again, not if he could be with someone like Ro. They embraced and kissed each other with hungry passion. Sam was surprised—she seemed almost like a different woman than before. No longer reticent, but insistent—

Gripping his chest and shoulders, she pulled him away from the sleeping Romulan and the beaming consoles. Shoving him urgently while she nuzzled his neck, Ro propelled Sam toward a dark alcove where an airlock was hidden away. There was nothing Sam wanted more than the feel of her all over him, but he knew it was wrong to desert their posts. It was also a bad idea to leave the Romulan alone, unobserved, in a place like engineering.

Insanely, against every urge in his body, Sam pried the passionate Bajoran away. "Ro, we can't do this now. Later—"

"How do you know there will be a later?" she insisted.

"There has to be—we'll *make* it happen."

"I'm afraid," she breathed, gripping him tightly. "A lot of them think I'm the one . . . the one who's been sabotaging the mission. If they come after me, will you protect me?"

"Sure," he told her with a comforting smile. "Why don't we tell the captain that we want to be buddies, like Tamla and Enrique?"

"No, no!" she said, gripping his hands. "Let's keep it a secret, just between us. I want to have a special signal to call you, if I need you."

"Okay," said Sam hoarsely.

She looked around the room, then fixed him with her large, radiant eyes. "From any station on the ship, I can send a general alert to every other station. If you see an alert for a meteor shower, come to the station of origin. I'll be waiting."

"All right," agreed Sam, squeezing her hands.

"I love you," she replied in a voice which sounded dark and husky.

Before the stunned human could reply, Ro Laren brushed his lips with the most gossamer of kisses, then reluctantly pulled away. She put on her poker face, straightened her shoulders, and strode purposefully through engineering and into the corridor.

Forcing his lungs to breathe and his legs to walk, Sam shuffled after her. He paused by the display table and stared at the closed door, wishing that he hadn't told her to wait until later. *Why did I send her away?*

"You're playing with antimatter," said the supposedly sleeping Romulan, never opening his eyes.

Sam scowled at Hasmek and started to disagree, but he couldn't. Ro's neediness played into his fantasies, but like most fantasies that came true, the reality was not altogether appealing. He had been hoping he could depend on Ro to get them through this mess, and now it appeared as if she might end up depending on him instead. *Ah, the downside of everything.*

"You wouldn't help *me* escape from this ship," said Hasmek with a sniff, "but I'm sure you'd help *her.*"

"Nobody's escaping," answered Sam with grim certainty, "until it's all over."

The acrid smell of cleaning solvents brought Ro Laren slowly back to consciousness. After her olfactory senses awoke, aches in her back, neck, and leg muscles followed, until finally she was forced to pry her eyes open. She found herself in total darkness.

When Ro tried to shout, she discovered that a thick gag stretched across her mouth; she couldn't reach the gag with her hands, because they were tied together. Instinctively, she kicked with her legs and found that they were bound together, too, and a length of freight cable tied her feet to her hands. Ro was in a fetal position, sitting up and barely able to move.

She tried to stay calm and assess the situation. Her headache and general fuzziness made her believe that she had been unconscious for some time, maybe hours. The smells, darkness, and cramped confines suggested that she was in the equipment locker at the rear of the dormitory. Despite her anger, Ro realized she was lucky to be alive, because she had been at the changeling's mercy. It had stunned her—on a heavy setting—but it could have killed her.

All this time, she thought in amazement, *it had been Taurik, the Vulcan.* The changeling must have been on Sam's crew since they left the collider as prisoners, out to mine Corzanium. No one knew about it, not even Grof. It had accidentally found itself part of the Federation's only plan to stop the artificial wormhole, and now it was going to sabotage the mission, from within. With the ability to look like anyone on board, even the captain, it could go undetected for as long as it needed.

I have to get out of here!

Ro squirmed, yanked, and kicked, but all she got for her efforts were more stabs of pain in her arms and legs. Plus she fell to the side and plowed ear-first into a cold metal bulkhead. Panting, fighting to remain conscious, Ro lay there in the abject, silent darkness.

I have to be patient, she told herself. *I have to think. Why did it keep me alive?*

One answer was that it was still taking prisoners, still finding slaves for the Dominion. Anther possibility was that it needed a living reference, which meant that it was out there, pretending to be *her!*

Ro lashed out frantically, but she only succeeded in twisting herself into an even more painful knot. She had to move slowly, in tiny increments, if she hoped to explore her cell. If there was anything in here that could help her, she had to find it.

"As long as you understand, Captain, the charge must be big enough to take out this entire panel of instruments as well as the circuitry behind this bulkhead." Enrak Grof indicated two key points on his meticulous diagram.

Captain Picard leaned across the table in the make-shift ready room and studied the plans. It all seemed so simple when laid out in black and white and perused at one's leisure. *Get in, place the charge, and get out.*

But they no longer had high-yield explosives to beam into the collider, so coming close wasn't good enough. They had to be exact, which meant that a team had to beam over to the catwalks and access tubes of the spidery structure and manually place the charge, whatever it was. Although he had considered this possibility before, it sounded especially daunting, now that it was their only option.

As if this problem wasn't bad enough, his mind kept slipping over to the saboteur. He couldn't help but wonder what harm their hidden foe was doing to the ship and the mission, while he sat in conference with this egomaniac, Grof. Nobody had contacted him in a panic—nothing seemed amiss—but the captain knew that the enemy's next strike could be decisive.

Picard reached for the padd and mustered a smile. "Thank you, Professor, excellent work. I think it's time to print up your schematics and make copies for Mister La Forge and myself. And I'd like to get you working on the escape pod with La Forge."

"Good idea, Captain." Grof checked his timepiece. "We only have eleven hours."

Picard rose to his feet, suddenly anxious to check on the rest of his crew. He led the way out of the ready room and down the corridor, past the cargo hold and engineering to the aft section. Here, on either side of the ship, were two small hatches. One was closed and marked by a red light, showing that the escape pod had been launched. The other hatch was wide open, and the sound of voices bursting from the pod was surprisingly reassuring to the captain.

He ducked his head, looked inside, and saw Ro Laren, Geordi La Forge, and Jozarnay Woil bent over a piece of machinery. The three of them barely fit inside the cramped sphere. Although the pod was intended to accommodate eight, that was with all the passengers strapped to the walls, hanging in zero gravity, not roaming freely. The escape pod had no artificial gravity, except now when it was still part of the ship. It didn't usually have all this extraneous equipment crammed into every spare centimeter.

Geordi patted the metal box fondly, then looked at

Picard. "Hello, Captain. I used the distortion amplifiers from our secondary emitters to make this jammer. It will block their sensors and make us look like a simple meteoroid. It's crude, but it only has to do one thing, and we can test that with our tricorders."

"Excellent," said Picard with a genuine smile. He glanced at the big Antosian. "I regret, Mister Woil, that we had to put you through the mind-meld, but our security is vital. How do you feel?"

The Antosian shrugged. "Fine. I don't feel any different at all."

The captain looked around. "Where's Taurik?"

"Oh," said Ro, "he wasn't feeling well after the procedure, so I suggested he stay in the dormitory and sleep."

Picard frowned, thinking it odd that the subject of the mind-meld felt great, but the Vulcan had to rest. Perhaps Taurik wasn't an expert at the procedure—there was no reason to think all Vulcans should be equally adept at it. He hadn't been particularly enthusiastic.

"What's all this talk about mind-melds?" asked a gruff voice behind him.

Picard turned to look at Grof, who so far had been kept in the dark about the most recent attempts to sabotage their mission. He didn't want the Trill to lose confidence and revert back to being recalcitrant and uncooperative.

"It's part of our ongoing investigation into the failure of the food replicators," he explained. "Nothing for you to concern yourself with." Picard gave each of the others a stern look, to remind them not to discuss it.

"Come on," said La Forge, "we need to finish

installing the transporter, then work on the outside of this thing."

Picard snapped his fingers and scowled. "I'm sorry. With the distractions, I forgot to set the scoop to pick up debris from the rings."

"That's all right," replied Geordi. "I alerted the bridge—they're doing it. I plan to stucco the sphere, using a molecular bonder and the transporter."

The captain nodded, certainly glad that he had brought Geordi along on this desperate journey. "Can you find something for Professor Grof to do?"

"Sure," answered the engineer. "Know anything about molecular scanners and pattern buffers, Professor?"

"Certainly, I used to program them in secondary school." The Trill muscled his way past Picard and entered the cramped pod. To escape the crowd, Ro leaned her body into the curve of the wall and studied a tricorder.

"I'm glad everything is under control," said Picard. "I'll check on engineering."

"Captain," called Ro, "don't worry about Taurik. He's going to call me when he wakes up. I know he's still my buddy, and I'll watch out for him."

"Very well," said Picard, grateful that he had Ro along, too. "We have less than eleven hours."

"I'll remind them," vowed Grof.

Picard backed away from the hatch and took the short walk down the corridor to engineering. When he entered, he was encouraged to find both Lavelle and Hasmek alert and at their posts. Sam came to attention, and the Romulan sat up with curiosity.

"At ease," he told them, as if that were even possible. "Is our status normal?"

"Yes, sir," answered Lavelle. "Not much has happened down here."

"How goes the search for our hidden enemy?" asked Hasmek.

"Slowly." The captain stepped into the room, letting the door shut behind him. "But the mission is progressing quickly, which is why I'm here. We have less than eleven hours."

"With no evidence," muttered Hasmek.

Picard ignored him. "Mister Lavelle, you mentioned that you had an idea for destroying the entire magneton collider, not just the accelerator room."

"Yes, sir," answered Sam, eager to share his plan. "I spent a lot of time floating along various parts of that monster, and there are air lines running through every centimeter of it—to feed the workers' space suits. I think you could flood those lines with hydrogen, which is part of the breathing mixture, and ignite it. With luck, you might blow the whole thing up."

Hasmek turned around, looking impressed. "Very inventive, Sam. I like it."

Picard cocked his head thoughtfully and lifted the padd in his hand. "I have Grof's schematics here, and I need to enlarge them and make copies. After you do that for me, take a look at them and see if you can find a way to implement your plan. At the very least, it would make quite a diversion, and we might need that."

"Sure, Captain, let me transfer it to the computer." Lavelle took the padd from him, crossed to his duty console, and jacked it in.

While Sam worked on Grof's files, Picard strolled around engineering, a room in which he hadn't spent much time since coming aboard the *Orb of Peace*.

Considering all this little ship had been through, its energy and propulsion systems were in remarkably good shape. Of course, they had been using guile to get around Dominion space, avoiding fights whenever possible.

He looked up and saw Hasmek watching him. The Romulan rose to his feet and walked slowly toward Picard, a troubled look on his face. "I've been thinking about our personal spy."

"Yes?"

"I don't understand what he's doing. I think he must be crazy, or suicidal. For example, taking out the food replicators. Isn't that suicidal?"

"It didn't prove to be," answered the captain. "It forced us off our mission and deeper into the Badlands—"

"Where we nearly got killed. We were very lucky to find someone who could help us." The Romulan shook his head. "Maybe he learned his lesson after that, because that was the last crazy thing he did."

Picard frowned thoughtfully at the one-armed Romulan. The destruction of the explosives and the subspace beacon had seemed so immediate that he hadn't thought much about the first incident. Taking out the food replicators was so bizarre that it had been difficult to accept as an act of sabotage . . . until more acts followed. Everyone needed food and drink. *Or did they?*

"And the death of the transporter operator," said Hasmek puzzledly. "I was asleep, but the rest of you were on duty. Who could have left their post, gone to the transporter room, done it, and gone back— without anyone seeing? Unless we have a ghost on board. No, I think her death must be unrelated."

Picard suddenly realized who could have done the murder as Hasmek described it—who could have flowed through the air ducts or slithered along the decks, who could have intruded into her body and caused death without leaving a mark.

A changeling.

It could look like any of them—*be* any of them. Lavelle had mentioned seeing a changeling in the Dominion prison.

"Captain," said Hasmek with irritation, "you're not listening to me."

"On the contrary, I've listened very carefully." The captain gazed at the Romulan's face, wondering if he really were a Romulan.

The changeling had to be Hasmek, Ro, or someone from Lavelle's crew—someone not from the *Enterprise.* After learning how changelings had infiltrated the Klingon high command, Starfleet had developed a complex medical test to ferret them out. They had administered the test to every officer, from ensign to admiral, but that didn't do them any good here.

Without Beverly Crusher, he had no chance of duplicating that test on the *Orb of Peace.* Even then, he doubted if they had the equipment and supplies needed.

"Captain, you are very distracted," said the Romulan with exasperation. "We'll speak later."

"I am distracted," agreed Picard, starting for the door. "But our conversation was enlightening."

"It was?"

"Absolutely. Lavelle, keep working on the diagrams."

"Yes, sir."

Picard walked out of engineering, and the door slid shut behind him. For a moment, he stood there, staring down a deserted corridor, aware that his nemesis could be the fire extinguisher, the grille of a vent, or the light above him. Fighting a changeling was almost too difficult to contemplate, and he hoped his suspicions were wrong.

But what if they weren't?

Chapter Twelve

GEORDI STOOD UP from his labors and wiped a sheen of sweat off his forehead. The escape pod wasn't built for manual labor, and the air circulation was poor. Woil was standing outside the hatch, taking radiation readings with a tricorder, and Ro and Grof were installing a transporter pad in the only empty square of bulkhead left on the curved inner surface. A transporter pad had been pulled whole from the main transporter platform, and they had to anchor it and get power to it.

"Since there won't be any gravity on board," said Ro, "we'll have to install some bars or handles for people to stabilize themselves. They'll have to put their feet on the pad, right?"

"Right," answered Geordi. "That's a good idea. There are extra handles in the lavatory."

"I'll get them," declared Ro, starting for the hatch.

"Wait a minute, the captain said people weren't supposed to be alone." Geordi looked disapprovingly at her.

"I have to go check on Taurik, anyway," insisted Ro. "He's my buddy, so I won't be alone after I get him back on duty."

"I don't know—"

"Oh, let her go," grumbled Grof. "Maybe then we'll have room to move around in here."

In a blink, the lanky Bajoran was gone. Geordi sighed and went back to work, thinking that it had always been hard to tell Ro Laren what to do.

Gasping for breath, the Bajoran stopped kicking on the walls of her dark cage. A lightheaded feeling came over her, and she sat still, meditating, until it passed. The raw pain on her wrists and ankles helped her to remain conscious. For the first time, Ro realized that the air didn't replenish well in this dark, smelly equipment chest, and she was in danger of using too much of it, too fast.

Besides, it was doubtful that anybody could hear her muffled kicks—here in the back of the second largest room on the ship, after the cargo hold. Nobody had any reason to come in here, except for her captor.

She wasn't going to kick her way out either. On her right was the outer hull of the ship, which meant that the nearby bulkheads, hatches, and doors were fortified. Having spent considerable effort and pain to get into a position to kick, she didn't want to stop; but Ro knew she had better save her strength and air until she had a real opportunity.

She tried to relax and tell herself to be patient—that she had been kept alive for a reason. She would have a chance to escape if she bided her time. Until then, she would have to stay alert and ready.

In her desperate squirming, she had found that her metal tomb was empty except for the residue of cleaning solvents and detergents, which she could still smell. In fact, the solvents were all over her clothes, adding to the itching and discomfort.

Solvents, she thought suddenly; *they wouldn't do anything for the bindings on her hands and feet, but they might loosen the glue on her gag.* Ro didn't want to think about the contortions she would have to go through to get her mouth on the floor of the narrow box, but she resolved to do it.

Captain Picard sat down at an auxiliary console on the bridge, ignoring the quizzical looks from Horik and Maserelli. He tried not to stare at them or wonder: *Are they really human and Deltan?*

He went back to his console, but after a few moments, he frowned in disappointment. The comm system would not allow him to track the whereabouts of every crew member, as he could aboard the *Enterprise.* He could only tell if their combadges were functional. There weren't even video logs of the various decks and stations of the *Orb of Peace* that he could use to trace the crew's movements.

Picard stood and stretched, feeling as if he should *do* something—make the rounds—question everyone again. But their mission was progressing, under an imposing deadline, and he couldn't afford to throw the ship into turmoil. As much as he disliked it, Picard was forced into a defensive position, waiting for his nemesis to make the next move.

But if time was running out for them, it was also running out for *it.* Their foe had to act soon to stop the mission.

His combadge chirped, and the captain answered it, "Bridge."

"Captain, this is Lavelle. I think I've found the atmospheric treatment center on Grof's drawings. We ought to be able to access the conduits there and flood the collider with hydrogen."

"Fine," answered Picard. "As soon as possible, I'll come down to engineering."

He started for the door and turned to Horik. "You have the bridge—maintain position."

"Yes, sir," answered the attractive Deltan.

After leaving the bridge, the captain paused at the top of the spiral staircase, wondering if he had left any loose ends. Everyone was busy working, except for Taurik, and it was time to roust the Vulcan and get him back to work. Picard wanted to make sure that everyone was occupied and no one was alone.

He descended the stairs and made his way along the deserted corridor. A sudden shadow on the bulkhead made him whirl around, but he saw nothing—except for a bulb flickering in one of the overhead fixtures. Picard took a sharp breath, thinking that he had better control his jumpy nerves if he was going to finish this job.

He walked slowly down the corridor until he reached the door of the dormitory. It slid open at his approach. Inside the large room, it was dark, except for a few dim lights on the ceiling. Ever since they had discovered so many bodies in the dorm, it had engendered uneasy feelings among everyone, Picard included. He put them aside in order to enter the cavernous room, but he kept his hand on the butt of his phaser pistol.

The room appeared to be empty, except for the pile of cushions in the center where Jozarnay Woil had been sleeping. No one lay there now—it looked deserted.

Picard paused to tug on his earring, wondering where Taurik had gone. He tapped his combadge. "Picard to Taurik."

"Taurik here," came the Vulcan's calm voice.

"Where exactly are you?" asked Picard.

"In the mess hall with Ro. She woke me up and insisted I get something to eat before going on duty."

Picard heard a thud that sounded far away, within the bulkhead. It was probably noise from Geordi's labors, he told himself, even though it sounded as if it came from behind him. Ambient noises could be confusing on an old ship like this, Picard knew.

"Captain," said the Vulcan, "we thought we could relieve the bridge crew for a few minutes, give them a chance to eat."

"Very well," answered Picard, "but I don't want anyone to be alone on this ship."

"Understood, sir. I am sorry that I was unavailable after the mind-meld. I am out of practice."

"That's all right." The captain walked through the dormitory, his footsteps clapping dully on the deck. "Picard out."

Back in the corridor, he felt more at ease, although he was convinced that this moment of relative calm wouldn't last long. Somewhere on the ship, someone was plotting their demise, and he had to find them before they took action. *But how?*

The only way was to be vigilant—to watch for them to make a move or a mistake. With grim determination, Picard resolved to keep making his rounds. He wanted to observe his crew of misfits, until he found the ultimate misfit.

*   *   *

Cursing with frustration and biting her gag, Ro Laren rolled over in her dark tomb and stopped kicking on the wall. She had been in an awkward position, with her face to the floor, when she first heard the voice. She hadn't reacted quickly enough, and now it was too late.

Her throat was burning from the solvents she had digested, but she had managed to coat her gag with the greasy substances. Now she bit with her teeth and probed with her tongue to try to loosen the gag over her mouth. It was working, slowly but surely, and her anguished grunts and cries were getting louder as they escaped from a gap between the gag and her upper lip.

Her lips raw, she worked her face muscles until they were as sore as the rest of her body. Gradually she freed her mouth and spit out as much of the rank taste as she could.

Ro slumped back against the wall, unable to really lie down in the narrow confines. She was exhausted, gasping for breath, but now she would be able to make more noise the next time she heard voices out there. There was little point in gnawing on her bindings, but she lifted her wrists to her mouth and tried anyway.

One way or another, I'm going to get out of here.

Picard stepped around the master display table to get a better look at Lavelle's large graphics. Normally emblazoned with schematics of the *Orb of Peace,* the screen now displayed schematics of the ten-kilometer-long magneton collider. Seen in three-dimensional, wire-frame vectors, the gleaming skeleton of the artificial wormhole was even more impressive. Picard felt a slight pang that they had to destroy this noble achievement, but that was the nature of war—destroy or be destroyed.

Several important areas were highlighted, including the accelerator room and the atmospheric controls for the air lines that snaked through the structure. Lavelle demonstrated how he could zoom in on the highlighted areas, showing greater detail.

"Very impressive," said the captain. "You and Professor Grof work well together."

Sam scowled. "As long as we don't have to be in the same room. But I will admit, he knows his stuff. I just took what I know and what he knows—and fancied it up."

Picard pointed to the atmospheric controls in the large junction of eight spidery spokes. "You're sure about the atmospheric controls being in here?"

"I've never actually been inside," admitted Sam, "but I worked on that module from the outside, when I first got to the prison. We had to carry all of our own air before we finished that junction; but afterwards, we had centralized air on every tether line. Grof could probably tell you more about it."

"I'm sure he could," agreed Picard. "But he's been working so cheerfully—for him—that I hate to do anything to spoil his mood."

Sam leaned over his table and smiled. "His diagrams filled in a lot of blanks for me. Now I feel I have the big picture of how that place works. Before it was all disjointed. I still don't want to go back there, but it's no longer a metal monster—just a machine."

"We're going to put it out of business," vowed Picard.

"I'm all for that."

The captain smiled. "I hate to keep volunteering you, so this is your choice—I'd like you to go with me and Grof on the demolition team."

Sam blinked at him, and the captain could see the

fear fighting with his sense of duty. "Over to the collider?" he asked, already knowing the answer.

"Yes. I always believe in having the most knowledgeable people along, and that means you and Grof."

"Taurik knows it as well as I do," Sam suggested hopefully.

"If he volunteers, he'll be in the meteoroid drifting along beside us. I need somebody good in that post, because he'll have to run the transporter and coordinate the mission. He'll also have to decide if it becomes impractical to retrieve one or more of us."

"Has Grof volunteered for this yet?"

Picard tugged on his earring. "No, I haven't really had a good time to present it to him. But it will have to be soon—less than ten hours to go."

"Can we really trust him?" whispered Sam.

The captain scowled. "I wish I knew who we could trust. Have any of the crew been acting oddly?"

Picard could see a moment of indecision flash across Sam's face, as if he would have to answer yes. Instead he shook his head. "Not that I've seen."

"Well, think about it," ordered the captain. "Our lives depend upon it. If you see anyone acting strangely, report it to me."

"No offense, sir, but we're *all* acting strangely. Some of us have been to hell, and now we're going back again."

"Does that mean you're going on the demolition team?" asked Picard.

Sam rubbed his eyes wearily, then smiled. "With you, Captain, it's always business first, dying later."

"Dying, only after you've exhausted every other possibility. I'd better check on the bridge."

As the captain strode through engineering, he

pointed to Hasmek. "Don't think I have forgotten you. I want to get you home, so that you can make a full report."

"Only Grof's report is going to get through," grumbled the Romulan, "but at least history will always know who was the Federation's greatest traitor. Believe me, Captain, if I were making a report, I would laud your determination in the face of adversity. I know from serving with you that the Federation's defeat will not come easily, even for the Dominion. I only wish you had more time."

"We'll make do." The captain headed out the door and strode briskly along the corridor to the spiral staircase. Things seemed to be going too well, as Ro occasionally pointed out. He hoped he ran into the Bajoran at his next stop, because he had a job for her to do.

Picard climbed the stairs and made the short walk to the bridge. As he entred, Maserelli stiffened at the tactical station. "Hello, Captain."

"What's the status of the target?"

"Quiet. They seem to be waiting, or down for the night. There is quite a bit of encrypted message traffic. If we had a full crew and lots of computer power—"

"Keep recording it; maybe we can decode it later." The captain looked around the bridge. Tamla Horik sat at the conn, her back to him, and the viewscreen showed the split image of the collider on one side and the drifting debris of Juno's rings on the other. Everything seemed to be in order.

"Were Ro and Taurik here?" asked the captain.

"Yes," answered Maserelli, "they relieved us for a meal break, then went back to the escape pod, I believe."

"Carry on." Picard left the bridge and briefly

patroled the first-deck corridor, which was truncated by the upper level of the cargo hold. There was little in this part of the ship except for a few cubicles, classrooms, and life-support systems. The more time he spent on the *Orb of Peace,* the more he realized that it was supposed to function as a space-faring monastery. Maybe someday it would again, thought Picard. A few cubicles were being used as makeshift sleeping quarters, but they were deserted now.

Picard went back to the staircase and descended to the second level, where most of his crew was busy working. The traitor on board was still keeping a low profile, still trying to hide his identity for as long as possible, which made Picard's job all the more difficult. If their nemesis waited to make an attack until they were close to launching the decoy, he could cause irreparable harm. They had to flush him out . . . soon.

Picard strode down the corridor, noting how deceptively quiet it was in this part of the ship, too. Finally he heard voices coming from the far end of the corridor, and he hurried his step. The hatch to the escape pod was open, and he peered inside to see Geordi, Grof, and Woil hard at work, wiring separate parts of the transporter pad.

Geordi saw him and rose to his feet. "We're on schedule, Captain. In another half hour, we should be able to start tests. Then we can work on the outside of the decoy."

"Good," said the captain, glancing around. "Where are Ro and Taurik?"

"Aren't they on the bridge?" asked Geordi. "Ro checked in from there and said she was on relief."

"I wish she'd come back," muttered Grof. "We're waiting for those handles she went to get."

"I can get them," said Geordi, moving toward the hatchway.

"No," insisted Picard, gently pushing the engineer back into the sphere. "I'll find her. I don't want anyone to leave their posts."

"What's wrong?" asked Grof suspiciously.

"Professor, I'll tell you as soon as I know." The captain stepped away from the hatch and tapped his combadge. "Picard to Ro."

There was no response.

"Picard to Ro. Come in."

Still there was no answer, and the captain frowned and tried again. "Picard to Taurik. Come in."

There was no answer, even after he tried repeatedly to raise both of them. In exasperation, Picard slapped his combadge and said, "Picard to bridge."

No response came to that summons either. Now all three men in the hatch stopped working, rose uncertainly to their feet, and stared at Picard.

"What's going on?" demanded Grof.

"The combadges appear to be malfunctioning," answered Picard.

"That's not it," barked Grof. "You suspect Ro of being behind the food replicators, and whatever else you're not telling me about. I'm no fool, Picard—something has gone seriously wrong, hasn't it?"

"There have been irregularities," admitted the captain, "but I don't suspect Ro or anyone else. As long as the work continues in here, our mission is on course."

"I don't believe you, Captain," declared Grof, folding his arms obstinately.

"Then come with me, Grof, and we'll get to the bottom of it." The captain's dour expression made it very clear that he expected the Trill to either help investigate or shut up.

"I'm coming," said Grof, handing his tools to Geordi. He lumbered through the hatchway and stood beside the captain.

"La Forge, continue your work, but keep this hatch closed and *locked*," ordered Picard in no uncertain terms. "Don't open it for anyone but *me*."

He scowled. "On second thought, don't even open it for me, unless I supply the password." Picard stepped into the escape pod and whispered one word into Geordi's ear: "Deflector."

La Forge nodded gravely. "Yes, sir."

Now the fear was out in the open, thought Picard, and it registered on the faces of all three men. The captain stepped into the corridor and shut the hatch. He heard La Forge bolt it from the inside with a clank.

Grof looked amused. "Captain, do you really think there's a *Founder* on board?"

"I don't know, but it would explain why someone we trust is trying to sabotage our mission." Picard took out his phaser and checked the setting, not even knowing if heavy stun would have an effect on a changeling.

"That's preposterous," said Grof. "Where could he have come from?"

"On the antimatter tanker with you and Lavelle."

The Trill chuckled. "Captain, I can assure you, a Founder has better things to do than stow away on a tanker with a bunch of prisoners."

"Does he?" asked Picard. "Didn't you say they were always observing us? Testing us. And what's more important to the Dominion than the artificial wormhole and its security?"

The Trill scratched his beard. "Well, I still say it's either the Romulan or that Maquis."

"Right now," replied the captain grimly, "I would very much like to speak to that Maquis. Come on."

With phaser drawn, Captain Picard led the way down the corridor. He checked a weapons locker and was dismayed to find it empty—looted of the Ferengi phaser rifles they had stored there. Also, two tricorders were missing. Fortunately, he remembered where he had hidden the Klingon disruptors they had taken off the dead Romulans. No one but he and Ro knew that he had placed them behind a wall panel in the transporter room.

If the disruptors are still there, then Ro isn't a traitor.

Grof continued to shake his head doubtfully as he strolled along behind Picard. "So how bad is it? What haven't you told me?"

"Someone disabled the subspace beacon and destroyed our explosives and fuses."

"What? *What!*" sputtered the Trill. "And you didn't think I would find that news of interest?"

"I also spared you from being interrogated," said Picard, "and for that you can thank me. What you were doing was vital, and I wasn't about to distract you. We can jerry-rig up explosives to use, and we'll fix the beacon later."

"I hope there's going to be a 'later.'" Grof shivered as he walked, suddenly looking much more fearful of their plight.

Picard stopped outside the door to the transporter room, which remained closed with lights blinking, warning that it was inoperative. He cautiously touched the panel near the door and stepped back as it slid open. The transporter room looked empty, as expected, and Picard slowly walked in. He noted the gaping hole in the transporter platform where a pad had been removed for transplant in the decoy. The control console was also open, and loose wires dangled from its disassembled components.

"Look at that," muttered Grof, "we destroyed our *own* transporter room. Didn't need any help."

Picard hoped that decision wouldn't come back to haunt them, but the deed was done—the transporter room was inoperative. He hurried behind the rear screen of the transporter platform.

"Captain, where are you going?" called Grof nervously.

"I'll be right out!" Picard quickly pried a wall panel off its hinges and reached into the dark recess. His hand hit upon cold metal, and he drew out one of the weapons—a Klingon disrupter. Green, sleek, and deadly-looking, the handle seemed to mold to his grip. He reached inside and felt two more disruptors, but he left them there.

When he emerged from behind the rear screen, Grof was very glad to see him. "Can't you tell me what you're doing?" he demanded. "I'm tired of being left in the dark."

"I was getting another weapon." Picard held up the disruptor.

"For me?" asked Grof with gratitude.

"I'm afraid not. We can't use this unless it's an emergency, because it has no stun setting—only heavy phase disruption."

"Sounds like a good weapon to use on a changeling," remarked Grof with a nervous smile. "How about giving it to me?"

"Only if there's an emergency." The captain stuck

the disruptor into his phaser holster and kept his phaser drawn. He tapped his combadge and said, "Picard to bridge."

No answer.

"Picard to Maserelli." As before, there was no response. "Our next stop is the bridge. And from now on, no talking."

"Uh . . . I'm perfectly willing to go back to work on the escape pod," said Grof hopefully.

Picard put his finger to his lips and hissed at the Trill. Then he motioned to the door and led the way.

In a defensive crouch, the captain cautiously climbed the spiral staircase. As soon as his head poked above the landing, he kept his phaser trained on the door to the bridge. Once again, nothing seemed amiss, but he knew not to trust appearances. Thudding footsteps announced that Grof had started up behind him.

Picard reached the upper deck and moved slowly toward the door. It opened at his approach, as if nothing were wrong, and he froze. He could see the soothing turquoise and golden lights of the instrument panels, and he heard the tiny blips and beeps of monitoring systems. On the viewscreen was the expected split image: collider in one half and the grainy ring in the other.

But everything was not as before, because Enrique Maserelli was not at his tactical post. It was deserted. However, Tamla Horik still sat at the conn, her back toward him. Very cautiously, his weapon leveled in front of him, Picard stalked onto the bridge of the *Orb of Peace*.

"Horik," he whispered when he was within a few meters of the conn. The bald-headed Deltan didn't move. She just kept staring down at her instruments.

He heard a sound behind him, and he whirled around to see Grof stumble onto the bridge. The Trill threw his hands up, afraid that Picard might shoot; but the captain waved him in and turned back to the silent helmswoman. Tamla Horik sat straight as an arrow, oblivious to him or her blinking instrument panel.

Picard's flitting glance scanned the bridge as he edged forward, knowing that the changeling could be anywhere—could be anything! Licking his dry lips, he moved within arm's length of the Deltan, but still she didn't move. It was all Picard could do to force his hand forward to shake her by the shoulder.

As soon as he touched her, she tumbled out of the chair and sprawled onto the deck. A phaser rifle which had kept her torso propped up clattered onto the deck beside her.

"Aaagh!" screeched Grof, leaping backward.

The captain bent over the Deltan and checked for a pulse or signs of breathing.

"Is . . . is she dead?" asked Grof nervously.

"No, but she's been heavily stunned," answered Picard. "She ought to be under a doctor's care."

"Oh, look, there's a weapon for me." The Trill walked forward and bent down to pick up the fallen phaser rifle. With a burst of intuition, Picard leaped to his feet, grabbed Grof, and wrestled him away from the rifle.

"Don't touch anything!" he barked.

Indignantly, Grof pushed him away. "Come on, Picard, do you still think there's a Founder on board? There may be an old-fashioned murderer running loose, but not a changeling."

Without warning, the door behind them suddenly opened wide, and the chair at a rear auxiliary station elongated into a silvery strand which shot out the doorway like an eel. Grof yelled, and Picard lifted his phaser and squeezed off a shot—but it was too late. The door slammed shut, as his beam bounced ineffectively off the deck.

While Grof pointed and babbled incoherently, Picard sat at the conn and tried to see if he could open the door or restore communications. As he feared, the console was completely locked, and he was denied access. The creature had allowed itself plenty of time on the bridge to wreak havoc and reprogram the systems.

Picard jumped up and ran past Grof to the door, but no amount of pounding or pushing would induce it to open again. They were trapped on the bridge, incommunicado, with the changeling running loose on the rest of the ship.

Chapter Thirteen

GEORDI LA FORGE PLUGGED in the last of the gel packs and sat back on his haunches. He tried not to look at the closed hatch of the escape pod, but it was impossible to ignore what was happening out there. The worst part was *not* knowing what was going on. With the combadges out, he felt disconnected, and the claustrophobia inside the cramped pod was much worse now that he knew they couldn't leave.

His Antosian shipmate, Jozarnay Woil, couldn't keep from fingering his phaser and glancing at the hatch. "What . . . what if we get *launched* in this thing?"

"Then we'll go on quite a ride," answered La Forge. "I imagine we'd let ourselves be captured rather than crash-land on one of the planets around here."

Woil shook his head vigorously and lifted his phaser. "No, not me! I'll *kill* myself before I fall into their hands again."

"Suit yourself," said Geordi, "but don't start shooting that thing off in here, okay? I'd like to live."

Woil shook his head and dropped his weapon hand. "I'm sorry, Commander. I'm a little edgy. What are we going to do if . . . if there really is a changeling out there?"

Geordi picked up a spanner. "Whether there's a changeling or a mugato out there, we're going to do our jobs."

Suddenly the door clanked. The manual bolt held tightly, yet they stared at the hatch, expecting it to open, anyway. The intercom crackled on, and a plaintive but familiar voice said, "Let me in! It's Ro!"

Both men looked at each other, but neither one made a move to open the hatch.

"Come on! That *creature* is after me! Open up!" They could barely hear her pounding on the thick metal hatch, but her voice came through over the intercom speaker.

With a trembling hand, Geordi tapped the blue panel beside the hatch. "Ro!" he shouted. "If you really are Ro, you'll know that when we were back on that ghost ship in Death Valley, it reminded me of something that happened to you and me in the past. What was it?"

A burst of static came from the other side. "Geordi, help! Let me in! It's right *behind* me!"

"Answer my question! What happened to us in the past?"

"Let's kill it!" shrieked Woil, jumping into firing position.

"Calm down," snapped Geordi. "We're safe in here. It's the safest place on the ship."

With weapons leveled, they crouched down and waited. Geordi wiped the sweat out of his eyes, missing the sweat seal from his old VISOR.

"I have you," said a strange, androgynous voice over the intercom. "All of you are locked away in safe places. Stay there, if you wish."

"What's your hurry?" asked Geordi desperately, trying to keep the thing talking. There was no response. "Hey! Are you out there?"

"I want to kill it!" declared Woil through clenched teeth. "Please, let me go out there and kill it!"

"No. We're not opening that hatch until we know it's safe."

"You could transport me out," said Woil with a gleam in his green eyes. "We wouldn't have to open the hatch. Come on, you want to test it, anyway, don't you?"

"Not at the moment."

The Antosian grinned in anticipation. "The next time it comes and tries to get in here, you transport me behind it, and I'll blast it to bits!" He hefted his weapon confidently.

"Yeah, good plan," said Geordi uneasily. "Let's make sure we've got the transporter calibrated first, or you'll end up in the middle of a bulkhead."

The Antosian grabbed a spanner and shook it with determination. "But I want to make sure we have time to kill it."

"Listen, we only have eight hours left!" snapped Geordi in exasperation. "If we don't finish this job, it won't matter what we do to that one changeling, because a whole *horde* of them will come streaming through the wormhole. Now get to work!"

"Yes, sir," said a sobered Antosian.

While his partner worked, Geordi tapped his combadge and tried to contact the captain one more time. When there was no answer, he began to think about what Woil had said. At the moment, they had the only working transporter on the ship, and that might come in handy before this long day was over.

Or it might make them a target.

Sam Lavelle paced the length of the nondescript engineering room, wondering what the heck was happening. Repeatedly, he had tried to contact the captain, Ro, or anybody in the crew—but the comm channels seemed to be dead. Nobody had contacted him either, and nobody had stopped by engineering since the captain's visit almost an hour ago.

Hasmek sat gloomily at the duty station. "I tell you, something's gone seriously wrong. I'm beginning to think that it's every man for himself."

Sam twisted his hands nervously. "Maybe they're just busy with the mission."

"Too busy to notice that the combadges aren't working?" the Romulan scoffed. "Too busy to drop by and tell us what's going on? What about those strange requests we got from the bridge? Diagnostics on the warp drive? Somebody wanted to power us up to get out of here. I can't blame them, but it wasn't a good sign."

Sam stopped his troubled pacing and nodded. The anonymous request to turn over engineering functions to the bridge had been highly unusual, and when Sam had asked for an authorization code, the comm channel went dead. That mysterious contact was the last they had heard from anyone else on the ship, and the silence was terrifying.

The Romulan rose to his feet, a look of determination on his ageless face. "I tell you, Sam, we're on our own. Whatever evil has plagued this ship has finally made a move to take over. Now what are we going to do about it?"

Sam shook his head, too concerned to come up with a quick, facile answer. He was also worried about Ro; the others might think she was the spy. He wouldn't tell Hasmek, but the first thing he had to do was to make sure that Ro was safe.

"Okay, I'll tell you what we have to do," said the Romulan. "Self-preservation is the first order of business, so we have to arm ourselves." The Romulan strode across the room to the weapons cabinet and grabbed himself a Bajoran phaser rifle.

"Hold it," said Sam, "the captain didn't want you to have a phaser."

"Well, you are welcome to report me," Hasmek replied with a grim smile. When he had difficulty managing the rifle with one hand, he tossed it to Sam, who caught it deftly in midair.

Hasmek grabbed a Ferengi phaser pistol and hefted it with satisfaction. "The second thing we have to do is get control of this ship. I figure that we can make a break for the Badlands if we wait for the Dominion to open their artificial wormhole. There should be a lot of distractions and unusual readings, and we just might make it."

"You mean . . . desert?"

Hasmek snorted a laugh. "This is more like running for your life. I can't operate this ship by myself, but the two of us could. If you have a better idea, I'm waiting to hear it."

In truth, Sam had no ideas at all, but he was all in favor of getting out of this room and finding out what had happened. They would be disobeying orders by leaving, but personal initiative was allowed when the chain of command had broken down.

He motioned toward the door with his rifle. "Lead on."

Hasmek tapped the door panel with the butt of his phaser, and both of them dropped into a crouch as the door slid open. The corridor appeared deserted, but they crept cautiously forward, weapons leveled.

After painfully breathing stale air and staring at darkness hour after hour, Ro Laren barely managed to stay alert. She began to fear that no one, not even the changeling, would come back to get her. It wasn't rational, she knew, but rationality was having a hard time staying in charge of her thinking processes.

Have to be ready, she told herself, *for the moment the chance comes to escape—to strike back.*

When Ro heard footsteps outside in the dormitory, she almost thought she was imagining it. Before, she had heard phantom sounds and started yelling, to no avail, so she didn't do anything right away. But then she heard a thud, as if someone had opened the door to her tomb.

"Help! Help!" she yelled hoarsely.

"Quiet," ordered a familiar voice. "I'm getting you out."

Ro fought down the temptation to cry out with joy, especially when a crack of dim light shot down from the top of the chest, momentarily blinding her. The first thing she could make out with her blurry vision was the bald head of her rescuer, shining like a beacon.

"Captain—" she whispered gratefully.

"Save your strength." Strong arms reached into the

narrow box and lifted her out. When the captain set her on the deck, she collapsed against his chest, and he gently lowered her to the floor.

Drawing his phaser, Picard adjusted the beam to a narrow pinpoint and cut away her bonds. He started to pull the tape off her face, but she caught his hand and said hoarsely, "Let me." It was painful, but she didn't cry out.

Ro rubbed her raw skin and tried to stretch her aching joints and muscles. "How did you know I was in there?"

"It told us." Picard stood up, holstered his phaser, and looked around the empty dormitory.

"The changeling told you?"

"It has what it wants. It's on the bridge, in control of the ship."

Ro stood uncertainly, trying to get the blood circulating in her stiff limbs and woozy mind. "What does it want, to disrupt the mission?"

"Yes, and it's doing a good job." Picard took her arm. "Can you walk?"

She nodded.

"The comm system is out," explained Picard, "but Geordi is still working on the decoy. If we can launch it, we have a chance. Anyway, it's the only safe place left on the ship. Come on."

Ro let the captain lead her through the deserted dormitory, but something in the recesses of her mind was screaming in alarm. *What if this isn't the captain?* she asked herself. *There's no way of knowing who anyone is—what's real or what's fake.*

She gazed at Captain Picard, who marched straight ahead, his jaw set with the familiar confidence and determination that she had come to know. Despite his convincing appearance, she would have to judge by his actions if he was really who he said he was. His grip on her arm suddenly seemed cold, alien, too insistent.

They stepped into the brightly lit corridor, and Ro winced from the light. Before she had a chance to acclimate herself, an angry voice shouted, "Halt!"

Ro and Picard whirled around to see Sam Lavelle and Hasmek training phasers on them. Each man had a distrustful, murderous glint in his eyes.

"Ro!" called Sam, stepping forward. "Are you all right?"

"Yes," she admitted taking a step toward him.

Picard pushed her back, but he never took his eyes off the drawn phasers. "Who's in engineering?"

"No one," answered Hasmek. "We got tired of not knowing what's going on."

"I can tell you what's going on," said the captain. "There's a changeling on the bridge—it has control of the ship."

"A changeling?" asked Sam in horror. "How did it get on board?"

Picard glanced at Ro, and she explained, "It came on board disguised as your friend, Taurik."

"Taurik?" Sam looked stricken. "What happened to the *real* Taurik? Where is he?"

"I presume he never left the prison," answered Picard. "We're glad to see you, but we need to get on with our mission. If you want to be helpful, go to the bridge and make sure the changeling doesn't escape. We're going to try to override his commands and get the decoy launched as planned."

Sam looked uncertain as he tried to absorb this devastating news, but Hasmek reached a decision. He yanked on Sam's arm. "Let's go to the bridge, and see if it's true."

When the young man was still reluctant to move, Ro gave him an encouraging smile. "Go on—I'll see you later."

Within moments, the two pairs were again headed in opposite directions—Ro and Picard toward the escape pod and Sam and Hasmek up the stairs to the bridge. Ro had a sinking feeling as she lost sight of them.

When they reached the escape pod, the captain motioned toward the intercom panel by the hatch. "Go on, tell them we're here."

That seemed odd to Ro, since it was the captain who should be making contact. But he stood guard in the corridor with his phaser drawn, so she cautiously tapped the panel.

"Geordi, are you in there? It's me—Ro."

There came several moments of uncomfortable silence, then a wary response from Geordi: "Were you here a few minutes ago?"

"No."

"I have a question for you. When we were on that ghost ship in Death Valley, what did it remind me of? It's something that happened to you and me in the past."

She smiled. "When you and I were out of phase, and we had a cloaked Romulan on board the *Enterprise.*"

"Ro!" came a cry of relief from inside the pod. "Just a second, and I'll open the hatch."

"No, wait," said Ro with a glance at her companion. "Captain Picard is with me. Ask him one, too."

She saw a brief look of concern cross the captain's face, but he squared his shoulders and waited for the question.

"That's easy," answered Geordi. "What's the password he gave me?"

She looked at the captain and awaited his response. When it didn't come for several seconds, her stomach knotted, and she started to back away from him.

"Captain, I'm waiting," insisted Geordi's voice.

"It's *him!*" shouted Ro.

The creature which looked like Picard gave her a smarmy smile and aimed his phaser at her.

In the next instant, when Ro was certain she was going to be killed, a column of swirling lights appeared behind Captain Picard. As Woil materialized, he raised a phaser and blasted the captain with a beam that blew off half his shoulder. The rest of his body liquified and retracted from the searing beam, but one long tentacle lashed out and wrapped itself around Woil's neck.

Ro lunged for the phaser pistol that had fallen to the deck. By the time she grabbed it and took aim, the blob-like changeling slithered across the deck and vanished into a cooling vent.

"Ro! What happened?" called Geordi's voice.

Keeping her weapon aimed at the vent, Ro crawled to Jozarnay Woil's body. One glance at the bloody pulp of his face and neck told her that the Antosian was dead. From the corner of her eye, she saw a strange lump of pulsing goo squirming across the deck, and she blasted it with her phaser. It turned as black as charcoal before disintegrating into dust.

Panting, Ro jumped up and pushed the intercom panel. "Geordi, Woil is dead, but he wounded the changeling—shot a piece of it off."

"He said he wanted a piece of it," replied Geordi. "Do you want to come inside?"

"No, I've got to find the captain, if he's still alive."

"Stand back!" ordered Captain Picard, as he aimed his Klingon disruptor at the door. Grof didn't need to be told twice—he scurried behind the tactical console. They had tried as many nondestructive remedies as they could to open the door and the comm channels, but their enemy had frozen them out. Only a complete rebuild of the ship's computer would fix it, and Picard didn't have the time or patience for that.

He glanced back at the two unconscious bodies lying in front of the viewscreen. Horik was still out, and Grof had found Maserelli hidden behind an access panel. They were both still alive, but barely. The changeling had apparently emptied the phaser rifle into them at full stun. Picard wasn't sure they would recover, but at least they had been found. *What about Ro and everyone else?*

He shook off questions that couldn't be answered in order to concentrate on the task at hand, for which the disruptor was the perfect tool. Wanting to damage the door as little as possible, the captain decided to cut a triangle at the bottom. He pulled the trigger, and sparks and motlen metal sputtered into the air as the disruptor sliced a diagonal line through the copper-tinged door.

Picard flinched from the sparks, but he kept a steady aim until the first diagonal cut was finished. Then he shifted the blazing beam to the other side and started a new diagonal gash. When the cutting was finished, Picard gave the triangle a swift kick, and it went skittering into the corridor beyond. He got down on his hands and knees and crawled through to the other side.

Picard knew he should expect anything, but he was still surprised when the barrel of a phaser rifle prodded his neck. "Drop the weapon and rise slowly to your feet," ordered Sam Lavelle.

The captain glared at the young officer. He thought about resistance until he saw Hasmek, standing on the other side of him, also aiming a phaser at his head.

"Drop it," ordered the Romulan.

"I'm not the changeling," insisted the captain.

"That's what the *other* Captain Picard said," replied Sam, waving his rifle. "Until we sort this out, put down the weapon."

"You morons!" bellowed a voice from inside the bridge. "That's Captain Picard! I've been with him every moment since Geordi vetted him."

Hasmek scowled. "Well, that sure sounds like Grof." He lowered his weapon a few centimeters.

The captain crawled through the hole and rose slowly to his feet. When Lavelle and Hasmek still continued to train their weapons on him, he stuck the disruptor in his belt and raised his hands. "Hold me if you want, but don't let it get away."

Lavelle shook his head in shock and disgust. "I still can't believe it was Taurik."

Picard blinked at him. "How do you know it was Taurik?"

"I told him," said a voice. They whirled around to see Ro's head emerge just above the landing of the staircase. Holding her phaser above her head, she climbed the rest of the way and walked cautiously toward them. *"That* is Captain Picard."

"How do we know?" Hasmek aimed his weapon at her. "And how do we know *you* are Ro Laren?"

She barely looked like Ro, thought Picard, with

soiled clothes and welts all over her face and wrists. His sympathy went out to her, but Hasmek had a point—anyone walking around by himself on this ship was highly suspect.

"There's no time for this!" insisted Ro. "Woil shot the changeling—there's a chunk of it on the lower deck. It's wounded, and we have to keep after it."

Lavelle and Hasmek looked at one another with confusion in their eyes, unsure what to do—unsure who to trust, except themselves.

"Lavelle," said Picard, "when you served on the *Enterprise,* there was one officer whose respect you were always trying to win, but never could. I can tell you who that officer was."

"Go ahead," answered Sam hoarsely.

"Will Riker."

With relief, Lavelle lowered his phaser rifle. "It's him."

Ro looked at Sam and smiled. "I had the same problem."

They heard grunting sounds and turned to see Grof trying to squeeze through the triangle the captain had cut in the door. "Will somebody help me?" he bellowed.

Picard and Sam pulled the Trill to his feet, as the Romulan finally lowered his weapon. "I guess I'll have to believe you people."

"Come on," insisted Ro, leading the way back down the stairs to the lower level.

A few moments later, they stood outside the hatch to the escape pod, inspecting Woil's body and the charred lump of changeling flesh. The captain had Geordi open the hatch and hand him a tricorder, and he scanned the changeling matter until the tricorder could identify it.

"Hopefully, you've at least slowed it down." The

captain turned slowly in a circle, intently studying the tricorder readings. Finally an audible beep and flashing lights told him that he was getting warm. "It's below us, in the torpedo room."

"Let's finish it," said Sam, hefting his rifle.

"Grof, Hasmek—you go with Geordi to the bridge. Try to get control of the ship, and get the combadges working. Ro and Lavelle, you're with me." The captain jogged down the corridor with his two former officers right behind him.

Moments later, they descended into the bowels of the ship, squeezing cautiously between the life-support ducts and pipes. Leading the way, Picard kept glancing at his tricorder, but he didn't need the device to tell him they were on the right trail. Gooey residue, like the slime from a snail, greased the deck and the torpedo rails.

They found the creature at the very back, slumped against an empty torpedo tube. Apparently, it had been thinking about escaping into space, but didn't have enough strength left to crawl into the tube. It looked vaguely humanoid, like an unfinished pewter mold of a human, but the shape kept ebbing and shifting, as if maintaining even this poor imitation was too great an effort.

Picard drew his disruptor, determined to end it here and now. Ro and Lavelle moved warily beside him, their weapons ready for action, but nobody got any closer than ten meters.

"Careful about opening fire this close to the hull and the torpedo," cautioned the captain.

A slit, which might have been a mouth, gapped open like a wound, and an eerie voice gurgled forth. "Still being practical, Captain? I had no idea that humans were capable of such sustained opposition. I didn't want to kill you, because I thought you could still be useful to us. Now I see I was foolish to let you live, but I wanted to know more about the weaknesses in our defenses."

"Why did you kill Lena Shonsui?" asked Picard.

"I caught her scanning me during a transport. She was too smart, too suspicious. I went through the wiring—" The voice trailed off. Picard stepped back from the silver blobs that splattered outward. For several seconds, the Founder struggled mightily to maintain any semblance of a shape.

"You might as well just give up. It's over," said Sam.

The thing laughed—or whimpered, it was hard to tell. "I'm dying . . . yes. But you won't destroy the wormhole. When I left the bridge, I put out a distress call. The Jem'Hadar are bound to see it."

With that, the creature rose into a serpentine rod and tried to slither into the torpedo tube, but Sam took swift aim and drilled it with a pinpoint burst. The beam cut the changeling in half. As the creature melted into a bubbling pool, it made an inhuman screech.

"Both of you stay here and make sure it's dead." Picard tossed the tricorder to Ro and dashed through the jumble of pipes and tubes. He had to get to the bridge.

The viewscreen showed a lone Jem'Hadar attack craft streaking toward them like a bullet. Picard could feel grim reality setting in among the shocked crew, all of whom were on the bridge, and he had no words to counteract the image on the screen.

"How long before they get here?" asked the captain.

Geordi furiously worked the conn. "Less than a minute, I'd say."

Grof slammed his fist on the tactical station. "And we've got no control at all! If we only had thirty minutes—"

"I'm sorry, Captain," said Hasmek somberly. "It's been quite an exciting trip, but it appears to be over."

"Are shields up?" asked Picard.

"Yes," answered Geordi. "It had to leave shields up to protect us from the ring debris."

Grof plied his console. "Stall them—I'll get to work on the computer. I can think like a Founder."

Picard gave the Trill an encouraging nod, but a moment later he was forced to turn back to the viewscreen. The dagger-like ship streaked toward them, its hull pulsing with blue and gold energy bursts, while they lay beached inside a sea of sand.

Chapter Fourteen

SAM NUDGED a small lump of the changeling with the barrel of his phaser rifle, and it crumbled to gray dust. All around them, the remains of the creature were drying up and crumbling. Ro had the only tricorder, but the thing sure looked dead to Sam.

"I think we can report to the bridge," he said. "This changeling is space dust."

"The readings so far agree with you," answered Ro. "But let's be thorough and finish the cycle."

"Okay." Sam crossed his arms and whistled a popular tune. The tones echoed pleasantly in the underbelly of the *Orb of Peace*, while Ro frowned and shook her head.

"That wasn't you, was it?" asked Sam wistfully.

"What wasn't me?" Ro barely looked up from her tricorder.

"At the height of the madness, you visited Hasmek and me in engineering."

Ro's spine stiffened. "And what did I do? I mean, what did *it* do?"

Sam grinned. "It gave me one hell of a kiss and tried to tear my clothes off."

"And you thought that was *me?*" Ro scoffed, and she looked both ticked off and mildly amused. "And you enjoyed it, I suppose."

"Since that first kiss, I've been hoping for a repeat," admitted Sam. "I guess I didn't hide it too well from anyone. But I knew something was wrong, and I sent it packing."

Ro smiled at him, looking relieved. "I can tell you, I would rather have been kissing you than be locked up in that tool box."

"Yeah," said Sam with concern, "you should get some first-aid on those bruises and cuts." He stepped forward and gently touched one of her wounds. She lowered the tricorder, and her stained, brusied arms wrapped around his lean body. They held on to one another tightly, like man and woman, like comrades in arms, like two people who needed a hug.

Their longing embrace was interrupted when the deck jolted under their feet. They staggered to maintain their balance, and Sam grabbed Ro by the hand. "What the hell's going on?"

The transport stopped shaking, and Ro folded up her tricorder and stepped away from him. "Maybe later," she said with disappointment.

"I hope there *is* a later," grumbled Sam, snatching his phaser rifle.

He followed her through the duct work and up the ladder to the second level. They climbed the spiral staircase and dashed onto the bridge, where the gloomy faces directed their attention to the viewscreen. Obscured by the dirt of Juno's rings, a Jem'Hadar attack ship sat off their bow, barely visible except for its blinking blue and gold lights.

"I guess the changeling wasn't lying," muttered Sam.

"What was that jolt?" asked Ro.

"Tractor beam," answered Picard. "As soon as they arrived, they informed us we were being 'rescued.'"

"Their tractor beam cut right through our shields," added Geordi.

"So their shields are down," said Ro.

"Yes," answered Geordi, "but we have no control over our weapons, even that one measly torpedo. We can't even activate our self-destruct sequence. We're sitting ducks."

As Sam watched the viewscreen, his eyes drifted upward to one of the Bajoran platitudes on the frame. It read, "Follow the Prophets into the Unknown." Sam imagined he would do that soon, because he had no intention of being a Dominion slave ever again.

"Captain Picard," he said, lifting his phaser rifle, "permission to resist capture."

The older man nodded grimly. "Permission granted. I'm sorry I led you into this, Sam."

"Think nothing of it, Captain. You gave me a chance to fight back—to be a Starfleet officer again—and that was how I wanted to die, not as a slave."

The *Orb of Peace* was jolted once more, and everyone staggered to remain on their feet. "We're moving!" yelled Grof. "It's dragging us away!"

"Everyone, keep working to get control of the ship!" ordered Picard. "Until they beam us out, keep working."

Suddenly, out of nowhere, a blazing light cut

through the dust of millennia and slammed into the Jem'Hadar ship. For a moment, Sam thought it was a plasma bolt, but he then remembered this wasn't the Badlands. Like a lightning bolt of divine retribution, another streak wracked the Jem'Hadar ship, and it exploded into a billion shimmering particles, which were quickly swallowed up in the rings of Juno. Within seconds, every visual trace of the Dominion ship was gone.

Along with everyone else, Sam gaped at the view-screen, unable to believe that they had been rescued once again . . . *by whom?*

"Were those photon torpedoes?" asked Ro in amazement.

"That's what they looked like," answered Geordi.

A small craft maneuvered slowly into view. It, too, was obscured by the debris, but it was a very familiar size and shape, like a breadbasket with skis.

"That's a Starfleet shuttlecraft!" exclaimed Geordi.

"With torpedoes?" asked a puzzled Ro.

"They're normally not so well equipped," said the captain with a smile. "But we did modify one for . . ."

"For the android cavalry," quipped Geordi. He grinned sheepishly. "Sorry, Captain. I didn't mean to interrupt."

"Quite all right, Mister La Forge. I couldn't have said it better myself."

A spontaneous cheer went up on the bridge of the *Orb of Peace,* and Sam clasped hands with Ro, then Hasmek, then Grof.

It was like a party by the time Data materialized on the bridge in a column of sparkling molecules. Hasmek drew his phaser at the sight of the yellow-eyed android, but Sam grabbed his wrist. "He's a friend."

"Hello, Captain Picard," said Data matter-of-factly. "I observed that you needed assistance. I trust my intervention was not unwelcome."

"Oh, it was welcome, Data. *Very* welcome." The captain warmly clasped the android's hand. "But what are you doing here?"

"I perceive your ship is in some distress, so I will make my answer brief. The *Enterprise* was forced to retreat from the rendezvous point, and I was left alone in a shuttlecraft to watch for you to release the subspace beacon. Unfortunately, I lost track of you soon after my launch.

"Pursued by Dominion vessels, I learned that I could elude them and their sensors by landing on extremely inhospitable planets, such as this one we are currently orbiting. For the last ten-point-seven days, I have been hopping from Class-A to Class-Z planets, trying to get as close as possible to the artificial wormhole, assuming that you would eventually arrive here. I spotted it three days ago. No doubt, we both chose this planet as an observation point for the same reasons: proximity and sufficient cover."

"Then you've been here all this time?" asked Geordi in amazement. "Why didn't you let us know?"

Data cocked his head slightly. "My orders were to observe, wait for the release of the subspace beacon, then alert the *Enterprise*. It was never my intention to interfere, until it appeared you were in extreme danger."

"Where is the *Enterprise?*" asked Ro.

Data shook his head. "I am afraid I do not know. She did not return to the rendezvous point. She could be in a starbase, undergoing repairs, or she could be a casualty of war."

There were grim faces at that frank assessment, but no one could stay glum after such a dramatic rescue.

"Data," said Geordi, pointing to the conn, "we had a changeling as an unwelcome passenger, and it locked us out of our computer. Will you take a look?"

"Certainly. It is good to see you, Geordi."

"You're the most beautiful thing I ever saw!" said the engineer with a grin.

"Thank you." Data sat down at the conn, and his fingers flew over the console, moving so quickly they were a blur. Diagrams and lines of computer code blazed across the screen as fast as the computer could display them. Hasmek and Grof, who had never seen Data in action, crowded around and gaped in astonishment.

Grof whispered to Sam, "I always thought a joined Trill was the most advanced being in the galaxy, but I'm not so sure anymore."

"He'll live longer, too," said Sam with a smile.

Suddenly, lights flashed on all the consoles, and reassuring blips and beeps filled the bridge. "The computer is repaired," announced Data, rising to his feet. "All systems are operational."

"What *are* you?" asked Hasmek, staring into Data's golden eyes.

"An android."

"I never expected to see an android out here."

"I can truthfully say I never expected to see a one-armed Romulan here either."

"How much time do we have left?" demanded Picard, hovering over the tactical station.

"Seven hours," answered Grof.

"Now that Data's here, that ought to be enough time," said the captain. "And having his shuttlecraft gives us a lot more options. La Forge, take Data to the escape pod and get the decoy finished. Explain the plan to him as you go. Ro, you have the bridge. For brief periods, use our tractor-beam to keep the shuttlecraft close by."

"Yes, sir." Ro slid into the conn seat and studied the instruments. Even beaten up, thought Sam, the Bajoran looked beautiful sitting in that chair.

"Hasmek, get the first-aid kit." ordered Picard. "See if you can get Horik and Maserelli back on their feet."

"Yes, sir."

"Lavelle and Grof, come with me to engineering."

"That's a good idea," said the Trill importantly.

Five minutes later, Sam stood hunched over the display table in engineering, looking proudly at the diagrams he had converted from Grof's basic schematics. The Trill was taking all the credit, of course, and Sam kept still, trying to concentrate on the mission.

"I tell you, Captain, it was a good thing you met up with me," bragged Grof. "I don't see how you could have gotten this far without my help, and now here you are—perched on the edge of success. You must be very pleased."

The captain gave him an engaging smile. "I am, and I know I couldn't have done it without your help. That's precisely why I want you to continue with us all the way through—to the final step. Professor, you've got to come with us over to the collider."

A look of horror twisted Grof's features and made

his spots darken. "No, no! I was going to say that now that we have the shuttlecraft, I can just *leave* with Data. There is no reaon for *me* to remain here. I'm a civilian."

"Like civilians aren't being killed," grumbled Sam.

The captain's smile faded, and his lips thinned. "Data will be with us on the mission, and so will the shuttlecraft. Whether you're with the demolition team or not, you'll be part of the mission. Your diagrams are excellent, but nothing compares with your firsthand experience of having worked there."

Sam blurted, "You're wasting your breath, Captain. He's a coward."

Both Grof and the captain shot Sam angry stares, and Picard said, "I don't think that attitude helps, Lieutenant. We're too close to our goal to let anything stand in our way, and I mean *anything*. If I have to do it without either one of you, I will."

Picard looked directly at Grof with those piercing eyes and high arched brow. "I've seen enough to know that you're no coward, Professor. Since we have a limited amount of explosives, we have to be accurate. You've come this far with us—I just wish you would see it to the end."

While Sam crossed his arms and waited, the Trill looked down at his hands. "I've tried to do my job against all the obstacles life has thrown at me, but this isn't my job! I never wanted this war. I always thought we could work out our differences with the Dominion."

"War is about making sacrifices," said Picard. "Are you willing to sacrifice the Federation? That's what it's come down to. If we don't stop them right here and now, we're finished. Professor, we stand a lot better chance of success with you along."

"I'm no soldier," protested the Trill. "I'm no good shooting a phaser or rigging charges—"

"No," said Picard, "you're our scout, the one who knows the territory. You just lead us, and we'll do the rest. With any luck, no one will shoot a phaser. We want to get in and get out, remember? And now that we have *two* ships, our chances of getting out alive have doubled."

"I didn't consider that," replied Grof, mustering some false cheer.

"Let's proceed," said Picard, leaning over the table display. "We're going to have two targets—the accelerator room and the atmospheric treatment center."

"What?" bellowed Grof, shooting a stare at Sam. "That's completely unnecessary. Did Lavelle talk you into that?"

"No one talked me into it," answered the captain with great restraint. "It makes perfect sense to have two targets, in case they stop one of us. If Lavelle is successful in flooding those conduits with hydrogen, they won't need more than a spark to set it off."

Grof buried his face in his hands. "You're determined to destroy everything I worked for."

"No, I just want to destroy the Dominion's ability to wage war in this quadrant. We'll build your wormhole again—only next time it will be for the cause of peace." Picard bent over the display and pointed at the highlighted accelerator room. "Armed guards—where are they?"

"Two at this junction," answered Grof with a sniff. "Two more on the other side, plus workers in the room itself."

"How many?"

"Three or four."

"What will they be wearing?"

Sam moved to a keyboard and began to take notes, as the tactical session stretched to almost two hours.

Sam could hardly wait for the escape pod to launch, because hanging from the bulkhead in an uncomfortable harness was no fun. He glanced at Picard, Grof, Data, and Geordi, thinking that they all looked miserable, except for Data, who had a contented expression on his face, as if he were just glad to be here.

Grof had shifted in his harness until he was hanging upside-down, with his feet in the air and a nauseated frown on his hirsute face. It was all Sam could do not to laugh at him, but then this was no laughing matter. Their departure had already been delayed twenty-five minutes, and there was no end in sight.

All except Geordi were dressed in yellow jumpsuits, like those worn by the Vorta technicians they were likely to encounter on the collider. They couldn't pass any kind of close inspection, but a fleeting glance in the hallway might not give them away.

The captain scowled and tapped his combadge. "Picard to bridge. We've got to launch—it will take an hour to get there."

"I know, Captain," answered Ro's brusque voice. "But the steady traffic away from the collider hasn't let up. In five minutes, it looks like there will be a window."

"It won't matter much if we get there too late," said Picard. "Launch in five minutes, regardless."

"Yes, sir."

Everyone but Data glanced at the captain, and Sam assumed they were all trying to draw strength and courage from him. Sam sure was. Captain Picard had that rare trait of making bravery and duty seem like second nature, not the struggle it was for most of them.

The captain noticed their hound-dog expressions and smiled. "We'll be cutting it close, but we have enough time. We've been over it quite a few times, but does anyone want to discuss the mission?"

Geordi snorted a laugh. "Do you realize, we're going after the biggest target in Dominion space in the smallest spacecraft we could possibly find."

"And look at our support vessels," said Sam, snickering. "A shuttlecraft and a passenger transport."

Now they were all chuckling, except for Data, who looked quizzically from one laughing man to another.

"And!" shouted Grof, "we're going to blow it up with an overloaded phaser and a couple of homemade grenades!"

The laugher died down at that remark. When his combadge chirped, the captain answered it softly, "Picard here."

"All you all right down there?" asked Ro.

"Yes, just having a moment of gallows humor. Are we ready to go?"

"We have thirty seconds left on our countdown. Good luck."

"I'll see you later, Ro!" shouted Sam.

"I don't know if you'll be that lucky," she answered dryly. "Bridge out."

Sam's grin melted from his face as he counted down silently to himself. The first thing he heard were hissing sounds, followed by a loud clank, then a rushing noise as they were launched. The centrifugal force pressed all of them against the walls of their spinning sphere, and Grof howled like a kid in a carnival ride.

Seen from space, thought Sam, it must look like a

video-log run in reverse, with a craggy meteoroid shooting from the side of a transport ship. The decoy streaked from the murky rings of Juno into open space and went immediately into warp drive on a preprogrammed course. Hopefully, thought Sam, all that waiting had been worth it, and they wouldn't be noticed by the Dominion ships prowling the area.

"Ah, it feels good to get out of that gravity," said Geordi, floating effortlessly in his harness.

"I must admit it does." Grof drifted contentedly, no longer any more upside-down than the rest of them.

"We really haven't got anything to do for an hour," said Picard, "so why don't all of you try to get some sleep. Data will wake us up."

Right, thought Sam, *as if we could sleep.*

He lay floating in the cramped sphere with two other humans, a Trill, and an android, thinking how much was riding on this ragtag band. Sam tried not to dwell on the forces arrayed against them, but it was hard when they were hidden inside a fake meteoroid because they feared those forces so much. At least they had the element of surprise, and pure audacity.

It was quiet inside the tiny craft as it moved through space on its inexorable path to destiny. Picard seemed to meditate, La Forge studied a tricorder, Data watched minute readings on the jamming device, and Grof began to snore. Sam finally closed his eyes and tried to rest.

"Wake up, Sam," said a gentle but firm voice, as a hand poked his shoulder.

"Huh?" asked the young man, his eyes popping open.

"We're here," said Picard simply.

Sam looked around at his floating cabinmates, and they were all busy, either working on the transporter, checking the makeshift explosives, taking tricorder readings, or double-checking the jammer. There was no viewscreen inside the crude escape pod, so they were dependent upon portable instruments.

"Five minutes until the first stop," announced Geordi. "Data and Lavelle, get ready."

"There's been no contact with the enemy?" asked Sam.

"The jammer has been active," answered Data, "so we have been scanned."

"And we're still here," added Geordi. "We're passing no closer than four hundred kilometers to their precious collider, and we look like a regular space rock. There's not much more we can do."

"The question," said Grof, "is how they'll react when we beam aboard the collider. I never took much interest in security—perhaps I should have."

"Hopefully," said Data, "this apathy toward security is a system-wide flaw."

"Their security is hardly lax," muttered Grof huffily. "After all, they *do* station a fleet of ships around the collider, even if most of them have pulled back. The Dominion expects an invasion from Starfleet, not five fools in an escape pod. And they probably don't expect too much of an invasion, with Starfleet reeling on all fronts. Ironically, Captain, your lack of resources may be your greatest asset."

"Let's hope we have enough time," said Picard, gazing at his chronometer. "According to you, Professor, another fleet should be pouring through the artificial wormhole in eleven minutes."

"Their shields have to be down," added Sam, "or they can't use it."

245

"That's what we're counting on." Geordi plied the transporter controls, then nodded with satisfaction. "Sam, you're first out, and Data will be right behind you. Get into position."

With a gulp, Sam unfastened the buckles of his harness and floated free into the center of the sphere. He grabbed the handrails they had installed at the last moment and swung his feet onto the transporter. When he was sure he could maintain contact with only one hand, he let go with the other and drew his Klingon disruptor. When fighting Jem'Hadar, it was advisable to shoot to kill. Besides, Sam didn't intend to be captured again.

"Just remember not to lose your combadges," said Picard to everyone. "Or we have no way of finding you."

Sam nodded grimly. "I'm ready."

"Coming into range," said Geordi, hunched over his instruments. "I'm locking onto a solid surface, and there's good atmosphere."

"What more can you ask?" Sam gripped his disruptor tightly and tried to keep from looking too afraid. *This is what I want,* he told himself, *a chance to destroy that monstrous slave pit!* Guiltily, he glanced at Grof, who was gazing down, unable to meet his eyes.

Sam looked at his partner, Data, who was carrying the bag containing the phaser set to overload, a few tools, and an emergency fire-starter in case the phaser failed.

"Energizing," barked La Forge.

Sam could feel the familiar tingle, and he made sure that his feet remained in contact with the pad. It wouldn't do to get scrambled and killed in a transporter accident now.

A moment later, he landed heavily on his feet on a gray metal catwalk suspended between metal girders and huge ducts. He looked around at the utilitarian chamber, the junction of dozens of spokes in the collider. With dismay, he realized that the instruments and valves were above him on a suspended platform. As far as he could tell, there was no way to get there from his position, except to jump twenty meters straight up.

A soft thud sounded behind him, and he whirled around to see Data materialize on the catwalk. The android took in their surroundings in a fraction of a second, then made a decision in the next fraction. He crouched down and leaped upward, catching the platform above them with his powerful hands. With ease, Data threw his leg onto the platform and hauled himself up.

So intent was Sam in watching this display of agility that he didn't see the guards until it was almost too late. With pounding footsteps, a detachment of Jem'Hadar soldiers came running in from a tunnel on the same level as the platform. If they hadn't stopped to form ranks, Sam would never have gotten off the first shot. He drilled the lead Jem'Hadar with his disruptor, and his chest exploded in a shower of sparks.

The other guards ignored Sam and fired directly at Data, who was the real threat. The android deftly avoided most of the deadly beams, and those that hit him scorched his clothing but left him unharmed. Nevertheless, Sam knew that he had to bottle up the enemy in the tunnel, or they would overwhelm Data with sheer numbers.

Running as he went, Sam shot repeatedly into the mass of Jem'Hadar guards, killing two more and distracting the others. He dove behind a large duct just as the Jem'Hadar shifted their attention to him and showered his position with a withering array of fire. Sam hunkered down, unable to move, as the catwalk and duct were blasted into metallic shavings.

He heard a rumbling sound, and he looked up to see Data grab the catwalk the Jem'Hadar were standing on and shake it like a blanket. Several Jem'Hadar tumbled off, and the others retreated into the tunnel. Sam sprang to his feet and killed two spiny-faced warriors who landed near him. Then he turned his disruptor upon the tunnel entrance, keeping the reinforcements at bay.

Data went calmly to the instrument panel and began to enter commands with one hand, while he spun a valve with the other. Sam kept firing nonstop at the advancing Jem'Hadar, until he noticed phaser beams coming from another direction, causing Data to duck for cover. He looked down and spotted a new detachment of Jem'Hadar filing onto a catwalk below him. They quickly formed ranks and fired at both of the intruders. Once again, Sam was forced to cower from the blistering phaser fire.

He wondered, *Is everybody having this much fun?*

Captain Picard and Enrak Grof beamed down to a quiet, nondescript corridor in the tail of the collider. This stretch of corridor was the only place cut off from Jem'Hadar view, according to Grof, and Picard was relieved to find it empty. Behind them stood a large hatch which opened to a space dock; blinking red lights alerted them that no ship was docked at present. Ahead of them, the corridor bent to the left, following the curve of the tail section. Beyond that, two Jem'Hadar guards waited at the entrance to the accelerator control room.

Grof bustled importantly past him, and Picard grabbed his arm before he could turn the corner. "Where are you going?" he whispered.

"I used to work here," hissed the Trill. "Maybe they'll remember me and let me pass."

The captain stared hard at Grof, thinking that it wasn't too late for him to betray the Federation and save his invention, and his hide. Then again, the less commotion they made, the better. If there was an easy way to get in, plant the grenades, and get out, they had to try it.

Picard nodded. "If you need help, shout. Then throw yourself on the deck."

"Aye, Captain," whispered Grof with a twinkle in his eye. Coming back to this familiar place, scene of his greatest triumph, had put the Trill at remarkable ease.

With his usual cocky assurance, Grof marched around the bend in the corridor, his footsteps echoing loudly. Picard sank against the bulkhead, his disruptor leveled for business, and waited.

Finally Grof's footseps stopped, and a voice barked, "Who goes there?"

"It's me, Enrak Grof," answered the Trill testily. "Surely, you remember me. I came here every day."

Picard edged closer to catch every word.

"You've been gone," said one of the guards accusingly. "You're not on the list anymore."

The captain impatiently checked his chronometer. Time was running out—they were down to less than five minutes, and there wasn't any time for small talk.

Without warning, an alarm pierced the air, and

Picard had to cover his ears to keep his wits. Their incursion had been discovered.

"Help!" yelled Grof. *"Help!"*

Crouching low to throw off their aim, Picard scuttled around the corner and opened fire with his disruptor. He shot everything that stood, hoping that Grof had hit the deck as ordered. Two Jem'Hadar lurched toward him, their bodies aflame, shooting wildly. Picard rolled to his right, jumped up and kept firing until they were down.

Grof no longer sounded so confident as he lay on the deck, pinned by a singed corpse, wailing in fear. Picard rushed down the corridor and dragged him out of the carnage. Their clean yellow jumpsuits were now covered with blood and white residue from the Jem'Hadar's neck tubes.

Picard shook the Trill until he stopped whimpering, then he had to scream over the sound of the alarm. "Get hold of yourself! Open that door and get us in there!" He pushed the Trill toward the door, which was locked by a blinking combination panel.

Grof nodded, took a deep breath, and mastered his emotions. He bent over the lock and began to work, while Picard vaulted over the bodies and hurried back to the corner. The enemy could beam into their position, they could come from the accelerator room, or they could even dock in a transport ship. Unless Grof could get them into that room, they would be trapped in this lonely stretch of corridor, with the alarm screeching in their ears.

Geordi floated over the small control panel of the escape pod, preparing to go in reverse and make another pass by the collider to pick up the demolition teams. It was terrible not having a viewscreen or even audio contact with his comrades, but they had to maintain comm silence. Geordi assumed the mission was going as planned. If not, it didn't much matter what he did.

Suddenly his little craft was severely jolted, bouncing Geordi around like a hamster inside a ball. Sparks spewed from the jammer, and he barely had time to grab an oxygen mask and pull it over his head before the air hissed out. Either he had hit something, or he was under attack! Either way, he was dead if he stayed in this can.

Geordi checked the range on the transporter and saw that he was still close enough to the collider—just barely. With no time to think, he flicked on the distress signal, which sent a coded message to the *Orb of Peace*. Then he grabbed the handrails and swung his feet onto the transporter pad. A two-second delay scrambled his molecules just as another Dominion phaser blast shredded the escape pod into gleaming strips of confetti.

Chapter Fifteen

SAM SHOOK OFF the fear and reminded himself that he had to save this part of the mission. After all, it had been his idea. He jumped to his feet and used his higher position to blister the Jem'Hadar below him. He kept running, finding better vantage points, while they remained pinned down. The Klingon disruptor in his hand wreaked terrible vengeance, and it seemed to have a mind of its own. At one point, it whirled him around to pick off a Jem'Hadar who had leaped across the broken catwalk and started after Data. The gray-clad figure plummeted down a long spoke into the depths of the collider.

Sam glanced up at Data and saw the android spinning huge valves in a blur of motion. He could only watch for a second before he had to turn his attention back to the Jem'Hadar guards below them.

Gripping the disruptor with both hands, he let it spit its red flame over and over again at the advancing guards.

When the bodies piled up on the catwalk below him, he turned his attention to the tunnel above. Only two Jem'Hadar remained from that force, and they were tentative, merely holding their ground. He used his disruptor to further weaken the upper catwalk, and a whole section of it came clattering down on top of those below.

Sam felt like a one-man wrecking crew as he swept the place with disruptor fire. He forgot about Data until a loud bang on the catwalk caused him to turn around and see the android. "Task complete," said Data as phaser fire zinged past him. "But Geordi is late."

They crouched down behind a large duct as the emboldened Jem'Hadar increased their fire. Sam thought about what Data had just done on that upper platform, flooding the tubes of the collider with hydrogen, then tossing in a phaser set to overload. It was like coating a roof with gasoline and tossing a lit match onto it.

"How much time until it blows?" asked Sam, breathing heavily.

"Two minutes and fifteen seconds. Geordi should have transported us by now."

Enemy fire blistered the duct, and it burst open with a geyser of steam, forcing both Sam and Data to dive onto their stomachs. They crawled along the catwalk, trying to get away from a frenzied counterattack by the Jem'Hadar massing below them.

"Where the hell is he?" moaned Sam.

* * *

Geordi dropped into the middle of a corridor and sprawled on his stomach as crossfire streaked over his head. He twisted around to see two Jem'Hadar fall back into the open hatch, then he looked in the other direction to see Captain Picard motioning urgently.

"Come on!" he yelled over an ear-splitting siren. Geordi didn't wait to be told twice—he jumped to his feet and charged after the captain. As he rounded the corner, a blue beam sliced off a chunk of the bulkhead, and he dove, skidding across the deck.

La Forge ended up at Picard's feet, and he looked up to see the captain, calm and steely-eyed, firing down the length of the corridor. "Grof, get us in there!"

Geordi looked back to see the Trill working frantically on a door panel. "They changed the codes! But I know how they think."

La Forge jumped up, drew his phaser, and wondered whether he would be more help to Picard or Grof. When another Jem'Hadar charged around the corner, firing blindly, Geordi joined Picard in blowing a hole through his chest.

"What happened to you?" asked the captain.

Geordi shook his head. "I got attacked, probably by the automated defenses. I went down with no warning, but I did alert Ro."

"We have less than three minutes," muttered Picard. "Grof!"

"I got it!" yelled the Trill. "I got it!" The door slid open with a pop, and a huge, ugly Jem'Hadar towered over Grof. They could see a red beam burn a hole through the Trill's shoulder and come out his back. He crumpled to the deck a microsecond before Picard's disruptor sliced the Jem'Hadar in half.

A yellow-suited Vorta bounded into the doorway,

firing wildly down the corridor, and Geordi almost regretted having to kill him. Two more Vorta technicians cowered in the control room, and Geordi shot enough phaser blasts to send them scurrying for cover.

The captain dashed forward and knelt down beside Grof, feeling for a pulse. After a moment, he told Geordi, "He's alive. Let's get him inside."

With each of them grabbing an arm, they hauled the wounded Trill into the control room and laid him on the floor. The captain motioned to the two remaining Vorta engineers to get out, and they gratefully scurried from the room. Geordi made sure the door shut after them, and he studied the unfamiliar controls, trying to figure out how to keep it closed.

After making Grof as comfortable as possible, Picard hefted his bag of homemade explosives and ran to a large window. On the other side of the window, several huge gleaming coils spun slowly, like a giant drill. That was the accelerator itself, thought Geordi, from which the whole incredible chain reaction began. Magneton particles sped faster and faster down the length of the collider until they bent time and space into the singularity called a wormhole. It was an incredible achievement, due in no small part to the man who lay bleeding at Geordi's feet.

La Forge watched as Captain Picard attached an explosive charge to the window. He was on his way to the instrument panels when the second door slid open, and two Jem'Hadar burst into the room.

The engineer opened fire from a crouch, killing one of them and forcing the other one to duck for cover behind a duty console. They didn't seem to want to shoot in the control room, and Geordi couldn't blame them, with their fleet about to come through the wormhole any minute. They needed this room intact, because there was no way for them to get word to the Gamma Quadrant to abort.

The door shut, and La Forge blasted the control panel with a phaser beam, intent upon keeping it shut. Now they were trapped in a room that was about to blow up.

As Picard fixed a grenade to a bank of delicate instruments, the Jem'Hadar jumped up and shot at him, shattering a large viewscreen. Geordi's beam caught the enemy in the shoulder and spun him around. Picard continued his work as if nothing had happened.

Taking a moment to breathe, La Forge looked down at Grof, who was squirming in pain. He tried not to think how unlikely it was that any of them would get out of here alive, especially with bombs set to go off all around them. When the wounded Jem'Hadar jumped up and started firing again, Geordi laid down blistering cover fire for the captain.

He heard angry pounding on the door behind him, and he could only imagine how many Jem'Hadar were trying to get in. Geordi glanced at his chronometer and saw that they only had two minutes left before all hell broke loose. He had a lot of faith in Ro, but it was hard to believe anyone could get them out of this alive.

Over the noise of the shuddering transport, Ro Laren shouted into the companel, "I'll run interference! Stand by on the transporter."

"Yes, sir," answered Tamla Horik from the shuttlecraft *Cook*. "Maserelli is on it."

"We're going right down its throat. Ro out."

Alone on the *Orb of Peace,* she hunched over the

conn, piloting the bulky transport through a sequence of desperate evasive maneuvers. The ship rocked every time it was hit by defensive fire from the collider, but the shields continued to hold.

Ro looked up at the viewscreen, watching the mammoth collider loom closer. It was about to engulf them like a whale swallowing a minnow. She switched views to the shuttlecraft, which hugged her stern like the tail on a kite while the *Orb of Peace* absorbed the brunt of the fire.

Hell of a pilot, that Tamla Horik. Too bad their original plan to dock with the escape pod at a safe distance had been blown to bits, along with the pod. Now it was up to her.

Ro saw ominous lights gleaming along the entire length of the collider, and there were no Dominion ships in sight. The ships were gone not because they feared the *Orb of Peace,* but because an untried wormhole was about to blossom open, right on top of her! *If that wormhole opens while I'm in it, my ashes might end up on the other side of the galaxy.*

The *Orb of Peace* shuddered again, and her shields dropped to eight percent. *This trusty transport deserves a better end than this,* thought Ro, *but maybe she always wanted to finish like a warship—in a blaze of glory.*

"Now!" she barked into the companel. "Get them *now!*"

Sam Lavelle covered his head as sparks and molten metal rained down upon him. He and Data cowered on what was left of the catwalk as Jem'Hadar troops converged on them from above and below. Sam returned fire, but he wasn't overly concerned about them—not when Data's phaser was about to explode in the hydrogen-filled air ducts. It promised to be a spectacular death for all present.

He looked at the android, who was lying on his back, gazing upward at the spindly girders and catwalks. Data was as calm as if they were lying on the beach at Atlantic City.

"Time left?" rasped Sam.

"Twenty-eight-point-five seconds," answered the android. "It has been a pleasure serving with you again, Lieutenant."

"You, too, Data. I couldn't have done this without you." Concentrated Jem'Hadar fire ripped up the catwalk, and a terrible groaning noise warned Sam that the metal had weakened and was about to crumble. He dropped his disruptor, shut his eyes, and hung on.

This is it!

Sam felt a tingling along his body, and he wondered if he had been hit. Suddenly hands grabbed him under his arms and yanked him hard; he started to fight against them.

"Quit struggling!" snapped Enrique Maserelli. "We're trying to save your butt!"

Sam opened his eyes to see Enrique and Hasmek pulling him off the small transporter pad of the shuttlecraft. They dumped him unceremoniously on the deck and turned to assist Data when he appeared a moment later.

"It's gonna blow!" shouted Sam.

"We know!" answered Tamla Horik.

Sam stared at the viewscreen and could see the collider light up like a glowing bar of steel. "Oh, my gosh," he muttered, "it's starting up!"

* * *

Geordi and Picard stood shoulder to shoulder over the fallen body of Enrak Grof, watching the door explode inward. Behind them, various instruments were beeping and blinking urgently, and the accelerator spun like a giant drill. The countdown to the wormhole had already started.

Picard and La Forge opened fire upon the first wave of Jem'Hadar who stormed the door, and three of them fell. At this moment, thought Geordi, it was pointless to hide—everything and everyone in this room was going to go in less than fifteen seconds.

Suddenly the captain began to glow and turn transparent. "I'll tell them you're here!" he shouted, his voice trailing off as he disappeared.

A reason to live, thought Geordi in shock. He dove behind a dead Jem'Hadar as a dozen live ones burst into the accelerator room. Grof disappeared in a flurry of sparkling lights, and two Jem'Hadar fired at the deck where he had lain.

Geordi scrambled away from the charges they had placed, and four Jem'Hadar rushed after him, trying to capture him alive. They tackled him, and the biggest one hauled him to his feet and smashed him across the mouth with a bony fist.

"Fool! You can't stop the Dominion!"

The pain brought Geordi to alert, and he saw a Jem'Hadar rip the charge off the accelerator window. Mustering all of his strength, Geordi ripped himself out of their grasp and flung himself to the deck as the first explosion ripped through the room, smashing glass, twisting metal, and turning several Jem'Hadar soldiers into burning totems.

Geordi felt the tingle along his body just as the second explosion bathed the room in flames. He felt the heat scorching his body, and then he was some-where else—on a shuttlecraft.

He stepped off the transporter into a very crowded cabin. "Captain," he said glumly, "they took the charge off the accelerator."

Picard nodded and looked around at the crowd of people. "Where's Ro?"

"The *Orb of Peace* is beaking up!" warned Horik at the controls.

"I've got her!" replied Maserelli, frantically work-ing the transporter panel on the tiny ship.

A moment later, a wild-eyed, singed, bruised Bajoran appeared on the transporter platform. Coughing violently, she fell into Geordi's arms.

"Maximum warp!" ordered Picard. "Now!"

There's no point setting a course, thought Geordi, *just get the hell out of here!*

On the shuttlecraft's small viewscreen, he saw a disheartening sight. It appeared as if the wormhole was about to blossom open, and the ghostly images of a hundred Jem'Hadar ships appeared in its cavernous mouth. *They were too late!*

Suddenly, the gleaming collider erupted in flame, and every seam and support burst open. The massive structure writhed like a ten-kilometer-long snake, and the ships in its mouth spun out of control, shooting outward like sparks from a campfire.

A monstrous rift opened at the twisted mouth of the structure; it began to grow exponentially, flowing outward like a tidal wave of light. Dominion ships that had escaped were sucked into the rift, and the collider buckled like a tin can. The crew stood shoul-der to shoulder on the cramped shuttlecraft, watching in amazement as the rift imploded with a blinding flash of light.

Fortunately, Tamla Horik never took her eyes off her controls. "Shock wave—brace yourselves!"

Geordi held onto Ro, who was still dazed, and Sam Lavelle covered Grof's immobile body. Hasmek gripped a chair with his lone hand, and Maserelli and Picard held onto control panels. Data merely widened his stance. When the shock wave hit them, the tiny craft was buffeted, but it held together.

Tamla's shoulders slumped foward with relief. "Shields down to fourteen percent, but holding."

"Yahoo!" shouted Enrique. "We did it! We did it!" Spontaneous but weary cheers broke out around the cabin.

Geordi was about to join in the celebration, until he looked down and saw Lavelle trying valiantly to stop Grof's bleeding. Sam pressed bandages against the awful wound as he grabbed a second hypo from a first-aid kit—but it was pointless. Even the Trill seemed to know his time was over. His trembling hand grasped Sam's wrist and halted his desperate measures. It grew very quiet in the cabin of the shuttlecraft.

"Sam! Sam!" Grof said hoarsely.

"I'm here," answered Lavelle, holding the Trill's hands.

"I can't see, but I heard the shouting . . . what happened?"

"We did it!" answered Sam. "We stopped them, and now we're going home. Just hang on—you'll be fine."

The Trill frowned. "Did we . . . did we damage it much?"

Sam looked at Geordi and swallowed hard. "No, no, it wasn't too badly damaged," he lied. "As soon as we capture it, we'll get it working again in no time.

You'll be there on the maiden voyage to the Gamma Quadrant."

The Trill nodded contentedly and closed his eyes. "Yes," he rasped, "I'll be there. Everyone will know . . . I designed it."

Captain Picard knelt down beside him. "Professor, I'm putting you in for a commendation, something I rarely do for a civilian. They'll not only know you're a great scientist, but a great hero of the Federation."

The Trill nodded. Then he winced with pain and gripped Lavelle's hand. "Sam, aren't you lucky—with me, you've got no messy symbiont to dispose of."

"You're not going to die," insisted Lavelle. "Come on, Grof, where's that old fire? You can make it home!"

"I'm going home," said the Trill softly. "I can see it! Thank you . . . my friend. May I call you my friend?"

"Yes, Grof, yes."

The Trill nodded with satisfaction. Then his body went limp, and his hand slid from Sam's wrist. Lavelle pounded on Grof's chest, trying desperately to restart his heart, and Picard finally had to pat the young man on the back.

"He's gone, Sam," said the captain. "Don't worry, he won't be forgotten. Now let's get everybody home."

"That will be difficult," said Data, who had taken the co-pilot's seat. "We have a Jem'Hadar battle cruiser following us."

Now it got really quiet on the crowded shuttlecraft, and Picard moved behind Data. "Can we reach the Badlands?"

"No, sir. At their superior speed, they will intercept us in approximately five minutes."

The captain slammed his fist into his palm. "Take evasive maneuvers and put out a Starfleet distress call."

"What Starfleet ship will hear us way out here?" scoffed Hasmek. "You're a perpetual optimist, Captain."

"Optimism has always worked for me," answered Picard with a wistful smile. "No matter what happens, this has been a job well done. We can all take considerable pride in today's work."

Geordi looked around and saw Ro and Lavelle consoling each other. Maserelli put his hands on Horik's shoulders, and even Hasmek looked resigned to death.

"We have one torpedo left," said Data.

Picard smiled. "We always seem to have only one torpedo. Ready it, and ready the self-destruct sequence." He looked around the cramped cabin. "Does anybody have a problem with that?"

"No," answered Sam, gripping Ro like a life vest. "We're ready."

"Who wants to live forever?" said Geordi hoarsely.

"In these remaining minutes," said Captain Picard, "I'd like to salute a fellow captain who had her first command go down in a valiant sacrifice. I'd like to salute that proud vessel, too—the *Orb of Peace,* and her captain, Ro Laren."

"Hear! Hear!" came several calls.

Ro, who looked burned, beaten, and half-dead, nodded wearily. "Thank you. I learned a lot. And thank you, Captain, for taking me back into Starfleet."

"Where you belong," added Picard warmly.

Out of the corner of his eye, Geordi saw Data cock his head. Then he conferred briefly with Tamla Horik in the seat beside him. Maserelli leaned over to eavesdrop, and a grin stretched across his face.

"Captain," announced Data, "our distress call has been answered by a coded message on a secret channel. It is the *Enterprise*."

"How close?" asked Picard, leaning forward along with everyone else.

"I am changing course now—we should reach them in time." The android swiftly worked the controls.

Geordi looked at Hasmek and smirked. "You see, it pays to be an optimist."

The Romulan broke into the first real smile Geordi had seen on him. "I should be able to get a promotion out of this. Maybe to a pleasant desk job somewhere. I'm tired of being a spy."

"We have to win the war first," muttered Geordi.

"Oh, you'll win," said Hasmek confidently. "I'm going to look like a genius for predicting this when no one else will."

"We are within range of the *Enterprise*," said Data. "From the course of the Jem'Hadar ship, it would appear they are not aware of the *Enterprise*."

"Slow down to impulse," ordered Picard, "and make them come out of warp."

"Yes, sir," answered the android, carrying out the order. "They are still following us."

"On screen."

The viewscreen shifted to the Jem'Hadar cruiser streaking toward them, glittering blue and gold along its sleek hull. Intent upon their prey, they disregarded the *Enterprise*, which flashed out of warp with quantum torpedoes and phasers blazing. The Jem'Hadar cruiser took the full measure of every weapon the Sovereign-class starship could bring to bear, and the shields around it glimmered like a halo. When the halo went blank, the *Enterprise* unleashed another barrage as she flew past the listing ship. The cruiser sparkled like a diamond in the sun before erupting in a monstrous cloud of gas and debris.

"Enterprise to *Cook,"* came a familiar voice over the comm channel. "Data, you're not alone."

"No, Captain Riker. I have the captain, Ro, and La Forge with me, plus several others. Nine in total."

"Great!" exclaimed Riker. "But we need to get out of here, because more enemy craft are on the way. No time to dock—set your self-destruct for two minutes, and we'll beam you over."

"Sam Lavelle," said Beverly Crusher with surprise as she helped him off the transporter platform. "Where did you come from?"

"It's a long story." He looked around at the happy reunions as Picard, La Forge, and Ro were reunited with Will Riker and the crew of the *Enterprise.*

"Are you all right?" asked the doctor.

"Yes." He heard a tinkling sound and turned to see Grof's body materialize on the transporter platform. Dr. Crusher instantly bent over the Trill with her tricorder.

"Dead," she concluded. "Who is he?"

"A brave man," answered Sam hoarsely. "A hero."

In the next instant, Hasmek appeared on the transporter platform, and Dr. Crusher looked askance at the one-armed Romulan as he stepped down. "You're not regular crew," she said.

"No, I'm special crew," he answered with a smile.

"Commander Riker, how did you know we were here?" asked Geordi suspiciously.

The handsome first officer grinned. "Outer patrols picked up a Talavian shuttlecraft carrying a fellow with an isolinear chip. It told us exactly where to look for the artificial wormhole . . . and you."

Sam looked down at Grof's body and smiled. "Your ego saved our lives, Grof. Thanks."

"We've got everyone," announced the transporter chief as Horik and Maserelli stepped off the platform.

Riker tapped his combadge. "Riker to bridge: maximum warp to Deep Space Nine."

"Deep Space Nine?" asked Picard with surprise and delight. "Did we win it back?"

"Two days ago," answered Riker proudly. "We've turned the tide in this lousy war, and the wormhole is safe! I hope your team did something to help?"

"Oh, I think we might have," answered Picard, nodding with satisfaction. "What about you and the crew—have you faced many hardships while we were gone?"

"It wasn't really that bad for us," admitted Riker with an embarrassed smile. "We spent a week at Starbase 209, undergoing repairs."

"Not bad," replied Picard with envy.

"I didn't save the universe, but maybe I helped one person," added Riker.

"Oh?" said Picard with a slight smile. "She sounds like a lucky young woman." The captain marveled at his first officer. Just like Riker to find romance under the most unlikely circumstances.

"I'd say more heroic than lucky. But with some very hard work on her part, it looks like her luck is about to change."

"I look forward to hearing all about her, Number One," the captain replied warmly.

As the others filed out, Ro grabbed Sam's hand and pulled him aside. For the first time since he had met her on the *Orb of Peace,* the Bajoran looked scared.

"What's the matter?" he asked.

"Everything is fine for you, but not for me," said Ro worriedly. "I'll probably end up in the brig over this."

"If you do, I'll personally break you out," Sam assured her. "And I'm sure I can get Captain Picard to help me."

Sam was with Ro eight hours later, when Captain Picard caught up with them in the lounge. They were in Federation space, only a few hours away from Deep Space Nine, and it felt good just to sit and eat. Sam was on his fourth helping of blintzes, okra, brie cheese, and trout almondine.

Ro watched him in amazement, shaking her head. "You'd better come up for air, Lieutenant, because the captain is on his way over."

Sam gulped down a huge mouthful just as Picard reached their table. "At ease," said the captain with a smile.

"Please sit down," offered Ro.

"Thank you."

Sam peered closely at the captain, thinking there was something odd about his appearance. "What's missing?" asked Sam. "Ah, it's the earring and nose ridges."

"I don't mind losing the implants," answered Picard, "but I rather miss the earring."

Picard smiled.

"I've asked you here today because I have something to say to each of you."

"What?" asked Ro suspiciously.

"First you, Ro. As much as I would like to simply restore your Starfleet commission, that is beyond my power. However, I have submitted a report to Starfleet Command about your recent efforts on behalf of the Alpha Quadrant. I would not be at all surprised if eventually, if you feel the path of your life leading back to Starfleet, there will be a place for you here. And if that is where your path leads you, I would be honored to serve by your side."

To Sam's surprise, there were tears in Ro's eyes as she thanked the captain for his words.

"As for you, Mr. Lavelle," Picard continued, "welcome back. I would not be at all surprised if a promotion was in your future."

"Actually, Captain," Lavelle replied, "I'm not sure whether my future is in Starfleet or not. I have some leave coming. . . ."

"At least several months," Picard said, "combining personal and medical."

Sam realized that Picard was way ahead of him. Ahead of both him and Ro, actually. "So I thought I'd take some time, see what life has to offer outside of a uniform."

"An excellent idea," Captain Picard said. "Any immediate plans?"

Sam smiled at Ro, and she smiled back. She— they—had already made a decision. Next week might still be up in the air, but they had begun to think about tomorrow. Sam answered the captain. "Going to find a farming planet, sir. Get some real earth under my feet, feel the sun on my back. Seems to me a fighting fleet could use some good, healthy, nonreplicated food now and again."

"Indeed it could." Picard looked thoughtful. "We're almost at Deep Space Nine. Even these days, it's still a crossroads. I'm sure you can find transport to someplace that suits your needs." The captain looked at them both, and to Sam it seemed he was pleased with what he saw. "You have both been handed a new life—no, you both earned a new life. Make the most of it."

Ro, her hand in Sam's, smiled at the captain. "We will, sir," she said. "It's a gift of the Prophets."

Look for STAR TREK Fiction from Pocket Books

Star Trek: Deep Space Nine®

Star Trek®: Voyager™

Flashback • Diane Carey
Mosaic • Jeri Taylor

#1 *Caretaker* • L. A. Graf
#2 *The Escape* • Dean W. Smith & Kristine K. Rusch
#3 *Ragnarok* • Nathan Archer
#4 *Violations* • Susan Wright
#5 *Incident at Arbuk* • John Gregory Betancourt
#6 *The Murdered Sun* • Christie Golden
#7 *Ghost of a Chance* • Mark A. Garland & Charles G. McGraw
#8 *Cybersong* • S. N. Lewitt
#9 *Invasion #4: The Final Fury* • Dafydd ab Hugh
#10 *Bless the Beasts* • Karen Haber
#11 *The Garden* • Melissa Scott
#12 *Chrysalis* • David Niall Wilson
#13 *The Black Shore* • Greg Cox
#14 *Marooned* • Christie Golden
#15 *Echoes* • Dean W. Smith & Kristine K. Rusch
#16 *Seven of Nine* • Christie Golden

Star Trek®: New Frontier

#1 *House of Cards* • Peter David
#2 *Into the Void* • Peter David
#3 *The Two-Front War* • Peter David
#4 *End Game* • Peter David
#5 *Martyr* • Peter David
#6 *Fire on High* • Peter David

Star Trek®: Day of Honor

Book One: *Ancient Blood* • Diane Carey
Book Two: *Armageddon Sky* • L. A. Graf
Book Three: *Her Klingon Soul* • Michael Jan Friedman
Book Four: *Treaty's Law* • Dean W. Smith & Kristine K. Rusch

Star Trek®: The Captain's Table

Star Trek®: The Dominion War

1252.01